PRETTY BROKEN DOLLS

BOOKS BY JENNIFER CHASE

Little Girls Sleeping
Her Last Whisper
Flowers on Her Grave
Last Girls Alive
The Fragile Ones

JENNIFER CHASE

PRETTY BROKEN DOLLS

bookouture

Published by Bookouture in 2021

An imprint of Storyfire Ltd.
Carmelite House
50 Victoria Embankment
London EC4Y 0DZ

www.bookouture.com

ISBN: 978-1-83888-898-5
eBook ISBN: 978-1-83888-897-8

PROLOGUE

The front door stood ajar. It bumped gently against the jamb in rhythm with the evening breeze. The screen remained wide open and was bent precariously around the aluminum frame. Pieces of broken glass from a shattered light bulb above had scattered across the porch, leaving behind a shadowy darkness draped across the front of the small house.

The neighborhood remained quiet; the light blue one-story cottage eerily so. No outside illumination or motion lights flooded the front area. The blooming climbing vines and perfectly manicured bushes were eclipsed by the darkness.

Headlights approached.

A small, dark vehicle pulled into the driveway. Waiting a moment before turning off the engine, a woman pushed open the car door and stepped out. The young redhead was dressed for the evening, in a sparkly blouse and tight black pants. Wavering a moment in her spiked sandals, she looked at the house in curiosity—and then in disappointment. Quickly grabbing a warm jacket from inside the car and slipping it on, she walked up the driveway.

"Jeanine, where are you?" she whispered and headed to the front door, ignoring the shattered light bulb on the step crunching under her feet. She knocked on the door. "Jeanine," she said, more loudly, leaning closer to the opening. "We waited for you… you missed a great party."

No response.

The front door pushed open, revealing a darkened interior.

"Jeanine?"

The woman hesitated but seemed to be pulled by an unknown force. She stepped over the threshold, not bothering to close the door, and moved through the living room. Confused by the darkness, she turned on a lamp sitting on a small table. The room lit up instantly. Everything seemed in place. The oversized beige couches with brightly colored throw pillows, the dark mahogany coffee table with neatly stacked magazines and books precisely centered appeared usual for Jeanine's house. It was always neat and organized.

"Jeanine?" the woman said again. "Are you here?"

The woman walked around and checked the kitchen and small bedroom, but there wasn't any sign of her friend. She eyed a piece of paper on the counter and decided to leave a quick note, scratching out that she had stopped by and asking Jeanine to call her when she got the message.

She suddenly noticed a strange high-pitched whistling noise coming from the other side of the living room. Curious, the woman moved closer to the sound. The back sliding door was slightly open. The crack was enough for the wind to invade and make a strange noise.

Her foot touched something. A tall turquoise vase that had been sitting on a shelf nearby was now lying on the carpet. It seemed strange to her that it had been knocked over. She bent down and picked up the vase, replacing it on the shelf.

She retrieved her cell phone from her pocket and tried calling Jeanine again. It rang numerous times and then went to voicemail where Jeanine's upbeat voice said, *"Hi, sorry I missed your call but please don't hang up. Leave a message and I'll get right back to you."*

The greeting was followed by a quick beep.

"Jeanine, it's Mandy again and now I'm standing in your living room. Where are you, girl? Everyone was asking about you tonight. Hey, and you left your front door open. Call me." She ended the call.

Mandy was about to head back to the front door to leave, but something stopped her—it didn't feel right—and instead, she stood at the sliding door staring out into the large backyard where dense rows of pine trees and acacia bushes huddled around the house's boundary. During the day, the property appeared green and lush, but now it looked gloomy and foreboding.

Mandy flipped on the outside light, but it only lit up the patio areas directly outside the house, and the extended wooded region still looked dark.

She pulled open the sliding door and the wind whipped through the house. It chilled her. Goosebumps scuttled up her arms. Worry now set in and she didn't know what to do. Redialing Jeanine's number, Mandy listened to it sound again and in unison heard the faint, far-off ringing of a phone somewhere in the distance.

She stepped outside, trying to decipher where the ringing was coming from. "Jeanine?" she said, noticing that one of the outside chairs had been toppled over and lay precariously on its side.

Moving off the stone patio and pulling her jacket more tightly around her, Mandy slowly trudged toward the trees, a bit wobbly in her shoes. She turned on the flashlight mode on her cell phone and moved forward.

She dialed Jeanine again. This time, she heard the distinct ringing of the cell phone coming from the trees—low at first and then it rang louder.

"Jeanine," she said, with barely a whisper. Her voice sounded oddly distant.

Looking down, she saw where there were crushed weeds and small broken branches as if someone had walked back and forth recently. Still, she kept moving forward, into the trees, swinging her cell phone back and forth which only illuminated a tiny patch of ground in front of her, creating dense shadows outside its beam.

Her pulse quickened.

Anxiety escalated.

Something fluttering on a bush caught her eye. She leaned closer, focusing. As she moved the cell light beam nearer, it revealed a piece of white fabric with a mother-of-pearl button still attached.

Mandy gasped.

It wasn't the fact that she had seen Jeanine wear that pretty white blouse on so many occasions, it was the droplets of crimson spattered across the fabric that shoved a spear of fear into her gut.

Thoughts of dread and horror-filled scenarios ran through Mandy's mind. Urgently, she pushed the redial button on her phone again.

The sound of Jeanine's ringtone rang in the darkness. This time it kept ringing and there was no cheerful message.

Mandy walked further into the dark realm of the trees, still hoping that there was a logical explanation. Stepping over old branches with loud crunching noises and sidestepping bushes just before reaching the back fence of the property, she managed to make her way to the sound of the ringing phone.

Everything went quiet.

Mandy stood a foot from the phone lying on the ground. It mesmerized her. She slowly bent down to pick it up. With a startled gasp, she stepped back, dropping the phone as she stared at her hand. It was covered in blood.

In a frenzied panic, Mandy ran past the phone and continued along the low wrought-iron fence. The flashlight feature dimmed and she couldn't see where she was going. Slowing her pace, she glimpsed something white and moving slightly.

"Jeanine? What's going on?" She spoke in a strained whisper.

Trying to catch her breath and calm her hammering pulse, Mandy approached. Her cell phone flashlight surged and shone brightly on the blood-soaked white silk blouse, now shredded from Jeanine's right shoulder. She reeled back at the sight of her friend.

Mandy couldn't tear her eyes away from the horror. Her throat constricted as her breath trapped in her chest. She staggered backwards, taking in the entire scene—unable to turn her focus away.

Her friend's upper body was impaled on the iron fence penetrating from her back through her ribs, and her throat was slit open. Her head flopped down, lifeless eyes trained on the ground. Her long brown hair fell forward, some strands sticking to the blood seeping from her chest. Her arms hung at her sides, legs crooked, like a marionette waiting for someone to pull the strings. Blood still dripped from her body, sliding down her arms to her fingertips before collecting on the ground—the wet crimson almost matching her fingernail polish. The body was shoeless and Jeanine's feet were dirty and bloody—as if she had been running through the woods barefoot.

It was the sight of Jeanine's face that made her sob in terror. Caked in grotesque makeup, making her look like a caricature of herself—a hideous broken doll. Red lipstick drawn heavy around her lips, dark purples for blush on her cheeks, and dark blues for eye shadow made her look like a circus clown instead of her friend.

Beside Jeanine's body, a necklace hung on the fence. It was a small locket that she always wore, which her mother had given her when she turned sixteen.

Mandy mouthed the word "Jeanine" but no sound escaped her lips. Realizing she still had her cell phone in her hand, she tried to dial 911 but fumbled a few times with the buttons before she heard the words, *"Nine-one-one, what's your emergency?"*

CHAPTER ONE

One year later…

Friday 1000 hours

Detective Katie Scott and Deputy Sean McGaven managed to get the search warrants they needed, along with a crew of police officers, to search the entire property including the Stantons' house, cars, barn, and storage areas. There were additional search warrants for the adjacent pond next to the Stantons' property and a large nearby pond owned by the state where many locals gathered to swim and fish and picnic on sunny days.

As Katie stood on the property watching the police and forensic personnel descend and fan out in search formation, she wondered if she had overstepped her authority—or her enthusiasm for such a huge search—but eighteen-year-old Jared Stanton was still missing after six months and she knew she wouldn't be able to live with herself if she didn't do all she could to find him.

She had her reasons for instructing the search, but what if it was just a hunch and he wasn't found?

What if this was just a waste of time and resources?

But her instincts screamed that Jared was dead, and that his body had been disposed of in a local pond; there would be no other way to get rid of a body that quickly and quietly before claiming that he had run away.

Katie and McGaven had constructed this theory based on evidence from their own examination, and the original investigation by Detective Alvarez six months ago when Jared Stanton was first reported missing. They knew that Jared and his parents had had an argument early in the weekend on Friday or Saturday. The reason for the argument wasn't entirely known. The fact that Jared's keys, phone, wallet, and his car were found at the property were indications that this wasn't a runaway teenager. It was highly likely he had been killed, either accidentally or out of rage, and his body disposed of nearby.

There was evidence of recent repairs, fresh paint, and alterations to the siding at one end of the barn, and two ATVs were missing. Things didn't add up.

The afternoon was cold and overcast, the grim sky lending an ominous weight to the scene, as the police worked their duties. Feeling the chill, Katie had gone back to the car and retrieved her warmer leather jacket and gloves. She zipped the coat up close to her neck to keep the cold away, but still felt shivers slide down her spine in anticipation of what they might find.

She knew that everyone from the department was watching her closely—she was still considered a rookie detective despite her accomplishments, and there were those who whispered about nepotism, which made her uncomfortable. If only they knew that her uncle, Sheriff Scott, was harder on her than anyone.

Katie walked down the same path she had taken with Amy, Jared's sister, only a couple of days ago and glanced up at Amy's bedroom window to see her in place again, looking down. Katie gave a wave but Amy didn't move from her position. Mr. and Mrs. Stanton were inside the house with a police officer and their attorney. They chose not to watch the search.

The walk around the picturesque property didn't have the same tranquil feeling it had a couple of days ago. The horses were grazing, but the darkness of the early afternoon made it appear more like the end of the day.

Over by the pond, McGaven was coordinating the dive team which consisted of two sheriff's deputies and Katie's fiancé Chad from the fire department, who navigated the motorized inflatable boat across the water. Chad was the dive and scuba instructor for the county, so he led the expedition while several uniformed officers stood around the perimeter and waited for instruction. A large police SUV retrofitted with a hoist winch was parked nearby in case it was needed.

The boat navigated slowly, chugging a few feet at a time, gently moving in a clockwise rotation, and stopping to let two of the divers search in each area for a minute or two before moving on. Bubbles from their respirators rippled the murky surface of the tranquil pond, which otherwise was smooth and glassy, reflecting the looming pine and eucalyptus trees surrounding it.

One diver would surface in his full scuba suit, bobbing like a seal in the ocean, and give the negative sign. A minute later, the other diver would surface and repeated the same signal—negative.

Nothing.

Katie kept her distance. Even though there were so many people surrounding her, supporting her, she felt isolated and detached. She kept her wits but her anxiety was always waiting in the shadows. Struggling with a sense of urgency welling up inside her, she took deep breaths and counted slowly, trying to relax her tight jaw and clenched fists. There was a fine line between anxiety and panic—more specifically, PTSD; something that had come home with her from the army barely more than a year ago, which had deeply impacted her life.

When she was first discharged, Katie didn't know whether to go back to police patrol at the Sacramento Police Department or stay at the Pine Valley Sheriff's Department headed up by Sheriff Wayne Scott—or Uncle Wayne, as she knew him. Katie decided on Pine Valley and was now heading up the cold case unit. She loved the work and the diversity of cases—and working with her strong and capable partner, Deputy McGaven.

The reality of watching a murder victim fished out of the family's large pond would be deeply disturbing, even to a seasoned professional. All Katie could do was wait and hope that her colleagues proved her instincts and experience correct.

She kept moving, hoping to keep her body warm. Glancing up at the top of the driveway, she saw a dark gray sedan parked on the street. She had noticed the vehicle earlier, and this time there was a man leaning against the side. Of medium build with blond hair and sunglasses, he appeared to be in his forties or fifties, and was distinguished-looking, despite his casual outfit of heavy navy windbreaker jacket and jeans. He stood like a statue, unmoving, watching the entire search take place.

Katie began to approach him, wanting to confront him about what he was doing there. She picked up her pace, but the man didn't make a move.

That's when she heard the commotion. Looking back, she saw one of the divers giving a thumbs-up sign. Chad yelled that they had found something, and a sense that was partial dread mixed with a strange relief flooded her body.

McGaven yelled across the pond to the men. "What do you have?" He then turned and called up to Katie, "They found an ATV!"

Katie felt a momentary sense of reprieve that it wasn't a body, and hurried to meet up with McGaven.

"They found it?" she said breathlessly.

"Yep. You were right," he said with a half-smile on his face.

"I knew it had to be close." She shivered.

"Those damn instincts of yours..."

They watched patiently as the crew prepared to pull the all-terrain vehicle from the deep, murky water. One of the search and rescue officers unwound the winch and tossed the heavy-duty hooks into the water. Then the diver disappeared underwater again to secure the hooks to reinforced places on the sporting vehicle.

As the churning winch began to pull, the ATV slowly emerged like a prehistoric animal out of the lake. One of the wheels was bent, so once it was dragged completely out, it was lopsided, dripping with muddy water. It appeared there were several dents in the side, and the top roll bar that was supposed to keep you safe was crushed inward and would probably have killed the driver—but there was no driver.

Katie shuddered as she immediately recognized the vehicle from several framed photos inside the house. She wasn't certain if she was happy or sad—perhaps a bit of both.

But the recovery crews weren't done yet—there was still more of the pond to search. Chad switched places with a teammate and they began the painstaking process once again.

"I think there's an umbrella in the car," said McGaven as drizzle started to fall around them.

"I'm fine," Katie said and pulled her hood around her head to keep her ears warm.

They heard several car doors open and close in the Stanton driveway and turned to see Detectives Hamilton and Alvarez exit a vehicle and walk down the path to meet them.

"Who called Hamilton?" said McGaven.

Hamilton was the detective in charge of any new homicide investigations. Katie had had some tense moments with him, but they had managed to keep their investigative relationship on a professional and friendly basis.

"Well, technically the sheriff did, but I requested it."

"Why?"

"Because I knew if there was a body found, we would need the help," Katie said.

"If Jared's body is in the pond, I think this is an open-and-shut investigation," he said.

"Hi, Detective McGaven," said Hamilton, nodding his greetings. "I see they found an ATV."

"So far," said McGaven.

"They still have almost half the pond to explore," said Katie, trying not to let her teeth chatter in the cold. The four of them stood watching the pond. They didn't speak for moment, keeping their eyes fixed on the divers and what they might pull up.

The rain gathered speed as a soft rolling thunder sounded in the distance. Clouds propagated in several shades of gray, pushing forward and gathering across the sky.

Chad's head popped up from the water suddenly and he gave the signal that he had found something, but not what it was.

Another ATV? Belonging to his dad?

Jared?

The other diver conferred with him a moment. Katie strained to hear the conversation and tried to read the body language. She waited anxiously.

Was it something?

Chad swiveled toward the shoreline and made a gesture at one of the police officers, who in turn hurried away to his patrol car.

Katie stepped forward to get closer to the pond, mesmerized by how gracefully Chad moved. She didn't care how wet she was going to get as the rain picked up momentum: she was chilled to the core anyway and more water wasn't going to make a bit of difference.

Chad made eye contact with her and he subtly nodded. Even in this terrible situation, she still felt the strong connection of love for him—her fiancé. She waited to make absolutely sure what he was implying was correct and he confirmed it with a grim expression. She knew what it meant.

Turning around, she spoke to the rest of the crew in a hushed tone. "Looks like we have a body."

McGaven confronted her. "You sure?"

"Yes."

Hamilton walked up. "Okay, we'll get the coroner, but for now let's pull the body up and out of this rain." Turning to Katie, he said, "Your crime scene awaits."

Katie looked at him, a bit confused—she wasn't sure if she had heard him correctly.

"That means you're working the crime scene—what there is of it," he stated. "You haven't let me down yet." Hamilton corrected himself, "You haven't let *us* down." He gave her a genuine smile, looking much more likeable as he relaxed his face.

Katie nodded and then looked at McGaven. "Back me up," she said as they walked to the south side of the pond—the closest to the recovery area—and waited.

She began preparing herself silently for what she was about to see. She glanced back at the house, expecting one of the Stantons to come running toward the pond screaming, but the house remained quiet—and no one came out.

She turned her attention back to Chad and the other diver as they pulled something to shore; it looked like a large black garbage bag. It was round, not the length and shape that would indicate a body. Could it just be a bag of debris?

To Katie's relief, the drizzly rain had stopped, but the rumbling of thunder continued to approach, gaining in volume. Taking off her warm mittens, she slipped on plastic gloves and knelt down, reaching her hand forward as McGaven used his body to block the view from the house and the neighbors.

Katie barely touched the bag but she felt something bristly. Flipping back the plastic, she revealed brown hair, then an ear, then the side of a young man's head. Katie gasped as she took in the grayish skin, concaved, shriveled, looking more like a rubber mask in a Halloween store than anything human. One eye was gone, but the other was blackened and staring out. It was the decapitated head of a man. A young man.

Katie drew her hand back in revulsion and turned away for a moment to compose herself. "It's a young man. It's… difficult to tell, but it appears to be Jared Stanton."

Several of the surrounding group members sucked in air but couldn't tear their eyes away from the horrendous site of Jared's face staring back at them.

McGaven retrieved his small pocketknife and handed it to Katie. She looked at him and reluctantly took the blade, not wanting to see more, but then sliced a small area on the opposite side of the construction bag.

It was just as she had thought.

Carefully, she turned back the bag, revealing the remains of a young man. His torso, arms, and legs were crammed inside—the dismembered limbs broken and crooked to fit into the bag. The water had done damage to the body and decomposition wasn't the same as it would have been if he were buried in the dirt. Jared Stanton's body and decapitated head were bloated and shiny, and Katie knew that now the skin was exposed to the air, it would soon slip off, turning black.

Katie took a few moments to try to ascertain what type of tool might have been used to separate his body. Jared's legs still had on jeans, his torso was wrapped in a T-shirt, and sneakers were on both his feet. She examined his head and neck to establish if there were any obvious clues to what had killed him—if there were any cuts, bullet holes, or traumas that led to his death—but nothing was obvious.

She immediately stood up and addressed McGaven and Hamilton. "The body needs to be taken to the medical examiner's office so it can be identified officially as Jared Stanton. We need to find out what was used to dismember him—and if there are signs of trauma, drugs, or poison in his body. This isn't the time or place to conduct any kind of examination, not in this weather." She swallowed hard and continued, "The ATV needs to be transported to the police impound so that forensics can search and document it, getting any VIN numbers to identify it."

She turned to Chad who was waiting in the background as far away from the body as possible. "I need the rest of the pond scoured for anything else that shouldn't be there, especially anything that could have been used as the murder weapon, and the other ATV."

There were two deputy sheriffs standing nearby. Katie summoned them. "I want you two to document anything in the barn that might be missing or might have been used to dismember the body, like a chainsaw, hand saw, knives, or whatever you can find, to assist forensics when they get here. Make sure that you keep any tools or items you find protected from this rain."

They nodded that they understood and left.

As Katie turned and began walking back up to the house, she eyed the blond stranger getting into his car.

"Hey, Katie," said McGaven, diverting her attention to him.

"Yeah," she said but kept moving.

"Where are you going?"

"Taking a break to take some notes on the events and begin our report," she said and hurried in the direction of the police vehicle.

Chad caught up to her. "Where are you running to?" he asked gently, knowing that every case took its toll on her.

"I'm fine. Just need to get the paperwork together for the sheriff."

"Hey." He took her arm and examined her face. "Take some time for yourself, okay?"

She forced a slight smile and nodded, not wanting to let him know how disturbed she was by the scene.

"See you later. Okay?"

It was clear that he wanted to kiss her but it would have been inappropriate at the crime scene in front of all of their co-workers.

"Bye," she said and watched Chad return to the group.

As Katie looked for the blond stranger, scanning the street in both directions, she spotted the car driving away.

Her cell phone rang. She wasn't going to answer at first, but it was the sheriff.

"Scott," she said, making sure that no one was near. She felt conspicuous when she talked with her Uncle Wayne.

"Anything?"

"Yes. A body and ATV have been found."

"Everything okay?" His voice was softer than his usual gruff sheriff demeanor.

"I noticed that detectives Alvarez and Hamilton are here."

"I sent them."

"I see."

"I need a report from you and McGaven, and then you can set this case free and let the detectives close it."

Katie stopped for a moment. It surprised her that he referred to "the case" as free.

The sheriff continued, "Alvarez will take over to make sure that everything is in order and he'll be working the entire homicide investigation from start to finish, since it was originally his case."

"That's it?"

"That's it," he said. "You've done your job—excellent work. You've had back-to-back cases lately and deserve a break. I don't want my cold case team burned out."

Katie sighed.

"Have the report on my desk no later than tomorrow."

"I will."

"And, Katie," he said.

"Yes?"

"Take some time for yourself," he said again. "When you've completed the reports on the Stanton case, take the rest of the day off and tomorrow." He sighed. "That's an order."

CHAPTER TWO

Friday 1330 hours

Katie drove into her driveway and cut the engine, relieved that she had finished all the necessary paperwork for the week. She sat for a moment, gathering her thoughts. It surprised her that she wasn't mad about the fact that she and McGaven didn't get to finish out the Jared Stanton missing person and murder case after the body was found. Mr. and Mrs. Stanton were taken into custody not long after the body was discovered.

She sighed and leaned back against her seat. It saddened Katie that the daughter, Amy Stanton, would have to be thrown into the mess of losing her family; first her brother and then her parents, to whatever fate they faced. Closing her eyes, she could still see the photograph of Jared Stanton's smiling face as he sat on his ATV—a time for fun and family now shattered and gone.

Katie stepped out of the car, pulling her jacket and briefcase with her. She hadn't realized how tired she was; her arms and legs seemed barely able to carry her body up to her house.

She found a small white box sitting on the porch. There was no name on the front but she opened it, and inside was a beautiful tropical plant terrarium. She had loved terrariums ever since she was about ten years old. The only person besides her parents who knew that was Chad. The note simply read: I thought of you. With all my love, Chad.

"Aww…" she said, "I love you too." Her heart was full and she couldn't quit smiling. She picked it up and carried it to the front door.

She was met by the deep barks of Cisco.

Opening the door, a black blur bounded around her before she could get inside. Cisco, a black German shepherd, had been her army partner for two tours in Afghanistan. No matter how bad her day was, Cisco made everything better. They had been through more together than she had with any human, whether friend or family—it was a bond that could never be broken.

"Hey, buddy," she said, dropping her jacket and briefcase on the kitchen counter. She carefully took the terrarium out of the box and set it down on the table. "I'm home early for once. What do you think of that? And the entire weekend." She scratched behind his ears as she went to the refrigerator to retrieve a cold soda.

The moment Katie opened the back-door slider, Cisco jetted by her and bounded into the yard, making his usual rounds. Katie smiled as she watched the dog run around, taking time to check out every bush and tree. The air was still cool but there were signs around her yard indicating that spring wasn't too far away. Birds were more active, weaving in and out of the trees. The acreage was greener, which would soon produce buds and then flowers.

Katie took a seat on her favorite porch swing, enjoying the moment. It was something that she hadn't done in several months. As she looked around, she was reminded, as so often, of her parents, who had been killed in a car accident when she was a teenager, leaving her Uncle Wayne to raise her. This was her childhood home, and every inch of the house and yard held warm memories.

Cisco ran up and gave two playful barks before running after a low-flying bird.

Katie laughed. His antics always brought a smile to her face. Watching him play helped her to decompress from the day and her current investigation.

Her mind wandered to Chad, her thoughts filled with wedding plans and beginning their life together. It was difficult to believe that she was going to be a bride. How her life would change... Wouldn't it?

Cisco, fully refreshed and relieved of the angst of being stuck inside, padded to her and easily jumped up onto the swing.

Katie petted the dog, but instead of relaxing, she found herself becoming edgy. It was unusual for her to have some time off and to find herself with no work to go to. Chad was working a forty-eight-hour shift at the fire department, and she wanted something to do.

Standing up, she said to the dog, "You want to go for a run?"

Cisco immediately jumped down and began his usual German shepherd whine in complete agreement.

Katie went inside to change her clothes. Running was something that helped her think and unwind, and that's what she was going to do.

CHAPTER THREE

Monday 0745 hours

Walking through the forensic division of the Pine Valley Sheriff's Department, Katie felt refreshed from the relaxing weekend and ready for the week. She saw McGaven's truck in the parking lot and knew that he was already perusing the top tier of the cold case files.

Katie and McGaven used one of the empty forensic offices due to the lack of room upstairs in the detective division. It suited them. The area was quiet and secure, giving them the sufficient space they needed to work through mounds of evidence and paperwork. It was an added bonus that the forensic evidence department wasn't far away.

Pushing the door open, she wasn't surprised to see her partner already hard at work.

"How do you always get here before me?" she said, shedding her jacket.

"It's a gift."

"I think it's the fact that you love this job."

"Maybe."

Katie's cell phone rang. "Scott."

"You here? McGaven, too?" the sheriff said in his gruff business voice.

"Just got here. And yes, Gav is here too."

"Good."

"What's up?" she asked, sensing he had something important to tell them.

"Can you come to my office?"

"Okay. We'll be there in five."

The connection ended abruptly.

"Well…" She slowly put her phone down.

"What's up?" asked McGaven.

"The sheriff has asked for us to meet with him—now. Well, actually, he ordered."

McGaven stood up, his height making him tower over Katie. "Let's go." He put his suit jacket on.

"Let's see what's so important."

Katie and McGaven reached the sheriff's office. Katie hesitated at the door, taking a breath to steady her nerves before knocking twice. There was always that terrifying thought that the cold case unit could be cut due to budget costs.

"Come in," came her uncle's voice.

Katie glanced at McGaven, whose expression was stoic and difficult to read. She opened the door and they stepped inside.

The sheriff wasn't alone.

"You!" said Katie, referring to the man sitting across from the sheriff. "Who are you?" She was shocked.

McGaven quietly closed the door, confused and not understanding Katie's reaction.

"I saw you at the Stanton residence. Who are you?" she insisted.

He was the man that had been watching the Stanton crime scene.

"Just take it easy," said the sheriff. "It will all be explained."

Katie stared at him and knew better than to say anything that she might regret.

McGaven took a chair but Katie remained standing.

"This is Special Agent Dane Campbell with the California High Crimes Task Force," the sheriff began.

Katie was surprised but still didn't trust the man, based on the way he'd so quickly left the crime scene as she approached him.

"He works high profile and serial murder cases, based out of Sacramento. Special Agent Campbell, this is Detective Katie Scott and Deputy Sean McGaven."

Campbell nodded. "Nice to meet you both." He smiled broadly at Katie.

McGaven gave his solemn nod in greeting.

"Special Agent Campbell," she said. "Can you please explain to me why you were at the crime scene on Friday?"

The sheriff looked directly at Campbell, waiting for an answer.

Campbell chuckled and calmly explained. "I was just briefing Sheriff Scott about everything."

"That's it?"

"Detective Scott, take a seat," said the sheriff.

Katie was about to say something, but dutifully, she took a chair and waited.

"I will let Agent Campbell explain."

The room became quiet with an uneasy silence. Campbell waited a few extra seconds before he began—as if he wanted to build more tension.

Katie kept her eyes directly on him, trying to get a read on him.

"We've been working on three homicides that we suspect are linked," he began, opening one of three files before him on the desk. The folder contained several photographs and reports. "Victim number one: Nancy Day, thirty-four years old, single, she taught Administration of Justice at a junior college in Placer County. She was found on a bench on the school grounds three years ago, throat cut, body posed, and her charm bracelet hanging in one of the trees like an ornament." He passed Katie a few of the photos.

She slowly thumbed through them, immediately noticing that the body position was indeed posed, reminding her of a doll or a character in a play. There was dramatic makeup in dark reds drawn around the victim's lips and eyes. Her long dark hair appeared combed and styled. It was clear that the killer wanted to express a message. But what?

"Who found her?" Katie asked.

"The first person who drove into Littleton College, who was the security officer by the name of Maynard Brighton. Luckily, after he called the police they were able to stop the students and faculty from seeing the crime scene. He has since been cleared of any possible involvement."

"Administration of Justice. That would be mostly people wanting to become police officers or paralegals, lawyers…" she said.

"Yes. Also county and state jobs as well."

Katie was intrigued by the crime scene and the potential motive of the killer. She looked at all the photos again—pausing on a close-up of the neck wound.

"Victim number two, Gwen Sanderson, thirty-one years old, she owned a small restaurant/deli called Gwen's Place, had a boyfriend in Sierra County, and was well liked by the community." He handed Katie the photos.

Katie passed McGaven the pictures of victim Nancy Day.

"Gwen Sanderson's body was found two years ago at a Western resort, Roy's Bed and Breakfast Dude Ranch, which was being remodeled and was closed for the winter," explained Campbell.

Katie examined the photos of the body attached to a wooden fence at the entrance to the ranch. The body was also posed like a broken doll, with dramatic makeup drawn on her face. Bruises were prominent. Her body was bloodier than the first victim's. Her throat was also cut, revealing a gaping hole.

Katie finally looked at Campbell and said, "What piece of jewelry was found? A ring?" She had seen the significant damage to her fingers, as if there had been a struggle.

"Very astute, Detective. Yes, it was an antique diamond ring her grandmother had given her on her twenty-first birthday. It was tied with a piece of red ribbon on the post next to her." He handed her the photo of the ring.

Katie saw that the ribbon was tied nicely and evenly.

"I'm familiar with how you and McGaven operate, retracing the crime scenes from the beginning," said Campbell.

"What do these cases have to do with us?" Katie looked at the sheriff. "These counties aren't our jurisdiction." She continued to study the crime scene characteristics.

"Do we have a cold case that is linked?" asked McGaven. He was clearly intrigued by the cases as he studied them.

Agent Campbell opened another file. "Third victim, Jeanine Trenton, twenty-seven years old, health care specialist, found impaled in her backyard in Raven Woods, in your Sequoia County, by her best friend, about a year ago."

Katie looked at the agent.

"Why wasn't she in the cold case files? I don't recall the name or case."

"Her case was tagged a couple of weeks after her murder investigation by the California Task Force as possibly linked to the other cases," said the sheriff. "The case had been put on hold after we had exhausted every avenue available. The case was transferred to the California Task Force."

Katie looked surprised.

"This case was before you came home," the sheriff said.

"I see," she said, handing back the crime scene photos. "I still don't see what this has to do with me and Gav. I'm sure that Special Agent Campbell has an entire team of investigators to work on these cases."

Sheriff Scott glanced at Campbell and said, "They've exhausted every avenue and have come to us for assistance. He has been impressed by our cold case closure rate and success—"

Campbell interrupted, "I've been authorized to recruit who I see fit and you, Detective Scott and Deputy McGaven, are who I've chosen to work these cases."

Katie's initial anger about how Campbell had presented himself had slowly dissipated, but she was still skeptical about his motives. Something seemed amiss about the entire situation, but she couldn't pinpoint what bothered her. Glancing at McGaven, he gave her a positive look, meaning that he was game.

"Wait a minute. Please forgive me for a moment. I assume I can speak candidly," she said.

"Of course," said the sheriff.

"What are the dates of the murders again? They are a year apart?"

Campbell nodded, watching her closely.

"I see. So you've reached the point where you've exhausted every avenue, have no new leads and now they are cold cases—but you're hypothesizing that the killer is going to kill again," she said. "By my quick calculation it could be anytime now. Is that about right?"

"Yes."

Katie looked to her uncle and it was difficult to read him. She sighed, making sure her pulse remained steady and calm. "My first loyalty is to the Pine Valley Sheriff's Department working our cold cases. It's Sheriff Scott's decision, not mine."

The sheriff smiled for the first time since the start of the meeting. "I agree with Agent Campbell and I will not stand in the way of these cases. The third victim is in our jurisdiction and is *our* cold case. That would be where you would start."

"Who will we be working for?" she asked.

"You will still report to me as usual," said the sheriff. "And Agent Campbell will be kept up to speed every step of the way. He will give you anything you need."

"Are we allowed to investigate our way? We will need everything you have on the cases—every note, photo, interview, speculation—*everything*."

"Of course."

"As with any investigation, we cannot guarantee the—"

"Of course, Detective, I'm well aware of that," he interrupted. "I wouldn't be here if I had another choice. But I have every confidence in you."

"Okay, this is settled, then, right?" said Sheriff Scott, looking directly at Katie.

"Can I use Cisco?"

"Of course."

"Who's Cisco?" the agent asked.

"My army K9."

Campbell smiled.

Katie looked to McGaven who subtly nodded. Looking at the photos now scattered across the sheriff's desk, she captured Campbell's gaze. "It's settled."

CHAPTER FOUR

Monday 1045 hours

Katie and McGaven waited while a courier wheeled three loads of boxes on a hand truck into the forensic lab, unloading them along the hallway next to their office.

"Wow," said McGaven, eyeing the boxes as they were stacked high.

"Looks like we've got our work cut out for us." Katie was amped to get started and began to dig through the files.

"How do you want to do this?" he said. "The boxes are marked by victim, date, and location."

"Let's start with Jeanine Trenton, as the sheriff suggested. She's in our jurisdiction and then we can move backwards."

"Sounds good," he said and grabbed two boxes, moving them into their office.

Katie did the same.

"Let's move the rest of the boxes into the storage across the hall," she said, hoisting more loads.

Within ten minutes, everything had vanished from the hallway and the boxes were put in order.

The cold case office was small but it sufficed, with two desks fitted in a T-shape. Two of the walls were filled with cupboards. A long counter with a sink occupied another wall, with several storage compartments underneath. Since they were in the forensic division, the offices were retrofitted with an area for forensic technicians to perform their specific duties, not for administrative assignments. A rolling whiteboard was pushed into one corner of the room and at the moment was wiped clean—ready for new information.

She and McGaven each had a box, marked "Trenton, Homicide, Raven Woods, Sequoia County." Katie opened hers and began sorting everything from the interviews—autopsy report, police reports, forensics, and photographs.

"You haven't really said how you feel about this," McGaven said, breaking the silence.

"It's another cold case."

"You know what I mean."

"It's a cold case," she repeated.

"Katie."

"Alright, yeah, this Campbell is a little sneaky and he strikes me as someone who follows his own rules and not the rules the rest of us have to abide by."

"You needed to get that out," he said and smiled.

"There's a ton of stuff here, but from what I can see, lots of duplicates." She sighed.

"Have you seen this?" he said and tossed over three photos of a house with boarded-up windows.

"Is that the Jeanine Trenton home?"

"Yep."

"Why are the windows boarded up?" Her interest had been piqued.

Flipping through some reports, McGaven said, "It seems that the house was vandalized not long after the murder, so they boarded the place up." He opened an envelope with a single house key. "How convenient."

"It hasn't been sold or rented? It's been a year."

"No. It had been willed to Jeanine Trenton by her grandmother, Ida Davies, two years previously. Completely paid for. Unfortunately, no one wants to buy it due to…"

"Someone being brutally murdered there." Katie finished his sentence.

"Exactly," he said, skimming through information. "I say—"

"We take a ride over to Raven Woods," she finished.

"Stop doing that," he said.

"What?"

"Finishing my—"

"Sentences. Isn't that what partners do?" For the first time since receiving the case, Katie smiled. "And it's your turn to buy lunch—and something better than a gas station burrito."

Dropping the files on his desk, he said, "Let's begin at the house as a starting point like we usually do—the crime scene," he said. "And what's wrong with those burritos?"

"I have to make a stop first."

"For?"

"Cisco."

CHAPTER FIVE

Monday 1350 hours

McGaven drove to Raven Woods, which was about half an hour from the department. He accelerated whenever he could, just out of habit as an ex-patrol officer.

Riding shotgun gave Katie some time to read through the investigation files in more detail. She tapped her finger on the photo of Jeanine Trenton's necklace hanging on the fence, hoping to decipher what the killer was trying to convey.

"Nice ring," he said.

"What? Oh," she said, looking at her own engagement ring.

"How's the wedding planning going?"

"It's going."

"You two still haven't picked a date yet? Where are you going for your honeymoon?"

"We're working on it. Still trying to figure out if we want a small, intimate wedding or something more festive. So many decisions."

McGaven glanced at his partner. His face clouded as he seemed to be trying to figure out what was bothering her.

A low whine came from the back seat, shortly followed by a dog face squeezing itself in between McGaven and Katie.

"Hey, buddy," said McGaven, scratching the dog behind his ears. To Katie, he said, "I'm glad you wanted to bring him today."

"I feel guilty leaving him home, but it can't be helped. And it's great that Sergeant Hardy from K9 allows me to kennel him whenever I bring him to work."

"Yeah well, he's a lucky dog. Right, Cisco?"

The jet-black dog let out a couple of barks in agreement.

They headed south through open mountains with slight rolling hills. It wasn't until they reached more heavily wooded areas that the sign "Raven Woods" appeared. They were about ten minutes from arriving downtown.

"What's the road we need to take?" asked McGaven.

Looking through the paperwork, Katie said, "One sixty-seven Fox Hunt Road."

"Did you leave a message for Agent Campbell?"

"Yep. I told him we were going to the house to have a look around."

"Think he's still in town?"

"No."

"Why not?"

"That guy high-tailed it out of here after dropping off all the information."

"Hmm."

"What?" she asked.

"He strikes me as a micro-manager."

"Maybe. But my money is on him being back at his nice big office in Sacramento by now."

"Agree to disagree."

Katie laughed. "Okay. That's such a weird term every time I hear it."

McGaven reduced his speed and turned off the main road, driving until he reached a faded sign indicating Fox Hunt Road. It was an older part of town with houses more than thirty years old, more acreage, and most properties seemed well maintained.

They crept along, the overhanging tree limbs making it feel dark. Looking for number 167, McGaven searched the mailboxes… 163… 165… finally coming to the end of the road.

Craning her neck, Katie said, "Is this it?"

"Matches the photos and address."

"Yeah, but it looks worse than when the photos were taken."

McGaven parked on the street across from the driveway.

Cisco whined, wanting to get out and work.

Still looking at the small house with boarded-up windows, Katie got out and stood on the road, taking everything in. "Stay, Cisco."

McGaven cracked the windows for the dog and exited the vehicle. He stood beside Katie as they scrutinized the house and property.

Katie studied the short single-car driveway leading up to the small, blue, one-story house. Heavy plywood and some metal reinforcement secured the home tightly. Katie noted the overgrown bushes and peeling paint. The drainpipes and gutters were disconnected from the corners and hung precariously. The fence was leaning and the gate stood open. The entire property appeared oddly out of place compared to the rest of the homes in the neighborhood—almost as if it belonged in a war-torn country. It was clear that it would be a hard sale if the house were put on the market.

"What do you think?" she said. "Can we learn anything new?" She began to think that they had wasted a trip.

"You can always learn something new," he said.

"Really?"

"Of course. You told me that at our first crime scene."

Katie chuckled. "Gav, you always keep me on my toes."

McGaven opened the trunk and retrieved a few tools: two screwdrivers, a crowbar, and two flashlights.

"Good idea." Katie took one of the flashlights. She adjusted her holster and gun, slipped her cell into her pocket, and shed her jacket. "From the looks of the yard, we may need a machete," she said, with some humor.

"I'll have to remember that next time I pack my gear."

They walked across the street and headed to the front door.

Katie stopped and listened. This was a routine approach for her when walking into any unknown area, knowing how important it was to listen and feel a situation and not just use your eyes. It was a tactic she had adopted in the military on so many occasions. She noticed that it was extremely quiet, even during the day—there wasn't the sound of any traffic and the road wasn't close to any freeway. She imagined the killer knew the area and used the quiet and seclusion to their advantage. The next-door neighbor was approximately a half-acre away and there were three large pine trees blocking the direct view of the house.

Leaning up against the fence were several bamboo poles that appeared to have been used for a sprinkler system instead of the usual PVC piping. A shovel and post-hole digger leaned up against a tree. There was a small narrow trench leading to the house, but that had long since been abandoned without any of the bamboo poles laid.

Katie focused on the cottage and walked up to meet McGaven, who was already looking at the door. He pried the metal away from the frame using the crowbar.

"The door is still intact and it looks like the key will work."

"I wish there was an easier way to enter than prying off the plywood," she said. Then she observed, "There's no garage." Thinking about it more, she said, "Let's go around the back. According to the reports, there is a sliding door. We can check out the crime scene area too."

McGaven followed Katie.

Normally they would split up when searching an unknown area and report back to one another, but this time they walked together through the open gate and headed to the backyard.

Katie recalled the photos she'd seen in the file of the backyard from the fence perspective and was surprised by how oversized it was in real life. It dwarfed the house. There was a small cement patio partially covered by a plastic corrugated roof attached to the house. Beyond this stretched a sizeable, rural backyard with apparently no landscape design—just untamed wilderness.

The weeds and dried bushes crunched underneath Katie's boots. "This is…"

"Like a jungle," replied McGaven.

"To say the least," she said. "According to the photographs, the body was found at the back part of the property—eastside. There should be wrought-iron fencing."

"Lead the way."

Katie tried to image how the killer had gained access.

Did the killer lie in wait in the house?

Did Jeanine Trenton know her killer?

She remembered the condition of the body: Jeanine's feet were cut and bloody as if she had tried to outrun her killer. Her shoes weren't found. She had been getting ready for a party, but she never left. The report revealed everyone else invited to the party attended—except two people. One was sick and the other decided to go to another friend's party instead. During Agent Campbell's thorough investigation, every person in Jeanine's life had been questioned and later dismissed as a potential suspect in the murder. Katie and McGaven had skimmed the information.

There was a group of large pine trees in a semicircle. Katie and McGaven squeezed around and immediately saw the black wrought-iron fence along the entire back part of the property. They turned east and stopped. A small piece of yellow crime scene tape was still tied around one of the posts.

"I think this is it," said McGaven.

"Yeah, it seems right." Looking from side to side, and then gazing out past the property lines, she saw a large farm acreage.

In the distance, cows were grazing. "The killer probably wouldn't enter this property from this area."

McGaven was quiet.

"What are you thinking?"

"The other bodies were posed in public places. But… why here? It's private."

"That bothers me too. And it's one of the reasons I wanted to see the crime scene area in person." She looked at the place which she estimated was where Jeanine's body had been impaled on the fence. "According to the autopsy report, she had more defensive wounds than the others, which means she fought her killer with everything she had."

"Maybe the killer didn't have enough time to take her body anywhere else?" he said.

Katie pondered that idea. "I don't think there's much out here that will help us."

"Except."

"Except?"

"We know that the killer might have been pushed to do something that they weren't expecting."

"And if this killer is indeed a serial killer, as Campbell's investigation suggests, they would normally become more practiced and comfortable with each successive attack—more confident about creating such elaborate crime scenes," she said.

"Something seems to have changed here."

"Let's take a look inside," Katie said.

As they walked back to the house, Katie considered what might have happened after the initial attack: Jeanine had tried to get away. If she was being chased the only way she could escape would be to jump the fence and try to get to another neighbor's house located behind the property. It was probably a few acres away. But why didn't she go next door or up the street?

"This slider is completely boarded up. Let's go in the front door."

"Okay," she said.

McGaven took a few moments to jimmy the metal bars loose and pry the plywood sheet from the front door.

Again, Katie was struck by how quiet the street and surrounding areas were. The screeching sound of the metal bars being pried loose overpowered the stillness.

She glanced to the car and could see the distinct outline of Cisco's head and ears—motionless and watching every move they made.

"Got it," said McGaven with a grin on his face. He had removed enough of the bars and boarding to create a narrow gap, through which he squeezed his tall body. The door was open and the key wasn't necessary.

Katie easily slipped through behind him.

Darkness greeted them.

McGaven flipped on a flashlight and Katie followed his example. It was almost entirely dark because of the coverings over the windows. Only tiny cracks of light peeked through.

Katie thought she heard Cisco bark once and then a strange hollow knock at the front. Straining to listen for a moment, she heard nothing except for her own shallow breathing and felt only her slightly accelerated heartbeat. Claustrophobia was starting to set in, one of her symptoms when PTSD surfaced. This wasn't an unusual reaction under unknown circumstances—which she worked hard to keep under control by regulated breathing and positive visualizations.

Katie moved in one direction and McGaven the other. The sweeping motions of their flashlight beams danced across the walls. They didn't reveal anything unusual.

Since the house was small, it was easy to see most of the interior by standing in the middle of the living room. There was still furniture, covered with white sheets. It looked like two small couches, a coffee table, two end tables, and a small dining table.

There was a faintly musty smell, mixed with something Katie couldn't immediately identify.

"I wonder what they are going to do with the house?" asked McGaven.

"It's a nice piece of property. Maybe someone will want to buy it and knock down the house, build a new one."

McGaven had a new thought. "Hey, where do you think her personal belongings are?"

"There's probably an attorney involved."

"I'll find out and see if we can have a look at her things," he said.

Katie and McGaven met back in the kitchen. Strangely, all the appliances had been removed, leaving weird gaps. The cupboards were still full of dishes, pots and pans.

"That's odd," she said and felt light-headed as she spoke. She wavered a bit, causing her to lower the flashlight.

"Katie?"

"I don't know. I'm not feeling well."

"Let's get outside and grab some fresh air," he said.

"Okay," she said weakly. She saw McGaven go to the front door but after a moment, he began pounding on it.

"What's wrong?"

"It's stuck."

Katie walked toward McGaven but her feet felt oddly heavy and the room began to spin. She fell to her knees. Trying to focus, she caught the distinct odor. "Gav, it's gas."

McGaven was swinging the crowbar, but the remaining metal coverings wouldn't move. He turned and saw Katie struggling. "Hey, I can smell it too." He took hold of Katie and steered her to the back sliding door. He stumbled too, obviously becoming overwhelmed by the escaping gas filling the house.

Holding her flashlight as tight as she could, she saw what McGaven was going to do. The slider was jammed and wouldn't budge. The only option was to smash the sliding glass door and then break the external plywood boarding. Katie leaned against the wall, trying to concentrate and keeping her mind conscious—fighting the unsettling disorientation. That's when she heard Cisco barking in rapid succession.

Someone was outside.

McGaven pulled his gun.

Katie realized what he was going to do and yelled, "No! The flash could ignite the gas." Her words seemed foreign and faraway.

Cisco continued to bark.

He swayed as he re-holstered the weapon. It was obvious that he too was fighting unsteadiness and confusion.

Katie used the opposite end of her flashlight and began pounding on the glass, spider cracks spreading rapidly.

McGaven swung the tire iron and with the third whack the glass shattered, pieces flying everywhere.

Kicking and smashing at the plywood almost seemed useless, but they kept trying.

Katie couldn't exert any more energy; her body was weakening and she fell to her knees, trying to catch any fresh air coming from outside. There was a tiny crack on the left side of the plywood where she could feel a slight breeze on her face. She desperately tried to bring oxygen into her lungs.

She turned to McGaven who had also dropped to his knees, but was still hammering at the wood—splintering it a little bit at a time. Pulling out her cell phone, she dialed 911 and was just able to say: *"Officers need help... 167 Fox Hunt Road..."* Katie looked down and saw her untucked blouse. Tearing a large section from the bottom into two pieces, she tied one around her nose and mouth, and then crawled to McGaven, helping him with his.

"Stay low," she said, remembering an army training exercise on poisonous gas.

He nodded. His eyes looked glassy as he struggled to stay conscious.

Katie rolled onto her back. She began kicking the plywood and was soon joined by McGaven. The large sheet of plywood began to break.

Cisco's barking became louder in between the kicking.

Katie saw Cisco's body through a small opening and his paws digging at the wood.

"Stay back, Cisco!"

Finally, the wood covering broke away. The fresh air rushing inside was the best thing Katie had experienced in a while.

Cisco leaped inside and began pulling Katie out. She turned and saw McGaven crawling on his hands and knees behind her.

They inched and crawled their way into the backyard to a safe distance with Cisco in the lead.

"Easy, Cisco. We're okay," she said, flopping onto her back, trying to take in as much air as possible.

The dog circled the two, licking one, then the other, until he seemed satisfied that they were okay.

Katie rolled onto her side next to McGaven. "You okay?" she said, coughing.

"I'll live."

Sirens sounded in the distance, approaching fast.

"Good," she said, relieved, as she stayed close to her partner and watched the natural color return to his face.

"You hear it too?"

"Yeah."

"Good to know," he said and flopped back on the ground.

CHAPTER SIX

Monday 1455 hours

Katie sat in one of the ambulances with an oxygen mask on, breathing easier and steadying her nerves. She was not only struggling with her anxious energy due to the stressful circumstances, she was also fighting back the anger. In her mind, she still saw Agent Campbell's aloof demeanor mixed with some well-placed compliments in the sheriff's office. And now she and McGaven had been sent into a precarious situation. Did he know it would potentially be dangerous?

Cisco had been returned to the police sedan—he sat stoically, watching the events unfold. Somehow, Katie surmised, in his urgent need to get to her aid, the dog had pressed the door remote control she had left behind, which had released the back door. She generally had it hooked to her waist when she was going somewhere alone, but since she had McGaven she felt it wasn't needed.

She watched as firefighters checked the entire house and found that the gas had been turned back on—it had originally been shut off when the house was boarded up.

Several deputies walked down the street and knocked on doors to see if anyone had noticed anything suspicious at the Trenton house.

"You feeling better?" the attendant asked.

"Much better," she said. Her focus had sharpened and her balance became normal again. Taking the mask off, she said, "I'm going to check on my partner."

The attendant nodded.

As soon as Katie's feet hit the ground, she felt like herself. In fact, she had a renewed energy. She saw McGaven still sporting his oxygen mask and quickly climbed into the ambulance and sat next to him.

"I'm feeling a bit of déjà vu," she said.

McGaven pulled the mask away. "I hate that expression."

"You okay?" she asked, ignoring his last comment.

"I'll live. Is Cisco okay?"

"He's fine. I don't know how he pressed the remote to release the back door, but he's special."

"That's true."

"They haven't said anything official yet, but I think someone tampered with the gas and helped to seal us inside."

"It speaks volumes," he said.

"Meaning?"

"There was something that they didn't want us to see."

"The killer?"

"Yeah, something."

"Something? Investigators have been all over this property and it's been sitting vacant for a while. So why now?"

"I don't know. Maybe they don't want any more investigators here. Maybe they don't want *us* to investigate."

"Us?"

"Katie, you do understand that there have been news stories about us, especially you, and how we solve and close cold cases. It's intimidating to killers out there."

Katie smiled. "I love your viewpoint."

"I'm glad."

"I—"

"Agent Campbell." McGaven took a few breaths from the oxygen mask.

Katie looked directly at him, her eyes wide.

"Something feels off about these cases… or maybe 'contrived' would be a better word."

"I feel the same way."

McGaven coughed a few times.

"You sure you're okay?"

"Yep."

Katie turned her attention to the house.

What was so imperative that the killer, or someone else, didn't want them to see?

"What?"

"I'll be right back," she said.

Katie went to the deputies and requested that they have forensics dust for any prints around the front door area. One deputy nodded and put in the call.

"Detective Scott?" said Fire Captain Anderson.

"Yes?"

"Glad you're feeling better. Any longer, and you and your partner would be in the hospital right now—or worse. Someone had jammed the front door with a stone."

"What about the gas line?"

"It had been tampered with recently and turned back on, but there wasn't anything in the kitchen to hook it up to. The gas caps had been removed, so it just flowed in."

"How can you tell?" she said.

"This house had the electricity and gas turned off more than six months ago, according the utility company."

Katie frowned. "What does it take to turn it back on?"

"The gas is on and available. It just depends if it's turned on for each residence. Someone would need just a wrench to reconnect it to the line."

"I see."

"So you're taking over the homicide case?" he asked with curiosity.

"Yes, we're looking into it."

"Good to know," he said. "Poor girl, she deserves some justice."

"Were you on the original call?"

He looked down. "Unfortunately. Not something you easily forget."

"No, it isn't. Thank you, Captain, for the update."

"If you need anything else…"

"No, we're good for now."

Katie took another look at the house. The windows were now open for ventilation and a couple of firefighters were still checking everything. Suddenly, she saw something underneath the eaves. At first, she thought it was some type of connection for cable or the internet. Then she realized it was a small security camera. Not wanting to bring attention to it, at least for now, she kept walking and returned to McGaven, making a mental note that she wanted to see footage from the camera and find out where was it streaming.

"What's up?" he said. He looked back to his usual self.

"Someone intentionally tried to gas us to death."

"Oh, is that all?"

"You're right. Someone really didn't want us here—they wanted to kill us, or at least take us out of the game."

"Game?"

Turning to him, in a serious tone, "You sure you're up for it? For this? No matter what it brings?"

"You bet. I always have your back. I want to catch this killer even more now."

"Me too." She smiled, thinking about some of the close calls they had experienced together. Their partnership was solid.

"What do you want to do?" He put the oxygen mask down.

"I think we need some solid, straightforward answers."

"From?"

"From the beginning."

"Agent Campbell." They both said.

CHAPTER SEVEN

Monday 1945 hours

"This is nice," said Katie as she took another sip of wine and relaxed.

"I know we haven't spent that much time together recently," said Chad as he returned to the couch with a glass. He snuggled in close.

"We both have jobs that require more than the nine to five routine. And that's okay. We can make it work."

Chad squeezed her hand.

"Okay, I've known you most of your life. And I know something is bothering you." Katie studied Chad with a sinking feeling.

"Just things going on at work," he said, trying to avoid her gaze. "You know what I mean."

Katie turned her body to face him. "You can tell me anything. There isn't anything that we can't overcome and work out."

Cisco sensed Katie's change of mood and came over to her, lying down at her feet.

"What is bothering you?" she said gently. "I've sensed it ever since you arrived tonight."

"Nothing that can't be discussed later."

"Oh no," she said playfully. "You don't get away that easily."

"What are you going to do—interrogate me?"

"I can… and I'll win." She took another sip of the wine, savoring the flavor and the quiet alone moments with the person that she loved more than anyone.

Chad looked down at his hands, hesitating. "I didn't want to ruin tonight."

"Ruin?" Katie was now concerned.

"Maybe that's not the right word. I have something I want to talk to you about."

"Okay," she said and set her glass on the coffee table.

"I went to that conference and met a lot of people."

"Yeah, the Firefighters' Association conference." Katie knew about it, but she was on edge now, seeing how much he was struggling with something.

"Well, I met with the Commander for the Los Angeles County Fire Department. His name is Ron Fairfield. We actually talked quite a bit."

Katie listened intently, trying to figure out his body language as he struggled to tell her something that was clearly extremely important because it was difficult for him to say.

"Well, to make a long story short… We talked about the job of fire investigator and it's been something that I've been interested in for a while."

Katie nodded. "Yeah, even when we were kids. Ever since the McClellan family house burned down, you wanted to do something important and investigate arson."

"Well, there's a training program that's very difficult to get into. You have to be invited."

"And you got an invitation?" she said.

"Yep."

"Oh, that's great! I'm so happy for you." She leaned in and kissed him, relieved that it was something positive.

"Wait a minute."

"What?"

"I start my training in a few days."

"Okay?" she said, surprised he hadn't told her anything about it before signing up.

"And it's for six months in Los Angeles."

"Oh," she said as her heart sank. "What about…?"

"Our wedding?" he said. "We will have to postpone it for a while longer. But we haven't set a date yet…"

"Okay," she said slowly.

"Katie, I've been waiting for something like this my entire life. And now I get the chance to train."

"I know," she said, forcing a smile. Inside, she felt abandoned. "You so deserve this."

"I've loved you my entire life, even when I was five years old. Every time I have good news or bad, you're the first person I want to talk to. I want you to be the first person I see in the morning and the last at night."

"We've been through a lot. Your mom's cancer and the death of my parents. We can get through anything." She made herself comfortable next to Chad. Not wanting to talk about it anymore, they passed the evening with the usual conversation. There was a subtle tension between them, but it wasn't about Chad going to LA. It was about a huge change coming, affecting their relationship. Katie wasn't completely convinced if they could survive the distance issue.

Katie's mood was downcast, which was unusual for her. She didn't feel like doing anything but going to bed after Chad left. She couldn't shake the strange feeling that her life was going to be turned upside-down. These unorthodox cold cases and Chad leaving for six months made her uneasy.

The evening turned colder and she snuggled in bed with Cisco at her feet. Katie slowly fell into a sound sleep for once, without killers, suspects, and flashbacks of her time in Afghanistan running throughout her dreams.

Her cell phone interrupted her peaceful slumber.

Katie jerked awake and automatically checked the time: the clock read 2:35 in the morning.

Picking up the cell, she said, "Hello?" her voice groggy.

"Katie?"

"Uncle Wayne? What's wrong? You okay?"

"I'm fine. You need to come to the fairgrounds through the west gate," he stated simply. It wasn't a request.

Katie sat up, fighting her sleepiness. "What? Why?"

"McGaven is on his way, as well as Special Agent Campbell. I expect you to be here in fifteen minutes."

"What is it?" she managed to say, bracing for the worst.

"Homicide. Another woman has been found. Signs indicate the same MO as Jeanine Trenton's killer."

"I'm on my way," she said, getting out of bed.

"See you in fourteen minutes."

The call disconnected.

CHAPTER EIGHT

Tuesday 0255 hours

Katie got ready to go in record time, pulling on a pair of jeans, T-shirt, jacket, and boots. She broke most speed limits all the way to the fairgrounds. Luckily, due to the early morning hour, the traffic was extremely light, making the journey that much faster. She opted to leave Cisco at home this time.

As she drove around to the west gate of the fairgrounds, Katie noted that this would be the entry point for the livestock areas. It was also next to the rides. She remembered the layout of the area based on her visits to the fair. She saw the flashing lights and a myriad of first responders and police cars ahead.

She eased her Jeep up to the gate and stopped where a deputy was stationed. He opened the gate.

Rolling down her window and showing her identification, she said, "Detective Scott."

The deputy waved her inside and motioned to the area where the other vehicles were parked.

Katie recognized McGaven's truck, her uncle's SUV, the forensic van, the medical examiner's van, fire truck, and several deputy cruisers. There was also another SUV that she didn't immediately recognize.

Still stunned by yesterday's events and the news that Chad would be leaving for six months, Katie pushed herself harder, trying to put everything behind her and focus on this victim. Her heart felt attacked but she wasn't broken.

Pulling up next to McGaven's truck, Katie cut the engine and quickly got out of the car. The lights she was seeing weren't from police cars or emergency first responders, but from one of the rides. She spotted her uncle.

The flashing lights were suddenly extinguished.

Katie walked toward the sheriff, but was met by McGaven. "Hey," he said.

"And again, you beat me here. Have you seen the victim yet?" she asked.

"No. It's like a closed set or something," said McGaven.

Katie waited a moment but the sheriff was speaking with officers and a young woman that she didn't know. She decided to jump ahead and have a look at the crime scene to see what they were in for.

But as she started walking, she was quickly intercepted. "Detective Scott," said her uncle. "I need to speak with you."

Katie was beginning to get impatient, but dutifully, she turned back to meet up with him.

"Yes?"

"I want you to meet Agent Dawn Haley," he said.

"I'm…" she began.

"Yes, I know you're Detective Katie Scott. Oh my gosh, it's so nice to meet you," said the perky agent, nervously moving around. She was petite, with shoulder-length brown hair that moved every time she spoke. She didn't seem to be dressed appropriately for a crime scene.

Katie studied her for a moment, unable to believe that this young woman, obviously a rookie—maybe thirty?—was at a homicide scene. "Nice to meet you." She turned to the sheriff. "When can I see the crime scene?"

"Agent Campbell and I have spoken and we're in agreement that you run the scene with McGaven, and Agents Campbell and Haley are spectators."

Katie wondered if she had heard him correctly and hesitated a moment before speaking again. "Uh, am I missing something here?"

"Not at all. The crime scene is yours. It appears to be connected to your cold cases."

Katie knew that look the sheriff gave when he wasn't going to answer any more questions and it was time to get to work.

"It's this way," said McGaven.

It was a relief to Katie to hear her partner's voice—something pulling her into reality and making her feel grounded.

Katie and McGaven walked past John Blackburn, the forensics manager, who was getting ready to work the scene when they were done. He nodded to them.

They reached the ride and approached the Ferris wheel—where two deputies were erecting a cordon—for a closer look.

"You ready?" Katie said softly to McGaven.

"As I'll ever be…"

"Turn the lights on like it was when we arrived," said a loud voice behind them. It was Agent Campbell, hanging back far enough from the crime area but close enough to see it. He was accompanied by rookie Agent Haley.

Katie walked up to the ride, remembering all the times she had ridden it during her childhood. Each car was painted a different color and was attached to a large wheel that would take the cars around in a full revolution. When you were at the top, you could see for miles. It had been one of her favorite rides as a child.

Another deputy went to the controls, turned the main emergency switch clockwise, and then pulled a lever. Instantly, the ride roared to life with bright colorful lights and irritating fairy-tale music, the jolly melody mocking the seriousness of the murder scene. The cars came around in turn, all empty—except for one where a solitary rider remained frozen in her seat.

"Stop!" yelled Katie. She raised her hands to halt the ride.

As it drew to a halt, she approached the car. The blaring music continued, which she found distracting. Reaching into her pockets, she retrieved a pair of exam gloves and slipped them on. As she came closer, she could see that the car held a woman, with long blonde hair, sitting up straight. It was eerie and surreal, and Katie was reminded of the feeling of walking into a carnival funhouse, half expecting something to jump out at her.

Her pulse raced and familiar heavy anxiety invaded her stomach, the feeling changing to a nervous energy.

Closer still, she could see the gaping hole across the woman's neck. Her head was positioned facing directly forward and her dead gaze fell directly on Katie. It was one of those looks that seemed to follow you around—almost as if the lifeless girl was condemning everyone at the location. It stopped Katie cold. She shook off the unnerving feeling and focused on the rest of the body inside the small car.

"Hey, could someone turn off the music?" said Katie. "And we need some lighting over here." McGaven handed her a flashlight and she flipped it on, beginning with the examination of the victim's face.

The exaggerated lipstick, rouge, and eye shadow created the same creepy appearance of the other victims, indicating the same MO. It didn't relate to the cause of death, but added the visual drama the killer wanted. The poor young woman obviously went through hell and ended up a killer's prize.

The music finally stopped, leaving a welcome silence.

Katie leaned closer. It was difficult to see at first under the greasy makeup, but her skin was grossly pale, almost translucent. This time the bright blood-red lipstick wasn't just an exaggeration around the natural lips, but was drawn in a downward curve that resembled a sad clown. The dark purple eye shadow went completely around her eyes, making her look like she had been punched in the face. The blush was a hot pink and smudged down her cheekbones in no special technique—but almost as an afterthought. Her forearms were sliced in a crisscross pattern that indicated defense wounds and several of her fingers appeared broken—disjointed and bluish. The victim had undoubtedly fought for her life.

Who are you?

How did you cross paths with this killer?

"This time the makeup doesn't make her look like a creepy doll, but as if she was beaten up," said Katie, trying to maintain her professionalism in the face of the heinous crime in front of her. "The killer possibly wants to draw attention to abuse?" She thought about the reality of the killer escalating.

McGaven studied the victim's face as well. "A warning of some kind?"

"Of things to come…" she said in a quiet tone.

Three construction lights on tripods went up and immediately illuminated far beyond the crime scene. It looked like daylight until you saw the dark edges just out of view.

Katie felt more conspicuous after the bright lights went on, as if she were on a stage—the killer's stage. There were many people watching the investigation unfold—specifically, watching Katie examine the victim and the surrounding area. She caught sight of John waiting patiently in the darkness to begin documenting and collecting evidence.

"Who was the first officer at the scene?" she asked McGaven. "And who called it in?"

McGaven left her side to gather information.

Focusing back on the Ferris wheel car, Katie noticed the victim's hair had been triple knotted and secured to the metal bar.

Unusual technique.

Why?

She surmised that the killer wanted the victim looking straight ahead.

At attention?

Eyes on the killer?

The victim's throat looked to have been cut with something extremely sharp, judging by the smooth edges of the gaping skin. The knife, or cutting device, was steady and sliced in a straight horizontal line.

Someone with experience in the medical profession?

Katie could ascertain that the blade went deep enough to cut almost through the vertebrae, but Dr. Dean would have to give the expert opinion.

McGaven returned with a heavyset deputy with the name Pendleton on his ID tag.

"Detective Scott," he said and nodded in respect.

"Deputy Pendleton, can you tell me about the call that got you here and what you saw?" asked Katie.

"We received a call from someone who didn't identify themselves but stated that there was a missing person found at the fairgrounds."

"Missing person?"

"Yes, ma'am."

"Did they say who?"

"No, ma'am."

"Any other description, like if it was a man or woman?"

"Negative."

"Dispatch couldn't tell if it was a man or woman?"

"The person whispered."

"Did you enter from the west gate?"

"Yes, it was already open."

"Unlocked? Or was the gate wide open?" she asked, realizing that the killer wanted the body to be found quickly—leaving the gate open was like an invitation.

"The gate was open."

"What did you see as you drove in?"

"Nothing at first, but I heard the music. I drove around and flashed the spotlight in every corner."

"And?"

"I was initially looking for the missing person, but didn't see anyone. Something didn't seem right. We didn't receive any details, whether it was a man, woman, or what they were wearing. Then my concern was that someone might be hiding—especially in the livestock areas. Or maybe that it might possibly be an ambush."

"Was the music going the entire time?"

"Yes. I'm not sure but it seemed to get louder—and not because I drove closer."

"Did you see anything unusual?"

"No, so I called in my position and moved toward the music." He took a breath. "I saw the Ferris wheel in motion with lights flashing."

Out of her peripheral vision, Katie saw Agent Campbell and his assistant agent move in closer to hear the conversation, but staying respectfully distanced. They leaned in to each other, obviously whispering. She ignored them and focused on what the deputy was saying. She had again that strange, prickly feeling of being part of a movie set, or a play.

The tall bright lights.

The focus on her, center stage.

The posing of the body.

Katie's mind raced and her heart was heavy as she thought about the victim.

Is that what the killer wanted?

To be the center of attention? The killer more than the victim?

"What did you do next?" Katie kept her tone professional but she was intrigued by the chain of events.

"I stopped in front of the Ferris wheel and stepped out of my cruiser. That's when I saw the vic and radioed immediately and requested backup. I didn't stop the ride because I didn't want to touch anything. I got back into the car to wait for backup to arrive to search the fairgrounds in case the perp was still here."

"Did you find anything?"

"No, ma'am. We finally turned off the ride and waited for you to arrive."

"Thank you, Deputy." Katie turned to address the group. "Okay, listen up!" she announced with all the calmness she could muster. "I want the entire fairgrounds searched. If a building or concession stand is locked, get the keys. I want search groups in teams of two. That means every building, every ride, and every stall in the livestock area. Be mindful that anything could be evidence, so don't attempt to retrieve or move it."

"What exactly are you looking for?" asked a deputy.

"Anything that might be related to the killer or victim. *Anything.* Something that is out of place or possibly planted, or dropped by the killer. But, specifically, there should be a piece of jewelry with a ribbon hanging somewhere, and some kind of knife. Please stay alert." She turned to Deputy Pendleton. "Can you organize the teams and report back?"

"Yes, ma'am," he said and smiled.

"Thank you."

The deputy hurried to the group of officers to coordinate.

McGaven leaned close to Katie. "You just made his day."

"What? Really?"

"You bet! If I was still on patrol and was asked to do that from a detective you might see a skip or two in my stride."

Katie smiled. "That I'd pay to see."

She turned back to the ride, taking a cleansing breath. Carefully moving around the compartments, she opened the ride car door so she could get closer to the body. Blood poured out like a light waterfall and spattered against the ground. Katie jumped back as quickly as she could but her boots and jeans took the brunt of it.

"You okay?" said McGaven.

"Yeah," she said sourly. "We now know that she was killed here and not somewhere else—because she bled out here."

With a feeble attempt, Katie tried to brush the blood away. It was no use. Her heart hammered and felt as if it would break. Remembering to breathe slowly, she tried to maintain her professional demeanor, but she couldn't shake the familiar feelings. She would have to continue the investigation saturated with the victim's blood until it dried or until she could make it home. Her immediate thought was that everyone was watching and assessing how she handled herself, so she forged on without hesitation. Her hands trembled slightly and she felt light-headed as she pushed away images of blown-up and bleeding soldiers from the battlefield. For some of them, she had been the last person they spoke to before death.

I can do this...

Katie carefully peered inside the car, not touching anything unnecessarily. The victim was wearing dark shorts and a sleeveless, light-colored top, which seemed odd, considering the temperature. It was too cold to wear such light clothing.

Was the victim dressed by the killer?

Before or after death? Planned or not?

Were the clothing pieces specific to what the killer wanted to convey? Summer? What was to come?

As if he'd read her mind, McGaven said, "She's dressed for summer. Is that on purpose, or a way of the killer trying to send us a message?"

"I'm not sure, but it is unusual for clothes to be chosen by the killer."

McGaven looked closer at the car and the body.

The victim was without shoes and her feet looked battered underneath all the blood. Two of her toes on her right foot appeared to be broken, judging by their odd position. They would know more when the victim was cleaned up and examined by Dr. Dean.

Katie took a pen and carefully moved the torn neckline of the top to see what appeared to be a heavily discolored area.

"Bruised?" he said.

"It looks like it."

"Maybe that's how the killer was able to get her into the car. Perhaps hitting her on the chest to either incapacitate or kill her. The killer could have partially drugged her... we'll have to see what the medical examiner has to say."

"We found something!" yelled a deputy.

CHAPTER NINE

Tuesday 0415 hours

The sheriff's deputy ran up to Katie and McGaven.

"What do you have?" said Katie.

"Shoes," he said breathlessly.

"Shoes?" she said.

"Yes, and blood."

"Show us."

Katie grabbed a walkie-talkie.

The deputy led them to an independent concession stand. It would have been easily missed on a general search. It was located between two buildings and in a darkened area. "Wait," he said. He turned on his flashlight and trailed the beam along the walkway. There were bloody barefoot prints leading away from the stand. Sitting in the ordering window were black, two-inch-heeled shoes.

"Let's get John over here to document this and collect evidence."

"I'm on it," said McGaven as he jogged back to the main area. "Anything else?"

"No. As soon as I saw this I didn't want to touch anything."

"Okay." Katie began to examine the area, waiting for John. There were some bloody fingerprints on the side of the food cart. She looked for any jewelry, but there was nothing.

"What have you found?" said John, as he approached with his gear and lights. One of the technicians, Rob, began taping off the area.

"Bloody footprints along the walkway, and fingerprints. Those shoes. I haven't found anything else."

John took his digital camera and began taking photographs for documentation.

"I'm going back to the main crime scene. I'll let you know when we're done with our initial assessment."

"Ten-four," he said with a smile.

As Katie made her way back to the victim's location, she heard a radio communication coming from Deputy Pendleton's radio.

"Found something at the livestock area," said another deputy.

Katie turned around and followed Deputy Pendleton. They hurried down adjoining rows of pens where large animals were housed. She was surprised that the searching deputies could find anything, given how huge the area was.

Katie spotted a couple of deputies waiting for her.

In the first pen—which was near the judging and presentation area—was a ring tied to a yellow ribbon. It swung slightly in the cool breeze. The dark stone was something like jade or a garnet, she wasn't sure.

It was like participating in a crime-themed scavenger hunt—never knowing quite where the evidence would be located. There was a playful quality about it.

Katie made sure she was on the correct radio channel before she requested the crime scene unit to cover this location. As she walked back to the primary location, several theories ran through her mind. It felt as if the killer was trying to make each scene bigger than the last. The fairgrounds were usually frequented by hundreds, if not thousands, of people during the season.

Maybe there's something important to the killer about this choice of location.

It connects with fun, family, and children.

But why a year apart?

Anniversary of something?

Katie knew that every passing year meant something to the killer. And as the victims were becoming more beaten-up and the throat-slashing neater and more experienced, it left her with a ton of evidence. Unfortunately, that's what the killer wanted.

She glanced around and observed everyone working—all except Agents Campbell and Haley.

"What's up?" asked McGaven.

"More evidence. Bloody fingerprints and bare footprints. John is working it."

Turning to her, he said: "Hey, what's up with you tonight?"

"Well, it's actually morning and soon the sun will come up."

"Something wrong?"

"It's a bit overwhelming and I'm still thinking about the gas incident," she said softly. "Now, it feels like all eyes are on us. Let's get back to work."

McGaven was going to say something, but held off.

Katie looked around for the agents and the sheriff, but they seemed to have disappeared and left the fairgrounds.

Katie and McGaven moved to a quieter and darker area as to not be overheard.

"We're not going to know any more until the vic is on the exam table and John has tested the evidence," she said.

"Who do you think did this?"

"You want me to rattle off a preliminary profile?"

"You bet."

"I don't like to do that, but there are some things that stand out to me."

"I'm not going to hold you to it," he said. "Just between you and me."

"I think the killer is someone who has endured abuse. The vic's body has some severe wounds. I think the killer has maybe gone through some horrific ordeal, or maybe someone close to them has—maybe someone they care about was murdered. The force is excessive, suggesting anger or rage—look at the severe damage to her arms, and what I assume to be broken fingers, as she defended herself." She paused to think about the entire area. "And they are creating these crime scenes in a way that makes sense to them—it's a way of working out their demons for everyone to see. Quite literally in our faces. Every year is telling—like an anniversary. Maybe it's during a time period where the inciting event or events happened."

"What else? I know you have more suspicions."

"Not really."

"C'mon, Katie, I can read you fairly well now—I know that you have more insights."

Katie glanced around to make sure that their conversation was still private. She looked at the dead woman as John documented the scene and the medical examiner's office waited to extract the body. She watched as the flash of the camera bounced around the area in a hypnotic display.

"And…"

"It all seems almost juvenile in execution. The over-exaggerated makeup and the long list of clues that don't really go anywhere—yet. We have more about motive, signature, and posed crime scenes. It takes time and energy to do this."

"So what's his motive?"

"The killer is playing with us."

"I would have to agree, but from previous crime scenes that we know of, there won't be another killing for a year."

"There's something different about this one. It seems more personal, more exaggerated with the sad clown face and the jewelry found further away from the body… as if the killer is working towards something. I can't pinpoint it." Katie watched as John dusted the Ferris wheel car for fingerprints and the technician dusted the area around the controls.

"Interesting. I like it when you describe your first impressions—it's telling and I can see where your intuition comes from."

"There's still a ton of evidence we need to sift through in all the cases to see what will fit the puzzle this killer has left for us," she said. "We need a lead to push us to the next level."

"But…"

Katie remained quiet.

"Something is weighing heavy on you…"

"My gut. It's just a gut instinct related to why and how Agent Campbell is here." She couldn't dismiss the way he kept checking up on her, or that he seemed to be watching her every move right now. "But the theater of the crime scenes is telling me that everything isn't what it seems. I think this crime scene indicates that the killer is escalating and that means it's possible that the next murder—and there will be another, if we don't catch them—could be sooner." She paused. "And there will be another victim soon."

CHAPTER TEN
Tuesday 1145 hours

Katie had been calling to talk to Agent Campbell, but he didn't answer, so she placed a call to the administrative assistant at his headquarters in Sacramento who said he was still in Pine Valley.

"I have his cell number, but there has been no answer. Can you give me the address where he's staying?" She eyed McGaven with a look of uncertainty. "Oh, you can. Please. Yes. I know it. Room number? Thank you." She ended the call.

McGaven drove toward the downtown area of Pine Valley.

"I'm a bit confused," Katie said.

"Confused? That's not a part of Katie Scott's genetic makeup."

She smiled. "No. It seems that Agent Campbell is staying at the Hobson Inn & Suites in Pine Valley."

Cisco barked suddenly from the back seat as they passed a cluster of pine trees with birds flying around.

"Isn't that a weekly place?"

"That's why I'm surprised. Why would he give us all of these cold case files and then stay here? Seems a bit off."

"Time off?"

"Maybe." Katie watched the landscape whizz by her window. "No… there's something else."

"You're still angry?"

"I don't like being played. And that's what this feels like. You aren't forgetting about the gas, are you?"

"That's what I mean. You're still pissed off."

"Aren't you?"

McGaven didn't say anything, but it was clear to her that he too was definitely angry about what had happened.

McGaven eased the sedan into a parking place at the Hobson Inn & Suites. They both sat for a moment staring at the inn. It comprised two large, dark-brown buildings, each with two stories, nestled in the trees. Even though the sun was shining, the motel crouched in the shade with lights illuminating the path towards it. It was a clean and tidy-looking building with only a half dozen cars parked.

"Ready?" said McGaven.

"As I'll ever be."

"Room?"

"Two-one-two."

"Let's go," he said and opened the car door.

"Wait," Katie said. "I can't let Cisco stay in the car any longer."

"Bring him."

"Cisco, *hier*," she commanded.

The dog jumped out, padded up next to her and waited. His ears perked up as he took in the surroundings.

"Hope Agent Campbell likes dogs…" said McGaven, more to himself than Katie, as he followed her and Cisco to the second level, quickly reading the room numbers.

They stood in front of room 212, pausing a moment.

Katie strained to hear any sound coming from the room but there was nothing, not even the television or a phone conversation.

She knocked twice.

Nothing.

She knocked twice again—this time louder. She was beginning to think that he wasn't there and they were going to have to come back later.

The door opened. Special Agent Dane Campbell stood in the doorway dressed in jeans and a black T-shirt—his perfectly combed blond hair was now messy. He looked more like someone who hung out at the beach than a special agent.

Campbell didn't seem surprised to see the three of them staring back. "What took you so long?" he said with an even tone and opened the door wider. He never blinked twice as Cisco entered with them.

Katie had thought about all the things she wanted to say to him, but when she walked into his one-bedroom suite she was stunned.

"Whoa," said McGaven as he looked around.

There were photographs of each of the three crime scenes organized in sections attached to the wall, along with detailed file notes including locations, maps, and every devisable means of escape imaginable. Reports were notated in specific colors, and certain details were highlighted. There were names and photos of people who were of interest in the case. There was different handwriting from all the investigators and police officers who had worked the cases.

"What is this?" she said.

Cisco took his cue from Katie's hand gesture to take up a comfortable position and jumped up into an upholstered chair.

"Detective, you don't recognize an investigation?" he said with some sarcasm.

"That's not what I mean. What. Is. All. This?" She gestured to the three computers, running what looked to her like surveillance equipment—it was clear that this case was part of something much more complex than he had led them to believe. One of the cameras was monitoring the Raven Woods house. "This is too much. We need some answers."

The special agent watched her with interest.

"Is that us?" asked McGaven who had been reviewing all the photos on the walls. "That's at the Stanton property." There were several photos of Katie close up.

"And why was there a video camera at the Raven Woods house? Why are you spying on us? You just asked for our help, but this has all been a…" She couldn't think of the right description. "Scam."

"Detective, this isn't a scam or a set-up or whatever you think. Let me explain."

"No. I'm calling the sheriff to get off this case. This is total BS."

"Please, let me explain."

Katie slowly lowered her cell phone against her better judgment. "Go ahead."

McGaven joined her and waited for the agent to clarify.

"Yes, we've been watching you for a while, but it's not what you think. You need to understand that these cases have been through a thorough investigation by many seasoned detectives, including myself—and I haven't been able to find any leads for months." He paused. "I needed to find the right people to work these cases. Someone who had a proven record, who understood more about these killers than most. You have been in several articles and on the news for solving several cold cases. You know how to work a crime scene, but some of your methods are a bit unconventional."

"What about the FBI? Profilers? I don't have the experience you need. I've only worked a handful of cold homicide cases so far," she said. "You could have just asked, instead of this shadow operation."

"This is more information than we're used to working with," said McGaven.

"The FBI and most homicide detectives have all been trained the same way—to put serial killers in certain categories. A white male between the ages of thirty-five and fifty-five—it makes us jaded, for the most part."

"Look, I don't feel comfortable with all of this and how it has transpired. And I haven't heard how these cases are even linked—with the exception of the way the victims are posed, the heavy makeup and the jewelry left behind."

"I know. If I were in your shoes, I would probably feel the same way."

"And, I don't have to work these cases."

"Yes, you do," the agent said. "You know you do because it's in your spirit—and it's your job."

McGaven turned his attention to the special agent.

Katie was annoyed as well as confused. This wasn't how it was supposed to work. She glanced at her partner and he seemed to be uncomfortable as well.

Katie looked at the video of the house in Raven Woods and realized it was live. "You knew we were there," she said and gestured to the computer screen. "You lured us to the house where we could have died from gas inhalation."

"No, that's not true. I knew you would go there, but I knew nothing about the gas. I swear."

"Show us the footage of when we were there," she demanded. "Now."

Cisco moved to Katie's side, sensing her mood change.

"Fine. You're not going to see anything that's useful or identifiable." He keyed up a few coordinates and found the correct section of the recording. They watched a person in a hooded sweatshirt approach the house, keeping their face away from the camera. It was unclear if the person continued onto the property or not.

"I had no way of knowing that this person would release gas into the house. It wasn't until later when I saw the firefighters and ambulances that I knew something was wrong. There was nothing that I could do. We'd put the camera there to protect the area and just in case the killer came back."

Katie watched the video again and it was true that the person was not identifiable. She turned away from the computer and took a closer look at the three homicides depicted so carefully on the wall. Looking at the faces of the people of interest, she noticed that some of them were in military clothing. Then she saw the close-up photos of her that must have been taken at her home and on her running trail.

"You've been following me for a while," she said, holding her anger in but feeling the creepiness of the entire situation.

"Like I explained, I had to be sure."

"To make sure that I could be trusted? Really?"

"I don't recall ever reading anything about stalking a fellow officer being a recognized job interview tactic," chimed McGaven.

"Look," said Campbell. "I understand how you both feel. But, I now know more than ever that you both are the perfect detectives for the job."

"Your flattery is a little too late," said Katie, as she made to leave.

"Wait," the agent said and gently took hold of her arm.

Cisco growled.

"It's okay," she said to the dog.

Katie and McGaven headed to the door.

"There's more to the investigations that you don't know. At least, not yet."

Katie sighed as her patience waned. "What is it?"

Campbell leaned against the desk. "Hear me out."

Katie waited.

"We have been able to find a link between all the victims. It was actually accidental and one of the junior detectives stumbled on it. It seems that all three victims were in the military for a short time. Even though they were all different ages, they have one thing in common."

"Being a homicide victim." Katie didn't hide her cynicism.

Campbell ignored her crass comment. "No, they were all part of the K9 military training program." He gestured to Cisco. "There were a total of eight women in the program."

"Are you sure?" she said slowly. Feeling a rush of heat and a slight prickle up her arms and down her spine, she steadied herself. She had never thought she would have something in common with a homicide victim, much less these three victims. It changed her outlook and now she wanted to solve the crimes more than ever.

"Positive."

Katie paused, looking back at the crime scene photographs.

"Were they all handlers?"

"Two were handlers like you—Nancy Day and Gwen Sanderson. Jeanine Trenton was a kennel manager and dog trainer."

Katie moved closer to the wall and took a longer look at everything. "So the military is the common thread?"

"That was one of the reasons why I thought you would be the perfect person to work these cases—with your military background in the same area as these women. Not to mention your success rate of cold cases."

"We didn't see any of this information in the boxes."

"No," he said and walked over to a desk, where he retrieved a flash drive. "Here. Everything we have is on there."

"Not in the boxes?"

"Just in case some paperwork gets misfiled."

Katie turned to McGaven who had been riveted to the new information just as much as she was. She gave him the look—he knew what she was asking and nodded in agreement.

"There's more, isn't there?" she said.

Campbell hesitated.

"These cases are about a year apart. Correct?"

"Yes."

"So that would mean this last case here in Pine Valley at the fairgrounds is on schedule?"

"Detective, you are very astute. That's why it's been important to have another set of eyes on these cases."

"While we wait for forensics and an ID to come in, we would need to re-examine everything on the Jeanine Trenton case—the autopsy, forensics, and reports. *Everything.* No restrictions."

"Of course. I wouldn't expect any less. In fact, I look forward to your assessments."

"Is everything about the victims' experiences with military K9 on this flash drive?" she asked. "I know the training facility here in California. Get us the clearance and information we need about the victims so we can talk to them."

"I'll see what I can do."

"No. That's not good enough." She glanced at McGaven, who she knew was on the same page as her. "Get us access and clearance to speak with the master trainer and the commanding officer." She walked up to the photos of each woman and studied them again. It struck her with angst that she had something of significance in common with them. Emotions were stirred up inside her about these cases and, sensing her anxiety, Cisco stepped up closer to her.

"I'll make some calls, ask some favors, and get back to you before tomorrow," he said. His expression changed a bit, showing more respect, as he watched Katie.

Katie looked to McGaven, the investigative wall, and then back to Campbell. "We're in."

CHAPTER ELEVEN

Wednesday 0900 hours

Once Katie arrived at work, she had a new perspective on the cases they were working. She had received text messages from Dr. Dean and John in forensics—both saying their reports were still delayed a bit due to the backlog. Statements and evidence were swimming through her mind and she needed to take a break. That was okay; for now, she wanted to take another look at the fairgrounds during the daytime and bring Cisco to run some track searches.

McGaven and John approached Katie.

"I just received the entire list of employees and any other person who had worked at the fairgrounds for the past five years and a list of employees at the Community Health Alliance. It's going to be a day of fun background checks."

"Wow, you've got the rest of your day cut out for you. I want to go back to the Sequoia County Fairgrounds and run some tracks with Cisco." She turned to John. "Would it be possible to get a small piece of the victim's clothing so that I can use it for scent work?"

McGaven walked to the office, opening the door. "Let me know if you need me." He smiled and went inside.

"Sure. I have the key to get in to the fairgrounds, too." John smiled. "I was going to run out to the county office and return it, but I could be persuaded to give it to you. Under one condition."

"What's that?"

"If I could tag along. You might need some documentation and it would be wise to get some overall shots during the daylight."

"What about the samples you're running and call-backs?"

"Rob is on top of it. I was going to run the errand to bring the keys back anyway. They also assured me that no one would be there—no security guards until this evening. There aren't any events scheduled until next month."

"Cisco and I would love the company."

After Katie picked up Cisco at the police kennels, they set off to the fairgrounds.

"So, what's the story with Lizzy?" he asked abruptly.

"Oh no, I don't have these conversations. If you want to know something about her, then ask her. I thought you two were dating?"

"We've been out for drinks a couple of times."

"So what's the problem?"

"She doesn't live here. She has a new job in Monterey, which is about five or six hours away. I've been in a long-distance relationship before and it doesn't turn out well," he said, looking out the side window.

Cisco stuck his big head out the back window so the wind could whip through his fur.

It was the first time that John had told her something private. She didn't know quite how to respond. "As long as you go in with your eyes open."

"Relationships are difficult enough without five hundred miles between you."

"Have you talked to Lizzy about this?"

"No. I get the feeling that she's looking forward to her new life on the coast."

"Of course, but..."

"Maybe it's best for us to just be friends. You never know who you're going to meet around the next corner." He watched Katie closely.

"True. But I think being open and honest is the best way to go, no matter where it takes you."

"Katie?"

She turned to look at John.

"Everything okay? I may be out of line here, but it seems that something is troubling you."

"You know, it's these damn cases. It's been extra stressful with the states cases and then two in our jurisdiction. It's quite a balancing act."

He nodded. It was clear that he knew something was up, but he was patient and wouldn't push his friend.

Katie pulled into the west entrance once again and was amazed how much less threatening it felt than it had yesterday. The fences, the livestock areas, and the carnival rides seemed old and outdated, as if they were long forgotten from another time.

John jumped out and unlocked the double padlocks, opening the large gate. Katie drove inside and he closed the gate behind them.

Cisco whined and ran back and forth across the backseat.

"Take it easy, Cisco," she said. "Soon, I promise."

John got back in. "Where did you want to go?"

"I know that there were quite a few sets of footprints around the livestock area and the perimeter, but I want Cisco to start a search where the body was, or ended up at, and work backwards, hopefully finding out how the killer entered and where they went."

"Sounds good."

"Finding a murder weapon would be nice," she said with skepticism.

John nodded in agreement.

Parking the Jeep near the fence area, Katie got out with a rolled-up map in her hands and examined it to get an overview. She wouldn't let Cisco out until she had a feel for the area; the wind speed, sounds, and any potential distractions.

John maintained a respectful silence while Katie worked, letting her get on with her job. It helped that he was also a veteran and was a Navy Seal; they had a mutual understanding of their experiences and skills.

Katie stood still for a minute, closing her eyes, to get a feel. She could hear traffic in the distance, some birds chirping in a nearby tree, a soft scraping sound that reminded her of a rusted metal sign swinging in the wind, and she could feel the breeze on her face.

She walked back to the front of the Jeep and unrolled the map of the Sequoia County Fairgrounds. "Okay," she said. "There are four major entrances and exits at each corner: north, south, east, and west where we entered. I noticed that there had been some recent construction, but I didn't see it yesterday."

"You're looking for where the killer entered."

"Yes."

"It would have to be by a car or truck," he said, scanning the map.

"But I'm not sure that they drove all the way to the Ferris wheel."

"Most people couldn't carry a body very far."

"But they could have forced the victim to walk to the Ferris wheel and get in a car. That was where she bled out."

John nodded and studied the sections of the map. "There are some emergency exits near the food areas."

"I noticed that. I know it's a big area, but it's really no different than searching in the woods."

"The search teams have been all over— won't that be a problem? And the night security guard, but he keeps to these areas, except when he does the rounds every hour or so." John pointed to an employee rest area near the restrooms.

"The scent should still be fresh enough, I hope, to stand out above the rest. What time does the guard come on?" she asked.

"Four to midnight."

"He leaves after midnight and no one is here after that?"

"Yep."

"The killer had to be here after midnight and then leave by 1:30 a.m."

"Seems reasonable."

"The victim had been dead for only about an hour or two before the first deputy arrived. I'm guessing, of course, but Dr. Dean will be able to pinpoint the time of death."

"I would agree with that. Rigor hadn't set in yet."

Katie rolled up the map and stashed it inside the car. "Okay, did you bring the piece of clothing?"

"Yep," he said reaching inside the car and retrieving a tube with ends that opened to let the victim's scent release from an item of their clothing without it being touched.

"I didn't want you to compromise the evidence, but I need it to give Cisco a scent. And then, of course, it goes into a doggie olfactory sensory computer and hopefully we'll learn something new."

John laughed. "I love that—doggie computer olfactory sensory neurons."

"Yep, I've coined that and you heard it here first."

Katie opened the back door and Cisco jumped out, wagging his tail and making his usual circles around them. She reached into the car to retrieve a long leash.

"You leash him?"

"Not always, but here I need to slow him down because of the cement, blacktop, metal on the rides, and the eateries. There's a lot of man-made stuff around, and it's not like it is in the forest."

"Interesting."

"There's not much wind today, so that's good. Just stay behind me, but you can fan out left or right."

"I want to video, is that okay?" he said readying the digital video recorder.

"Sure, anything that might help with the case if Cisco finds something. Just so you know, Cisco will passive alert, meaning he will become agitated but will sit as the signal."

Katie took the heavy-duty tube and began playing with Cisco, so he could get a good scent from the T-shirt the victim had been wearing. She ran with the jet-black dog, waving the tube so the scent wafted into the air, and ultimately in his senses.

"Okay," she said and handed the tube back to John.

After attaching the leash to Cisco, Katie led him to the Ferris wheel next to the car. There was still some crime scene tape and the blood had dried on the ground. Katie wrinkled her nose, remembering how it had soaked her trouser leg.

"Cisco *such*," Katie commanded—the German word for 'seek', pronounced 'suuk'.

Immediately, the dog began to sniff the area all around the Ferris wheel car. Katie let out a few more feet of the leash. Cisco moved in a zone pattern, taking in the scent. He clearly got the scent and after less than a minute he sat, giving two quick barks.

"Good boy. Now *such*," she said again, gently pulling on the leash.

This time Cisco's nose was in the air as he moved toward the left then, dropping his nose to the ground, tail down, he weaved back and forth until he picked up the scent and speeded up.

Katie knew that he was on to something and hoped that it wasn't some type of rodent. Every handler had those thoughts, but the dog knew exactly what he was doing. She saw John in her peripheral vision as he followed in the least unobtrusive way, recording the track.

Cisco led them to the east area at the entrance and spent some time there, but didn't alert. He then moved at a fairly brisk pace, making Katie run to keep up. They went around two food stands and crossed in a straight diagonal line to the livestock area. The dog hesitated around some wooden troughs and Katie thought he had lost the track, but then he picked the scent up again. His energy perked as he moved faster to get to the end.

Katie repeated her search command again to keep Cisco engaged and moving forward. Cisco went up one row and then down another, never veering from the straight lines. He ended up at the area where the ring hanging from a ribbon had been found. Cisco sat waiting.

"Good boy," she praised. Turning to John, "He led us up to where the ring was located. Back near the food areas, he seemed to get confused, but he was getting cross scents. It means that the scent went back and forth."

"That was amazing."

"It does mean something important. It further proves that the killer and the victim walked in here and she was killed on the ride. Otherwise we would see blood in other places and we haven't, with the exception of the bloody footprints." She unhooked Cisco and he ran around in glee.

Katie and John walked back to the Jeep where Katie drew Cisco's track on the map. It became clear what the victim's last minutes were.

"Wow," said John. "That tells the story."

"Part of it, anyway. Not who the killer is…" Katie had a thought. "Do you have another fifteen minutes?"

"Sure. What's up?"

"Let's take the killer's route and I want to have a look at the area under construction. Some of the rides are being updated as well." Looking for Cisco, she saw him sniffing areas around the chain-link fencing. "C'mon, Cisco." The dog looked up and happily followed them.

Katie and John took the walk from the eastern entrance, which led to the Ferris wheel. Then they followed the route from the ride around the eateries and to the livestock area where the ring was found.

"Seems plausible," she said. "But how did the killer get in? Did they have a key or did someone leave it open?"

"Let's take a look," he said.

As they walked back to the eastern gate, Katie noticed that the fencing and surrounding areas were old and worn. It was next to the area under construction.

"Wait," she said. Walking to the construction zone, she found heavy-duty white-and-blue tarps along with plywood covering the areas where the games would have been.

Cisco seemed to be extremely interested in the smells.

Katie entered underneath a tarp. The smell was oppressive, with a noxious scent of plastic and paint. The tarps helped to block out the light and created a darkened, creepy atmosphere. A slight pressure affected her ears like she was inside a soundproof room.

"John," she said.

He didn't respond.

"John!" she yelled.

No response.

She walked back to the entrance and squeezed between the tarp. "John?"

"Yeah," he said and walked up.

"You didn't hear me?"

"No."

"Check this out." She went back inside the area and was once again hit with the stagnant air.

"Stinks in here," he said.

Cisco brushed up against her leg.

Katie saw two wooden doors facing toward the parking lots outside. She retrieved her cell phone and popped on the flashlight mode. Aiming the light around the doors, she noticed that one of them had scrape marks.

"What do you make of these?" she said.

"I've seen this a million times. This is what is left behind when someone pries open a door or window. I've compared my fair share of tools to impression evidence from burglaries. More than I can count."

Katie turned her attention to the area and searched for something that would make that type of mark. She noticed a few tools lying on the ground in the corner—a long screwdriver and a piece of copper.

"Could something like these cause that impression?" she asked, pointing to the tools.

"It's possible. I'll go get my portable forensic case."

Katie nodded in agreement. She took the opportunity to look around, but nothing seemed obvious. But the slight soundproofing was interesting and could account to why the security guard might not have heard the killer and his victim enter. It would also give the killer time to observe the area, making sure that it was entirely vacant. Maybe the killer had entered on several occasions to scope out the area.

John returned and approached the doors and tools as if they were a crime scene. He photographed and collected the potential evidence. He used the dental stone commonly used to retrieve footprint impressions, to make an imprint of the scrape marks around the door.

"I think that's it," he said.

They walked back to Katie's Jeep. She was lost in thought, imagining how the killer entered the fairgrounds and how they had killed and posed the victim. And lastly, adding the ring and ribbon evidence for one last detail.

"I know you and McGaven will find the killer," said John.

Katie let Cisco back into the Jeep and shut the back door. "What makes you so sure?"

"Because you always do."

CHAPTER TWELVE

Wednesday 1335 hours

After Katie brought Cisco back to the police kennels and returned to the office, she found McGaven buried in paperwork in front of the computer.

"That looks like fun," she said.

"Loads." He turned, his chair creaking underneath him.

Looking up at the board, Katie realized she needed to begin to add their findings. "Any luck on those lists?"

McGaven let out an exhale. "It's longer than I thought it would be—I have this dreaded feeling that I'm searching blind here. There have been tons of employees at the fairgrounds. Some seasonal. Others just part time. Lots of names."

"You might want to add burglary or breaking and entering to your search parameter."

"Because?"

"I'm going to have to extend my list of people to contractors and subcontractors who have worked there in the past year or so." He keyed in search parameters and sat back. "Oh, I had a thought."

"And?"

"Well, I thought that the Ferris wheel might be something important. A symbol or of special significance to the killer."

She nodded. "Meaning?"

"I thought it might give us some insight into him, or her. Why the Ferris wheel? Why not the merry-go-round or one of the other rides?"

"Go on."

"I did a few searches. And for instance, did you know that the Ferris wheel is the fourth favorite ride at fairs and amusement parks?"

"No, but I'm not surprised."

"Anyway…"

"What's the first?" she said interrupting.

"The carousel or merry-go-round."

"Hm."

"The Ferris wheel was introduced at the Chicago Expo in 1893." He printed a piece of paper, grabbed it and continued, reading the copy. "So I went darker."

"I see." Katie listened intently.

"I checked to see what type of tragedies have happened at fairs over the years. And why they happen. It's said that the main reasons for accidents are negligence, not following the rules, health issues, and acts of God— like weather, when, say, a transformer blows up because of lightning."

"So you think that the killer might have experienced something that went wrong at a fair or amusement park?"

"Maybe, but it makes you wonder why they would choose the Ferris wheel."

"It could be for dramatic effect. There's been no connection to fairs and amusement parks with the other victims, but," she said, "dig a little deeper and see if anything happened to a child or something of the sort. I seem to remember a fire or something when I was about twelve or so."

"That's a long time ago."

"Funny," she said, wrinkling her nose.

"I'll poke around in between other searches and see what pops up."

McGaven went back to work.

*

Katie hurried home with some goodies from a deli and all the ingredients for cosmopolitans. It was going to be a low-key get-together for the girls, since they all had to work in the morning, but they had been talking about meeting up for a while and they all had openings in their schedules for tonight, so they booked the block of time.

Her friend Denise from the sheriff's department records division—who was also McGaven's girlfriend—and her army friend Lizzy were going to be there at 7:30 p.m.

Katie burst through her front door carrying several bags with Cisco in tow. "Okay, Cisco, we have half an hour to get ready. Think we can do it?" She wasn't expecting a reply, of course, and put things in the refrigerator before jumping into the shower to wash the day from her body, surprised that she felt refreshed and energized after a trying day of revelations.

Quickly drying her long hair, she decided to keep it down. She applied light makeup. Pulling on a pair of jeans and a casual top, Katie was just about ready when she heard her doorbell.

Cisco gave a high-pitched bark because he already knew who was at the door.

"Coming, coming." She opened the door and both Denise and Lizzy stood there patiently waiting—each with bags of goodies. After they hugged and chatted and complimented each other on what they were wearing, the ladies settled into the kitchen.

"So you and Gav had an interesting day," said Denise. Her perky personality matched her short haircut.

"Did he tell you?"

"What? What?" chimed Lizzy.

"Of course. We don't keep any secrets from one another." She helped to unwrap some deli rollups and unpacked potato salad. "Oh, this looks good."

"I'm so thankful that Gav was with me."

"What?" Lizzy said again. "I'm missing something here."

"It seems that Detective Scott here is getting some very interesting information about these new cases," Denise began. "Not to mention they got stuck inside a boarded-up house the other day, and someone decided to turn the gas on."

"What? That's crazy. You guys okay?" Lizzy looked worried. She absently pushed her bangs from her eyes.

"We're fine. At least, I am."

"Don't worry; Gav is just fine too."

Lizzy petted Cisco as he stayed next to her. "And this guy?"

"Cisco was in the car, but he did come to help us."

"What do you mean?"

"Somehow, he managed to press the remote I left in the car and release the back door."

"What?" said Denise. "You're kidding?"

"Nope."

"Such an awesome smart boy," Lizzy gushed. "I wasn't as lucky to bring my dog Billy home, but he got another handler and is doing his duty." She looked a bit melancholy as she stroked Cisco.

Uncomfortable, Katie said, "Lizzy, I have to warn you—this case I'm working… All the victims have been ex-K9 handlers. You will take care, won't you?"

Shocked, Lizzy paled, but then laughed. "Don't worry about me—I'm stuck in the office most of the time. And I'm going back soon anyway."

Happier, Katie finished a round of bright pink cosmos. "Here we are, ladies, just as I promised."

"Wow, haven't had one of these in a while," said Denise.

"Yeah, well, I'm only good for one tonight," laughed Lizzy.

"Okay," Katie began. "Here's to friends, love, and living every day to the fullest."

"Cheers!" they all said in unison.

"This is fantastic," said Lizzy.

"Oh, I agree."

The ladies chatted and laughed as they ate and drank.

Katie opened her closet and pulled out a garment bag hanging at the end. She could hear Denise and Lizzy laughing about something in the kitchen. She glanced at the photograph of her parents on the chest of drawers and wished that they could be at her wedding. If only she'd had more time with them before that fateful car accident took their lives. It was bittersweet that she had Uncle Wayne to walk her down the aisle.

Katie carefully laid the pink bag on the bed. Unzipping it she revealed a beautiful wedding dress with a lace bodice. She took a breath. It had belonged to her mother, but it was still just as stunning today as it was on the day her parents were married.

She choked back the tears and focused on her own wedding day. As she had promised her friends, she slipped on the dress. It was almost a perfect fit, with a few alterations it would be flawless on her day. Nerves hit her. Anxious energy pummeled her stomach. She felt jittery. She hadn't told her friends that Chad would be leaving for six months. There was no sense putting a dampener on the evening—she would tell them soon.

Walking down the hallway, she made a grand entrance. "Well, I promised I would show you."

Denise gasped. "Oh, sweetie."

"You are gorgeous in that dress," said Lizzy.

"Stunning."

"Beautiful."

"Okay, that's enough!" Katie said. "You're embarrassing me now."

Both women approached Katie, admiring.

Lizzy said, "Your parents would have loved you in this dress. It would have meant the world to your mom."

"They would be so proud of you."

"Do you think it's… well, up-to-date enough?"

"It's perfect," said Denise.

Lizzy nodded. "Absolutely."

Cisco got in on the action, circling Katie several times.

They laughed.

"Where is Chad?"

"Working."

"Well, he's going to flip when he sees you walk down the aisle."

After her friends had left, Katie went to bed almost immediately even though it was earlier than her normal bedtime. She was exhausted from the events of the day and her body and mind basically shut down. Cisco felt her weakness and snuggled in next to her. They both fell fast asleep.

Katie tossed and turned. Her sleep was restless, her dreams disturbing. It wasn't uncommon for her to dream about her past and the battlefield, and sometimes the victims in her cold cases appeared to reach out to her in a supernatural way—but tonight was different. It was as if someone or something was trying to warn her—pulling at her, struggling to convince her. She felt the heavy burden of premonition that something bad was going to happen.

CHAPTER THIRTEEN
Thursday 0745 hours

Katie looked forward to visiting the military dog training facility in Sacramento. It was where she had received her preliminary training for six weeks before she traveled to Afghanistan for the final advanced training with Cisco. To Katie's surprise, Agent Campbell came through for them and they were granted entry to view the facility and to speak with Sergeant Anthony Serrano. Katie drove there with purpose and high expectations of what they might uncover. Looking through most of the flash drive yesterday, it was becoming clearer that the K9 angle took center stage. That realization made the motive of the killer hit close to home for her.

"Thinking about your training?" said McGaven, interrupting her thoughts.

"It seems like such a long time ago. So many things have happened since then. But the training was memorable."

"Good or bad?"

"Mostly good. Everything turned out great, of course, but it was tough—actually, very tough at times. It would have been easy to wash out."

"I wonder if our vics had the same experience?"

Taking a turn off the freeway, Katie sped up to make several traffic lights. "Everyone was on the same page on how demanding it was, but just at different levels of training."

She turned down a road where a sign read: "Military Training Area." She slowed the sedan and drove into the civilian entrance where there was a booth and a heavy gate. Signs were posted everywhere stating, "Warning: No Admittance and Only Military Personnel Beyond this Point." Nothing could be seen of the facility—not the buildings, nor the dog-training areas. It was like a prison institution, with tall, impenetrable walls.

"I feel like I'm somewhere I shouldn't be," said McGaven as he searched the area.

"Most people don't know that dog training is performed here."

Katie pulled up to the security booth as a military police officer gestured for her to stop.

She put down her window. "I'm Detective Katie Scott from the PV Sheriff's Department. We have an appointment with Sergeant Serrano." She handed the officer her badge identification along with McGaven's. He disappeared for several minutes before returning and giving Katie back the IDs.

"Here are your ID passes," he said, handing her two laminated visitor passes. "Be sure to check your weapons and leave them in the trunk before entering the facility. Go straight and make the second right. Follow the signs for the K9 training until you reach the main office."

"Thank you."

He nodded. "Ma'am."

The gate lifted and Katie slowly drove through and followed the instructions.

As she made the second right and headed toward the K9 training area, they could see chain-link fencing with razor wire and several large buildings and kennel areas. She followed the signs and everything became familiar to her. She remembered arriving by bus with the other recruits. It was an exciting time and she would never forget the first time she met Cisco.

*

She walked through the long line of kennels, the walls ringing with the echo of barking dogs, jumping and pawing their doors on both sides. There were many German and Czech shepherds and Belgian Malinois breeds. An extra-loud banging at the end of the row piqued Katie's curiosity and she moved closer. She saw a dark face staring back at her when she approached. A black face with yellow wolf eyes and an expression of pure drive and curiosity gazed back at her. The dog barked and banged his paw against the door. She couldn't keep her eyes away from him as she slowly put her hand against the kennel door. Cisco gently licked her palm. At that moment, she knew he was the dog she wanted to train and to ultimately become her partner.

"I don't think you want him. He's washed out with two handlers," said the trainer. "Not sure what we're going to do with him."

"What's his name?"

"Cisco."

The beautiful jet-black dog barked as if it was an introduction.

"He's the one," said Katie as she moved closer to the kennel. "He's the one I want to work with."

Katie felt a flutter in her stomach as she remembered her first meeting with Cisco and their first day of training—rocky at best. The ups, downs, and the complete rush of feelings when they breezed through the obstacle courses and scent work. But as time went on, they proved to be one of the top military explosives K9 teams.

She pulled into a visitor's parking place and cut the engine.

"You ready?" she said. It was more for herself than McGaven. Emotions and memories from her time training were flooding back to her and she needed a moment to compose herself.

"You bet."

They got out of the vehicle, taking their weapons and securing them in the trunk as instructed.

Clipping her visitor's pass to her jacket and making sure she had her small notebook, she walked to the office area, followed by McGaven.

Several recruits were walking about and as they moved closer to the check-in desk, dogs could be heard barking.

Katie felt goosebumps pimple up her arms and part of her wanted to be back out in the training area. It was where her skills were constantly being pushed to another level and it was where her bond with Cisco was formed.

Katie reached the check-in desk staffed by three military men. "Excuse me?"

"Yes, ma'am. What can I do for you?" One of the men eyed her visitor's badge as well as her detective badge.

"I'm looking for Sergeant Serrano."

"And you are?"

"Detective Scott."

He nodded and went into a back office where he picked up a phone. She couldn't hear what he said, but he glanced back at her and McGaven several times.

He returned. "He'll be here shortly."

"Thank you," she said. Looking out the window she saw several training areas where agility courses were set up with jumps, box tunnels, and ladders, both vertical and horizontal. There was another larger training section behind a chain-link fence in the distance.

Within five minutes, a tall, slender, dark-haired man approached. He had the usual crew-cut hair and serious pace. He sported dark sunglasses.

"Detective Scott?" he asked.

"Yes. And this is my partner Deputy McGaven."

"Nice to meet you both," he said and shook their hands.

"I appreciate your time," she said.

"Not a problem. Today is a slower day. Besides, I'm happy that I can possibly help with your homicide investigations." He opened a gate and gestured. "Please, this way. You'll be able to see the layout of the outside training facility."

"Well…" Katie stammered. "I've actually been here and was a part of the training program."

Sergeant Serrano smiled. "I'm quite aware of who you are."

Katie turned to him, surprised.

"I've been briefed by Special Agent Campbell and Sheriff Scott. Campbell sent over the names of the recruits."

"I see," she said, trying to compose herself, before she dove right into the questions she really wanted to ask. "I noticed that there are fewer training teams than in my time. Is that true?"

Katie and the sergeant watched four separate K9 teams run through obedience drills one at a time.

"Your assessment is correct. Our intake has become smaller. Partly due to budget."

"Really? I remember that there were quite a few people wanting to be in the training program. It's difficult to get chosen."

They continued walking past the training areas.

"The truth is, the government has pulled resources and the competition is fierce for the few positions." Serrano opened another gate and waited for them to walk through."

"From everything I've read, aren't these K9 teams extremely effective in maneuvers, bomb recovery, and even terrorist retrieval?" said McGaven.

"Absolutely."

"But it's political," said Katie.

"Also, many military branches are now overloaded with older and retired canines that the handlers can't or won't take. It poses a whole host of other problems—even though there are civilian rescues and independents that take retired military dogs. Just not enough. So as you probably know, it puts this type of training in the political arena."

"I see. I was very lucky to bring Cisco home. Actually, Sheriff Scott was instrumental in his homecoming."

"I'm glad to hear that," he said and took a moment to observe Katie.

"We wanted to know anything that you could tell us about our victims. We know that one connection between the women is that they were all involved with the K9 military unit. Two were handlers and the most recent was a trainer and kennel manager."

"Yes," he said. "I'm only aware of two of them. The first, Nancy Day, was before my time here, which has been a little over three years now."

"What can you tell me about Gwen Sanderson and Jeanine Trenton?"

The sergeant paused a moment as they watched a decoy and attack procedure in progress with a sable German shepherd.

Katie sensed that he was hesitant about giving personal information. She gently pushed some specific questions, hoping to get some insight. "Sergeant, were they at the top of the class? Did they pose any problems? Any disciplinary actions? Or did anyone have any problems with them?"

"Gwen Sanderson was good. She had all the right skills, but she lacked the discipline. My biggest concern was that she would not be able to handle the extreme conditions once out in combat."

"Did she work well with a group or team?"

"Most of the time. Let's just say she had to be reminded." He watched another dog team as the handler released a tan Malinois.

"Sergeant, I know you are limited in what you can tell us— that there's a fine line between military inquiries and local law enforcement investigations—but rest assured that we are trying to learn as much about these women—these victims—as we can, so that we can begin to understand why they were butchered and left like a prop in a sadistic play." She tried to appeal to his sense of duty.

The sergeant turned to face Katie and McGaven. It was clear he was struggling with military ethics, or something more personal, but he seemed to relax. "I was told that I couldn't give you any official paperwork, but that doesn't mean I can't give you an opinion or names. So ask."

Katie decided to keep her questions short and to the point. "Did Gwen Sanderson ever have any discipline problems?"

"No."

"Was she here at the same time as Jeanine Trenton?"

"Yes."

"Did she ever complain that someone was bothering or harassing her?"

"No."

"Did she graduate from the training?"

"Yes."

"Jeanine Trenton." As she began, she noticed the sergeant light up. "You knew Jeanine Trenton?"

"Yes."

"I understand she was a dog trainer."

"Yes. She was very competent and had some experience before applying for the position. She put in her tour here at the kennels as a trainer. She had the opportunity to be a handler abroad, but she turned it down."

"Was she ever written up for any disciplinary issue?"

"No."

"Did she confide in you or someone else that anyone was harassing or bothering her?"

The sergeant hesitated.

"Please, Sergeant, anything might be helpful to us." Katie had the distinct feeling that the sergeant knew Jeanine Trenton more than just as a fellow army officer.

"Since she was a trainer, she encountered all types coming through this training facility. Both men and women."

Katie noticed the tension in his words. "What are the average numbers of recruits dropping from the program?"

McGaven kept quiet, allowing his partner to take the lead in interviewing the sergeant. He decided to venture away from Katie, watching the training.

"Average?"

She nodded.

"About twenty percent—give or take. It's for a variety of reasons, as you probably know, from recruits not liking what training is really like to personality clashes with both personnel and canines."

"Sergeant, I'm getting the impression that you knew Jeanine Trenton on a more personal level. Can you tell me what your relationship with her was?" She watched him closely.

His jaw clenched and he averted Katie's gaze. "I admit. I liked Jeanine. She was a hard worker and had an exceptional way with the dogs—something that you can't teach."

Katie listened.

"We went out a few times socially, but she became distant. I tried to get her to confide in me, but she wouldn't."

"Your thoughts about what would make her distant?"

"I got the impression that it was something with the training—someone who was bothering her—or worse. She began to hold back and not be as committed as she was before. She still did her job, but it was like her heart wasn't in it anymore."

"Anything else?" Katie pushed.

He shook his head and wouldn't open up.

She reached into her pocket and retrieved a business card. "Here's my card and my direct cell number. Please call me anytime if you remember anything."

He took it and popped it into his pocket. "Thank you. I'm sorry that you are burdened with these murders, but I'm glad that you're the one working them."

Katie blinked, not quite knowing what to say in response. She still felt that he knew more than he was letting on, but perhaps a little more time would be what the sergeant needed to confide in her.

"Do you have a moment? I would like to show you something," he said.

"Sure."

Katie made a gesture to McGaven who had been chatting with one of the trainers. He caught up to Katie and the sergeant and they walked into one of the buildings, housing several classrooms and storage areas.

As they reached a long hallway lined with bulletins, training lists, and photos, the sergeant stopped and turned to them. "I thought you'd like to see some of the best alumni K9 teams that we felt deserved special attention." He smiled and indicated some of the photos.

"Wow," said McGaven studying each one. "Private First Class Katherine Scott and K9 Cisco. Great photos. I think I like you in army fatigues." He smiled.

Katie stepped up and saw photos of her training with Cisco. More memories flooded back. She remembered those days like they were yesterday. Cisco had been difficult at first, but then they managed to get over his initial hard-headedness and became a great team. Then there was the photo of her and Cisco when they had graduated and were headed to Afghanistan. It was like stepping into a time machine.

"Look, she's speechless," said McGaven.

"It brings back so many memories." She turned to the sergeant. "Thank you for showing me these photos."

"Of course. I just wish I'd been here during your training, but I was working at the K9 facility in San Diego."

"We won't take up any more of your time, Sergeant," she said. "I meant it: if you think of anything about Gwen Sanderson or Jeanine Trenton, please call me."

"I will, Detective."

Sergeant Serrano watched Katie and McGaven leave.

Once back at the police sedan, Katie and McGaven retrieved their weapons before exiting the military training facility. They had more than a two-hour drive back to Pine Valley.

As Katie drove through the security area, McGaven said, "What do you think?"

"I'm not sure."

"Oh, I think you have an idea."

"Maybe."

"C'mon, tell me."

"I don't have solid proof, but I think it's fairly obvious that Sergeant Serrano was having a more serious relationship with Jeanine Trenton that he let on—based on the way he spoke about her."

"And?"

"And, did you notice that they video some of the training?"

"I didn't see them doing that today."

"They usually video when the training is coming to an end—and you're either going to graduate or wash out."

"I see where you're going with this."

"We need to see any video with Gwen Sanderson and Jeanine Trenton," she said. "I'll contact Agent Campbell."

"Don't forget about the first vic—Nancy Day."

"On it," she said. Inserting her cell phone in the car holder, she ordered from her hands free device, "Dial Agent Dane Campbell."

You're either going to graduate or wash out…

CHAPTER FOURTEEN
Thursday 2045 hours

Katie arranged herself on her sofa with her laptop and a clean notebook. After eating takeout from her favorite local Chinese restaurant, she was ready to dive into the two first cases to see for herself what happened to these two women—since she didn't have enough time at the office. She wanted to fully understand the revelation of what Agent Campbell had dropped into her lap, still astonished by the chain of events.

Her mind wandered to Chad. His face. His laugh. Their time together. She wondered what he was doing and she missed him dearly. They had been through so much together, to be separated now was almost unbearable. They hadn't said their official goodbyes yet.

She decided to send him a text: *Miss you. Hope everything is going well xx*

She leaned back against the couch pillows to let everything simmer in her mind. A fire was slowly burning in her fireplace, the flames lightly flickering, making the room feel cozy and safe. She didn't feel sleepy, quite the contrary: she wanted some answers, especially after speaking with Sergeant Serrano. She didn't know if it was the visit to the K9 training area or the fact that Chad was gone—but she felt melancholy.

Even though she had Cisco, she still had her firearm to hand. It was the police and military training that made her extra cautious.

Her security was engaged and running properly; it was just an added precaution, making her feel safer.

Cisco sensed her emotions were downcast and was, as always, at her side in case she needed anything. He circled a couple of times before finding the right spot to snuggle down into on the couch.

Katie tried to push away her feelings about being alone now that Chad had all but left for Los Angeles. Her heart felt broken. Nothing was permanent, but it still felt like her world was falling apart, one aspect of her life at a time. She was also saddened by the Jared Stanton case, wishing that she could have done something to change the outcome.

Cisco's light doggie snores interrupted her downhearted thoughts. She smiled as she watched him twitching his paws and legs, wondering what kind of dream he was having—happy or sad.

Taking a few more bites of her chicken and vegetables, she turned her attention to the cases.

Katie had transferred files from the backup flash drive into her laptop yesterday and now she waited as the files popped up on her screen.

Each victim's report was in a file and from there it was divided into seven subcategory files: background, autopsy, police reports, victimology, forensics and crime scene, interviews, and miscellaneous notes. It appeared that everything was the same as the physical boxes they had received.

Katie pressed "Victim #1, Nancy Day," and her overall investigation loaded up. She clicked on background information and began to reread through the lists and notes, putting asterisks alongside anything of interest.

Nancy Day, 34 years old, single, taught Administration of Justice for Littleton College* in Placer County. Brunette, average build, green eyes, no surgeries, no medical issues or prescriptions, no *mental health issues, no close family relationships, slightly reclusive, had $67,000 in savings*, rented home, conservative spending patterns, paid bills on time, vacation once a year, had worked a total of four jobs in her life: fast food restaurant, went into army as K9 handler*, worked as admin to a law firm, and then got her teaching degree to work at the college.*

Went into army to pay for her college. Well-liked by staff and students at Littleton College. No write-ups or bad behavior. Parents still living, not close*. Mom is restaurant/bar owner. Dad is an architect. Unhappy with daughter about army enlistment*. Sister married with two children—not close—no contact* in four years. Single. Dated two men, not at same time, over a three-year period, Darren Straight and Paul Wheeler. Both cleared of any involvement in her murder.

Katie sighed and sat back. "Not much to go on. Ordinary. Quiet," she said quietly. "Why were you targeted? How could someone get to you? Motive?"

Cisco grumbled.

Nothing stood out in the police reports and interviews. Katie made a few notes as she read through everything so that she could refer back to them later. Nancy Day's body was found in front of Littleton College, murdered and posed dramatically before anyone arrived. She was found by the security guard, who was later cleared of any involvement.

The victimology report did an analysis of a typical day and week for Nancy Day. The criminologist pinpointed the likely times and places where she could have been most vulnerable—especially if someone was paying attention or following her. These were at her home during the nighttime and working late at the college after students and most teachers had already gone home. Her death ended up being at the latter.

Who would have access to Nancy Day and want her dead?

Students? Teachers? Ex-boyfriend? Family member? Stranger fixation?

The theatrical staging of the crime scene would indicate that the killer wanted to embarrass her or show her to be a certain type of person—perhaps they wanted her to be exposed at her place of work. Revenge. Hate. But they didn't completely go all the way. They could have had her nude in a compromising position—but they stopped short.

The forensic reports didn't show anything tangible, such as fingerprints or fluids. The crime scene photos were presented well and showed Katie everything she needed to know at this point.

Katie quickly made notes and added more questions so she could get McGaven up to speed. From everything she had read, Nancy Day was average and had led a very quiet life.

Gwen Sanderson, 31 years old, petite, brunette, brown eyes, suffered from diabetes, owner of a small restaurant/deli called Gwen's Place, had significant debt $110,000, known to harass people in public places, went to anger management classes, boyfriend (Joseph Alda), on-again/off-again relationship, no drug usage, non-smoker, liked by customers, liked by community, adoptive parents died in auto accident, no siblings or family noted, worked many jobs before owning restaurant: restaurant, maid, clerk, babysitting, dog walker, etc. Left home at 18 to join army to get away from parents. Was military K9 police—discharged early (military file sealed). Washed out?

"Hmmm, problem child," said Katie.

She read through all the reports and one thing stood out to her: Gwen was murdered and her crime scene posed in a place that she had never visited. Her body was found secured to the front entrance on a fence at Roy's Bed and Breakfast Dude Ranch, which had been under construction during the winter months. No one was working on the ranch at the time of her death. The second aspect that stood out to Katie was that the staged scene was much more heavy-handed with the makeup and the level of violence. As if the murder could have been committed by someone else trying to make it appear like the Nancy Day crime scene.

Possible.

Katie read the forensics report and studied the crime scene photos. Everything appeared to be rushed and have an amateurish aspect to it—similar to the fairgrounds scene. All the crime scenes resembled one another. The exaggerated application of the makeup. There were spots of makeup on the clothes and her arms. The placement of the jewelry seemed like an afterthought, as if the killer was trying to make their motive known. That made Katie pause as she thought about all three victims and their connections. However, the Nancy Day signature with the makeup was less pronounced than the others as if the killer wasn't sure how much makeup to apply to accomplish the level of theater they had wanted. It was as if it was the first time the killer had applied makeup.

The characteristics that stood out to Katie connecting all four crime scenes were: posing of the victims in demeaning positions like broken dolls; a dramatic quality to the crime scenes —almost playful, like a game; items of jewelry hung like trophies that the killer didn't take; excessive makeup; battered chest, and then the final blow in each case, slicing the throat to let the victim bleed out. It showed control, a need to embarrass, humiliate, abuse, and then kill. The three victims were also linked by the lack of forensic evidence.

Anger. Revenge. Hate.

Katie made more notes and skimmed some of the sections again. Once she had a grip on the crime scenes and forensics she could update McGaven in the morning. She gave her eyes a rest, leaned back on the couch, and allowed herself to fall asleep.

CHAPTER FIFTEEN
Friday 0755 hours

Katie arrived at the Pine Valley Sheriff's Forensic Department and made her way to the cold case office carrying two large cups of coffee. She pushed open the door and wasn't surprised to see McGaven already working. Usually he was pecking away at the keyboard, but this time he was reading the lengthy reports from the Jeanine Trenton murder with a highlighter pen in his hand.

"Morning," she said.

He nodded. "Mornin'," but then realized that she had coffee. "Is that—?" He happily accepted it.

"Yep, your favorite."

"Occasion?"

"Nothing in particular."

"I thought you'd be late."

"Why?" she said, putting her jacket on the back of her chair. "Am I ever late?"

"No, not really."

"What's all that?"

"Going through the reports. I've also searched the missing persons database but I can't find anyone who matches our Jane Doe even though the 911 caller said she was missing."

"Perhaps she's not really missing."

"Seems that way. A way to get the police out there. And I've been thinking about the third victim, Jeanine Trenton."

"Yeah, I've been thinking about her too."

Katie sat down and leaned toward McGaven, sneaking a peek at which reports he was so engrossed in. "And?"

"I realized, after reading most of the reports, that there's quite a bit of repeated information—some of it is worded differently but it basically means the same thing. I think Agent Campbell has had more than a couple of people checking out this case. I mean, a *lot* of other people."

"Interesting," she said, more to herself than McGaven, taking a sip of her strong black coffee. "Remind me again what conclusion they came to? Suspects? Who might have committed the crime?"

"Okay, it came down to a few people—the usual leads."

Katie rolled her chair closer to her partner and eyed the highlighted sections.

"First, Mandy Davis, the so-called best friend that found the body."

"Okay."

"Look, here, she said she arrived at the house after Jeanine didn't show up at the party. But there are inconsistencies of time and how long it took her to find the body."

"It was a horrible crime scene. Maybe she wasn't sure."

"And they had a falling-out in their friendship two months before the party."

Katie skimmed the interview. "It's possible they made up."

"And…"

Katie read what McGaven was reading.

"They seemed to have an issue with a boyfriend."

"Hmm… Looks like her friend Mandy was upset after she caught Jeanine with her boyfriend, Brady Randall."

"That's not good. Where was the boyfriend?"

"He has a solid alibi. He was at a conference in Indiana at the time. Verified by the hotel, conference people, and he was seen on security cams."

"That doesn't mean he couldn't have had someone else kill her. Who were the other possible suspects?"

"I guess there was some issue at Community Health Alliance where she worked as an assisting nurse for those who are on assistance or social security."

Gulping more than half her coffee, she said, "What kind of issue?"

"It was a lot of back-and-forth talk, but from what I could gather, it sounded like a hostile work environment," he said and flipped through more pages. "There's background on the staff, but it reads like a boring book. Nothing that stands out."

"So our victim stole her best friend's boyfriend and her work place was antagonistic." Katie leaned back. "That could open up a whole host of other suspects—for all kinds of reasons—hate, revenge, jealousy. So what about neighbors?"

"Most are retired, except for next door. A Mrs. Sadie Caldwell who is also retired, but she's…"

"What's wrong with her?"

"She's on record for calling the police on two occasions because of a loud party."

"Not a big suspect list." Katie was disappointed that after all the manpower and time that had gone into the investigation, this was all they had come up with. "So what did the profiler have to say?"

"How did you know there's a profiler?"

"That's just how these types of investigations go. And *please* don't tell me 'a white male between the ages of thirty-five and forty-five, single, blue-collar worker, no arrests except for something like trespassing or fighting in a bar, etc.'"

McGaven smiled. "Pretty close."

Katie let out a loud sigh. "Agent Campbell is correct. They are all trained to investigate the same way, to not to see outside the box—for lack of a better phrase." She frowned, thinking about killers' motives.

McGaven handed her the pages he had highlighted.

"Let me see," she said and skimmed through the information. "It is like they kept repeating the same things… like they didn't have anything better to do. Making the report look bigger."

"You can see how they've hit a dead end."

"Let's start at the beginning," she said. "We have already spent time with military K9 training, but while we have to wait for information on our victim at the fairgrounds let's dig deeper into Jeanine Trenton. When we went to her house, all of her personal belongings were gone. I'm still waiting to hear back from the attorney."

"We might learn something new."

"Until we get an ID on the vic from the fairgrounds, let's dig in here."

"I'll contact Mandy Davis then," he said, searching for her phone number. "It's good to talk to the best friend and she's had some time to think about everything too."

"I'd like to know if she knew anything about the sergeant at the K9 training facility."

"Sounds good."

Katie reread the reports as McGaven spoke to Ms. Davis, and made several inquiries about Jeanine Trenton's belongings. She wanted to know what John in forensics had to say about the crime scene. She made arrangements through Agent Campbell for John to receive everything that was collected and also the photographs of Jeanine Trenton.

"We can speak to Mandy Davis at eleven thirty," McGaven said.

"Great." Katie slowly shuffled the paperwork around on her desk.

"What's bothering you?"

"No weapon found. No clear idea even of the type of weapon."

"Nope."

"It's strange. Now, we haven't completely gone through the two previous homicides yet. But… did you notice that it seemed very textbook with Jeanine? Originally the suspects were the closest friend, boyfriend, and people at work were antagonistic. It could be anyone."

"Good point," he said. "But that's what we're here for."

"There's something not right about this case. I get the distinct impression that we're missing something—or something is being withheld from us."

CHAPTER SIXTEEN

Friday 1100 hours

Mandy Davis worked in an office building downtown as an administrative assistant for a real estate broker. She had not wanted to meet with them initially, but McGaven had managed to convince her, explaining that it was routine. She insisted that they meet at the park, which was next to her work premises.

The morning was still chilly and overcast, so Katie paced back and forth to keep warm. The park was small with two rows of immature trees and bushes strategically planted and benches along the walking path. It was clean and pleasant. The space seemed generally used for running or walking workouts. As they waited, Katie looked around and noticed that most people who passed by were oblivious to what was going on around them.

A tall woman with long, flowing fiery-red hair approached, puffing on a cigarette which she quickly discarded before meeting with them. Dressed in a tan suit, she looked professional but it was clear that she was nervous—anxious about speaking with them.

"Mandy Davis?" said Katie.

"Yes."

"Ms. Davis, I'm Detective Katie Scott and this is my partner, Deputy Sean McGaven."

She nodded at them.

Katie noticed that she fidgeted with her hands and nails frequently.

"I'm sorry it's so cold, but I didn't want them to talk at work. You know…"

"Of course," said Katie as she gave McGaven the subtle signal for him to ask questions.

McGaven gestured for them to sit down on a bench. "Ms. Davis," he began.

"Please, call me Mandy." She began to relax a bit. Her shoulders eased downward and she stopped fiddling with her hands.

"I'm sorry to have to ask these questions about your friend Jeanine since you've answered them before. But we're here as cold case detectives and we want to hear from you in person, since you were the one that found her body. Are you feeling up to a few questions?" he asked.

Smooth, thought Katie as she took a backseat to the interview. She stood about ten feet away watching the cityscape, but still hearing the conversation, glancing every once in a while to observe body language.

"Yes, I'm fine," she said, her voice calm.

"I understand that you were both to meet at a party."

"Yes."

"When did you decide to go to Jeanine's house?"

"Well, she was usually late so I didn't think much of it at first. Time had got away from me when I realized that Jeanine didn't show up. It wasn't like her to completely blow it off. You know?"

McGaven patiently listened and nodded, letting her continue.

"I called her a couple of times but she didn't answer…"

"You called her from the party?"

"Yes, and then once when I was driving."

"Did you have any idea that something was wrong? Had Jeanine confided in you that maybe someone was bothering her?"

"No. She wasn't happy at work, but she had said that she was looking for another job—a small medical facility, she said. That's just it. She didn't tell me anything—nothing that indicated someone would want to harm her. I can't…" She stopped. "I'm sorry, but it's taken me a while to sleep through the night after finding her…"

"Please take your time," he said. "We just wanted to clarify a few things. I promise I won't make you go through every horrible detail."

She nodded. "Okay."

"If you can please think back to that night. When you arrived, what did you see?"

"Um, when I got there it was about eleven, maybe eleven thirty. I pulled into the driveway and it was dark. Very dark."

Katie knew the police report had said it was closer to 12:30 a.m. She watched Mandy's mannerisms when she answered McGaven's questions.

"Dark outside or inside?"

"Both."

"What about next door?"

"I don't…"

"When you drove up, did you look next door? And was it light or all dark?"

"It was dark. I'm pretty sure. The neighborhood was dark, but Jeanine's house didn't have her usual motion lights or flower-bed lighting, and there wasn't any light from the inside that I could see."

"What did you do?"

"I walked up to the porch and…"

"And what?" he gently pushed.

"It's funny, I didn't remember it at my initial interview with the police, but something crunched under my shoes. I remember thinking that I didn't want to cut my feet because I was wearing sandals."

"What do you think was crunching under your feet?"

"I don't know, something like glass, I guess."

"Could it have been a light bulb?"

She looked confused.

"For example, from the outside light?"

"I guess."

"Okay, what else did you see?"

Mandy looked at a couple walking by as if she knew them but she then quickly looked away. "The door was slightly open and her screen looked broken. She was very particular about her house and her things, so I guess I thought it was strange."

"Why didn't you call the police right then?"

"I didn't think there was anything wrong. I know now, of course, I should have gone back to my car and called 911, but…"

"I know these questions are tough even after a year, but any small thing you might remember that you didn't think at the time was important could be very helpful to us."

"Of course. It's okay." Her voice was shaky.

"Did anything seem strange or disarrayed once you were inside?"

"What do you mean?" Her demeanor changed, and there was a definite edge to her voice.

"Like, was there anything out of place? You said that Jeanine was a tidy person."

"Um…" she stammered. "Well, I remember a green vase, maybe it was blue, I don't know."

"A vase?"

"Yeah, it was on the floor and it seemed strange—out of place."

McGaven moved a bit closer to Mandy, his expression sensitive and understanding—intended to make her feel more secure. Katie watched him and knew that he would be outstanding in any area of law enforcement. She was lucky to have him as a partner.

"I don't know, the place just gave me an uneasy feeling," she said.

"I'm sorry, I have to ask you about this. It was in the statements that Jeanine was dating your boyfriend."

Mandy remained quiet, almost stoic, as she sat there. Her jaw clenched. "I know what you must be thinking. The original detective asked me about this too…" She pushed her wavy hair back. "Yes, she dated my boyfriend after we broke up. I don't know why everyone gets this wrong. Brady and I broke up, and then he started dating Jeanine."

McGaven paused. "It had to put a strain on your relationship with Jeanine."

"No… well, yeah, it did for a bit. But we had known each other for a while and our friendship was more important." She looked away as she spoke. "They only dated for three months anyway."

"What about Jeanine's experience in the army?"

Mandy shrugged. "I don't know much. I mean, I knew that she was in for two years."

"Working as a K9 trainer," added McGaven.

"Yeah, I guess."

"She never talked about it?"

"Not really. She loved dogs and would foster sometimes, but that's all I know."

"Was she dating anyone at the army training facility?"

She shrugged. "Not that I know of. She was pretty quiet about her time in the army."

"Does the name Sergeant Anthony Serrano mean anything?"

"No. I've never heard that name."

"I see. One more question, for now. Can you think of anyone who might have wanted to hurt or take revenge on Jeanine? Anyone at all?"

"No," she said. "I've thought about this ever since… ever since I found her that night. Oh God…" she trailed off.

"Anything you tell us is confidential, I promise you," said McGaven as he appealed to her sensitivities.

She wiped a tear away. "Like I said, I've thought about this a lot. She said that she was having trouble with her next-door neighbor, but nothing that would make her… murder her."

"What did she say about the neighbor?"

"It's what she didn't say. When I would come over, she would usher me inside because she didn't want the neighbor to see us. At least, that's what she said."

"Anything specific?"

"No, it was little things."

"Like?"

"She made sure her curtains and blinds facing her neighbor's house were always closed. She would hurry me inside and close the door quickly, locking it immediately. Just little things like that."

"If we have some follow-up questions, may we call you?"

"Of course," she said. Then Mandy took McGaven's arm. "Please, please find out who did this. I miss her every day."

McGaven stood up. "We are doing everything we can. Thank you, Ms. Davis."

Mandy hesitated for a moment, as if she wanted to tell them something more, and then decided against it. She turned and headed back to work.

Katie joined McGaven.

"What do you think?" she said.

"She's evasive and telling partial truths. She seemed hesitant with questions that were more routine and averted her eyes when she explained what happened."

"You think she's hiding something?"

"Yes, but it's something that she doesn't want us to know. My guess, it's something personal."

Katie glanced at a few people passing by. "I think she tried too hard to put suspicion on the neighbor."

Katie received a text message from John. It said: *No prints or evidence at the Trenton house.*

"What's up?" he said.

"John couldn't find any fingerprints at Jeanine Trenton's house." She was disappointed. Although it would be too easy.

"Too bad. Just means we need to keep digging."

They briskly walked back to the sedan and got inside to get out of the cold.

Katie drove out of the parking lot, heading to the Community Health Alliance where Jeanine had worked, to see what they could find out.

"So," said McGaven. "We have the best friend who can't commit to the exact time that she came over, tried to make it seem like when her best friend dated her boyfriend it wasn't any big deal, and tried to divert suspicion to the neighbor. That about right?"

"Just about." Katie rolled what Mandy Davis had to say through her mind and found herself unconvinced that she was telling them everything.

"We have our work cut out for us."

McGaven received a text. "Looks like we have been given the green light to take a look at Jeanine Trenton's personal belongings."

"Well, let's make that our first stop," said Katie.

CHAPTER SEVENTEEN
Friday 1305 hours

After Katie and McGaven picked up a key from Daniels & Smith, Attorneys at Law, they headed to the storage facility to have a look at Jeanine Trenton's personal belongings. Her things were being held in probate until the state could sell everything, including the house. She had no immediate family, but the probate attorneys were doing their due diligence in case there was a family member not listed.

Katie and McGaven had received permission to look through Jeanine's belongings as part of the murder investigation, and anything they took would be factored into the probate.

As McGaven drove to the storage unit, Katie remained quiet. She was thinking about the military K9 facility and wondered what experiences Jeanine Trenton had had there as a trainer. It was clear that Sergeant Serrano had feelings for her, but there was no mention of it to her best friend. Why?

"I wonder what secrets are going to tumble out?" said McGaven.

"We'll see."

"Why are you so quiet? That big detective brain of yours working overtime?"

She laughed. "Something like that."

"I bet you're trying to figure out the killer's motives and why they are so screwed up."

She shifted her weight and moved her attention from the window to her partner. "It's really difficult to stay focused on this killer when there are three previous cases."

McGaven didn't respond, but it was clear he knew exactly how Katie felt. His face and jaw tightened.

"This may sound strange…"

"What?"

"Somehow this case—these cases—seem personal. It's the K9 training. It's a part of you—probably forever."

"I never thought about it like that—but you're right."

"Yeah…" He took the turn into the storage facility and stopped at the entrance to key in the code. The black gate opened wide and McGaven drove in. "Sometimes I may just surprise you."

Katie smiled. "Every day on the job you surprise me, Gav."

McGaven eased around several buildings until he found "E." He parked outside and they both exited the vehicle.

"We're looking for E121," he said.

The entrance on the bottom floor was a plain metal door. There was a simple sign above, reading "E110–E130."

Katie pulled the utility door open and the fluorescent ceiling lights automatically lit up as they entered. The outside door shut behind them, making a distinct suction sound. They walked down a long hallway. As they passed through, the lights extinguished, leaving darkness behind them. The temperature was quite a bit cooler than the outside air and became stifling. Since there were no windows to indicate if it was light or dark outside, it had a creepy vibe.

"I think this is it," Katie said and pointed to a medium-sized storage unit on the left. "E121."

McGaven retrieved the key, unlocked the padlock and pulled up the roll-up door. "There it is."

Looking inside the locker, they sighed. There were boxes stacked from floor to ceiling and it would take a bit of time.

"Well," Katie said. "At least they are clearly marked, so let's find the personal items and forget the rest. We don't need to look at the dishes, pots, and pans."

McGaven shed his jacket and began to pull out boxes of interest. Twenty minutes later, they had only a total of ten boxes to view.

"That's not so bad," she said, with her hands on her hips. "I'll take five."

McGaven sliced open the tops of the boxes with his pocketknife.

For the next fifteen to twenty minutes, Katie and McGaven carefully emptied boxes, examined the contents, and then repacked them.

Katie felt keenly aware of the intrusion by going through Jeanine's private things as she viewed personal letters, birthday cards, and individual pieces of jewelry. "Anything?" she said, glancing to McGaven.

"Nope."

Katie had been through three boxes already and was just about to pull the last item from the bottom of the fourth box. It was a navy-colored journal. With no picture or lettering, it was just a plain book. When she opened it, she viewed handwriting and some simple drawings. She noticed that the last entry was a week before Jeanine was murdered. "Gav."

He was busily repacking one of the boxes.

"Gav," she said again.

He looked up. "What do you have?" He moved closer to see the journal.

"I'm just skimming but she was very honest and detailed when she wrote her entries."

McGaven read over her shoulder. "Let's bring it with us."

"Yep."

A couple of photos dropped from the back of the journal. Katie bent down and picked them up. They were of Jeanine during her time in the military, pictured with some of the dogs. Bright-eyed, smiling, she appeared to be loving her job. "It looks like Jeanine was very happy training dogs in the military."

"I wonder what happened? Why didn't she stay?"

"I don't know. Sergeant Serrano didn't give any indication," she said. She slid the photos back into the journal. "See if you can find any photographs or memory disks." She thought she should have pressed him harder.

"On it."

Katie and McGaven searched for anything that might prove useful, but didn't find anything other than the journal.

After returning everything to the storage space and securing the lock, they left the facility.

Katie was now behind the wheel as McGaven skimmed through Jeanine's journal.

"Listen to this," he said and read out loud: "'I love working at the CHA, but I don't know how much longer I can take the hostile environment. No matter what I do, tackling them head-on or ignoring them, it's always the same. Lately it's been aggressive and I'm afraid that they might try to harass me at my house.'"

"That sounds serious," she said.

"It does," he agreed. "And her handwriting starts out neat and then gets messier as if she was struggling to write that particular entry."

"Interesting. I'm glad that we're on our way to the health center now."

"Let's see what shakes out."

CHAPTER EIGHTEEN

Friday 1530 hours

The Community Health Alliance building was in the older part of Pine Valley and it helped people who were on assistance and social security. It covered all areas of care, including health screenings, family planning, and child health services. The building had been occupied by many businesses until the health care facility took over eight years ago.

"Listen to this," said McGaven as he read from Jeanine Trenton's journal. "'I can usually take the crap from some of my co-workers, but today was the last straw. I've decided to give my resignation first thing Monday to Angela Norton. I have a few prospects and I really need...'"

"Really need what?"

"That's it. That's the end of the entry. And it's dated two days before her death."

"She never got the chance to give her notice," said Katie.

Katie drove into the area and was able to find a parking place. The parking lot was in desperate need of a fresh paving. Stubborn cracks and various potholes littered the area. It was a sterile building that needed some type of landscaping to soften the sharp lines of the construction and to help make it more inviting.

Katie cut the engine and remained seated, staring out.

"What?" said McGaven drinking a large iced tea. They had stopped for a quick bite before taking on the challenge of talking with employees at the facility.

"Not everyone still works here since Jeanine Trenton was murdered."

"No problem. There's many ways we can go. Track them down or just go by the previous interviews—unless of course something stands out. Then… we'll take it from there." He looked at his partner. "What's really going on?"

"Do you actually think we're going to find anything new? There've been so many investigators working on these cases."

"We can always find out something new. And we're going to do it our way. I think something will surface."

"You're right. That entire command center with Agent Campbell just makes me wonder."

"You mean the command center or the agent?" He noisily finished his drink, sliding the empty cup into the holder.

"What's that supposed to mean?"

He laughed.

"What?" she said.

"Katie, I've known you a while now. We've been through—well, let's just say a lot."

"And?"

"And you can be tough, incredibly intuitive, and dense at the same time."

"Was that supposed to be a pep talk?"

"You're missing the point. You are so in tune with everything about cold cases and people relating to the investigation, but you fail to see things that are on a more *personal* level."

"Gav, what are you getting at?"

"You can be thick sometimes… you never seem to notice when men are intimidated by you—not just your smarts but your looks."

"So you're saying Agent Campbell was intimidated? Right. He's arrogant and controlling. His job is probably at stake and that's why he's so desperate that he came here when the big FBI didn't get anywhere with their own investigations."

McGaven raised his eyebrows in a look that meant "See, I told you so."

"Okay, I'll admit it. If you call me out on it, I'll deny it. He seemed to be interested in me—for the investigation. So? He's a good-looking man—if you like that type."

McGaven laughed again.

"I'm engaged," she said and flashed her ring. "Why are you bringing all this up? Other than to embarrass me."

"You need to take *everything* into consideration and make it work for you. Enjoy your life more."

Katie opened the door. "I'm not entirely sure why we're having this conversation, but it's noted. Okay? I get your meaning, that I need to pay attention to personal things sometimes…"

"Good," he said, smiling as he got out of the car.

The sun had managed to make its debut, peeking through the clouds and warming the air. Katie felt the heat on her back as they walked toward the entrance. She had become an expert in taking even, deep breaths and not drawing the attention of McGaven or anyone else. Calming her nerves, she readied herself and hoped that they would learn something new.

There were two people, a man and a woman, waiting outside, dressed in long, quilted royal blue coats, which seemed odd. It was chilly but not cold enough to have such heavy jackets. Averting their eyes, they didn't look directly at her. She thought they were a couple, but they seemed more like siblings, based on their mannerisms. They appeared to be agitated.

Katie and McGaven walked past and entered through the double doors.

Almost immediately, Katie was struck by the stifling air inside, which had the musty undertone of a basement, as if they were entering a garage that hadn't had any ventilation in a while. The old tile flooring was chipped and she detected unevenness as she walked. Everything was beige, including the floor and the walls, which made it feel more institutional than medical.

There were at least a dozen people sitting in plastic fold-out chairs patiently waiting. Several children were playing in the corner with toys. Some of the women looked up and watched Katie and McGaven walk towards the check-in desk. A couple of men were immersed in their cell phones and didn't pay attention to them. It was obvious that they were cops—their guns and badges were visible. The sustained looks were directed more at Katie than her tall partner.

A short woman with dark hair was at the front check-in counter. She coordinated clipboards with filled-out applications and medical histories.

"Yes?" she said, almost on cue and without looking up. "Take a form and fill it out, then bring it back."

"I'm Detective Scott and this is Deputy McGaven."

The woman's gaze darted at them. "What can I help you with?" she asked, her tone mistrustful.

Katie could see that her name tag read "Rita" and decided to take a friendly approach. She realized that many people, especially in struggling economic areas, didn't trust law enforcement and it made her sad.

"Rita," she said. "We're here to talk to two of the employees, if that's possible."

"What is it about?" she said suspiciously.

"It's about a previous employee, Jeanine Trenton."

Her demeanor softened as her shoulders slumped forward. "Oh, you haven't found the killer yet?" she said, with some hope in her voice.

"That's what we're working on and we just wanted to ask a few more questions. Do you think that would be okay?"

"I'm sorry, it was a real loss losing Jeanine and in such a horrible way. She was one of the good ones. Who do you need to talk to?"

Katie glanced at her notes. "Angela Norton and Virginia Rodriguez."

"Oh, Angie, she's here."

"What about Virginia?" said Katie.

"Uh, sure. She's here today too." Her tone was stilted.

"Would it be possible for me to speak with them?"

"Come with me," she said.

Katie looked to McGaven and he nodded for her to go ahead—he hung back and casually began to check things out.

Katie followed Rita down a long hallway past several closed doors that she assumed were private offices as well as exam rooms. They continued, rounding a corner where they took stairs to the next level. Katie's boot heels made a ringing noise against the metal as they climbed the staircase.

That familiar tug at Katie's stomach tried to get her attention as they climbed in the stuffy and claustrophobic stairwell—the building was clearly old and in need of an update. Pressure seemed to build in her chest, causing her breathing to become shallow and stilted. Whenever she was in a tight area with dim lighting it made her nervous, and she tried to keep her wits and panic in check.

"Sorry, it's a bit rickety, I'm afraid," said Rita. "But it's the only area where we have extra administrative offices. We needed every square foot downstairs for medical offices and exam rooms."

Katie smiled in response, keeping her focus on her breathing.

"Here we are," Rita said.

The door read: "Administrative Director, Angela L. Norton."

Rita knocked on the door.

"Yes, come in," came a voice on the other side.

Rita poked her head in and said, "A detective is here and wanted to ask a few questions about Jeanine."

"Of course, please come in." She eyed Katie a bit suspiciously.

Pushing the door wider, Katie entered the small office, which had no windows. The walls were lined with metal filing cabinets, with more folders on top waiting to be filed. There was a desk in the middle of the room with a computer, printer, and another large stack of files and paperwork.

"Thanks, Rita," said the director. She was a tall, slender woman dressed in a sweater outfit and had a gold chain with glasses dangling around her neck.

Rita shut the door quietly behind her as she left.

"Hi, Ms. Norton," said Katie. "I'm Detective Katie Scott from the Pine Valley Sheriff's Department."

"Pleased to meet you, but I'm saddened that it's under such unpleasant circumstances. I still can't believe she's gone."

Katie thought she detected an east coast accent, but wasn't sure. "My partner and I—he's downstairs right now—are cold case detectives. And we've been given the Jeanine Trenton case."

"Please sit down."

"Thank you." Katie spotted a metal chair up against one of the filing cabinets and slid it in front of the desk. She sat down. "One of the things we do when we receive a cold case investigation is speak with some of the people who knew the victim—and in this case worked with her."

"What can I answer for you?" she said.

Katie immediately liked the director; she appeared to be honest and her body language indicated that she was genuine. She was relaxed and patient, not uptight and suspicious. "Well, firstly, can you tell me, what were Ms. Trenton's responsibilities here? The report said she was a health care specialist."

"Yes. She was like a nurse's aide and was responsible for many things. She would jump in if someone was late or didn't show up. Unfortunately, we have a high turnover of staff here."

"Why is that?"

"Well, the pay is low and it's not very glamorous. Since we are a community health facility that means many times we don't get paid for services, and that means we are understaffed and without everything we need. But we manage to get by every month." She patted the pile of files on her desk.

"Did Ms. Trenton ever confide in you about something or someone that she was having difficulty with?"

Director Norton's face tightened and she hesitated.

"Please keep in mind I've read all the interviews and police reports, so there's nothing that I haven't been made aware of," Katie gently reminded her. "I just want to hear from you—from your personal experience."

"Well… there was a group of nurses that were abusive to Jeanine. They constantly belittled and undermined her, even though she was an amazing worker."

"Did she ever discuss it with you?"

"No, she was quiet and took it. It was obvious, but she loved it here. She wanted to help. You know she could have worked anywhere, but she wanted to help the needy."

Katie made a couple of notes. Her impression of Jeanine Trenton changed a bit as she listened to the director describe her.

"But most of the girls are gone now. I think she was waiting them out."

"Did she ever talk about her time in the army?"

"Not much. I knew about it, of course, through her application, but she didn't say much. Although thinking about it, I do remember she mentioned it once and her eyes would light up when she spoke about the dogs."

"Did anyone ever talk to her about it?"

"Not that I know of."

Katie was hoping for more information, but she had a clearer picture of who Jeanine was and knew that she would have probably really liked her.

"What's the matter, Detective?" asked Director Norton as if she sensed Katie's slight frown.

"Jeanine sounded like a very nice person, a hard worker, well liked—with the exception of a few women here at the time…"

"That's a fair assessment."

"I know there's something I'm missing."

"Such as?"

Katie shifted in her seat, not sure if she should say anything to the director. "There wasn't any talk, or gossip, about someone harassing her at home, maybe?"

"No, nothing that I can think of—"

There was the unmistakable sound of a gunshot from the first floor.

Katie jumped up from her chair and quickly went out to the staircase and listened. She heard voices yelling and then McGaven instructing someone to drop a weapon. She raced back into the director's office where she was standing with a shocked look upon her face.

"Call 911. And tell them shots have been fired. Let them know two police detectives are already here and in need of assistance. Got it?"

Director Norton nodded and quickly picked up her phone.

Katie raced down the stairs, almost stumbling before she reached the bottom. Pulling her weapon, she stepped into the hallway, looking both ways. The shot had come from below, in the vicinity of the entrance and waiting area.

Two nurses came out of a room to see what was going on. The worried expressions on their faces clearly evident as they looked up and down the hallway.

"Stay inside, lock the door," she told them. They obliged without any questions.

Katie hurried down the hall, listening intently, stopping at the corner with her gun held out in front of her. She moved slowly at first, and then continued on when no one appeared.

It was strangely quiet.

Her main concern was the safety of those in the waiting room and her partner. She knew that McGaven was capable and would do whatever it took to protect the people.

Reaching the end of the hallway just before the reception area, Katie slowed to a stop. She saw Rita on the floor in a crouched position. Her eyes were wide and face pale.

Katie caught her attention and made a motion with her hand to move back into the internal rooms.

Rita crawled until she was out of sight and then got up and hurried down the hall to safety and wait.

"No! Someone is going to pay!" yelled a man's voice.

"Take it easy. I'm sure we can work this out," said McGaven calmly with his gun drawn but not aimed at the man. "Just put the gun down."

Katie inched forward and spied around the corner, relieved that her partner was okay and was calmly confronting the situation in the waiting-room area. She saw the man that had been sitting out front when they arrived, now without the heavy blue coat. He had a handgun and was waving it around while pacing. It was clear that he was under pressure and felt that someone was responsible for his distress. She didn't see the other blue-coated person and wondered where she could be.

Pulling back, she looked down the hallway in both directions to check no one was around. Her instincts told her that she needed to assist her partner. There was no other way around to get into the waiting area. The other door was the emergency exit and it would be locked from the inside.

"You're going to arrest me! Me! I didn't let her die! They did!"

"Tell me what happened. We can straighten this out," said McGaven, still sounding composed and measured.

"She's gone! Someone is going to pay!"

Another gunshot rang out.

Katie was ready to move forward when she saw that the man had shot at the ceiling. He wasn't going to kill anyone, she thought.

"That's not the way to do it," said McGaven.

The man was still pacing, fretful and highly strung.

"Put the gun down before someone gets hurt."

Katie crouched low and scanned the area. From what she could see, there was a maintenance door near where the man was pacing.

She turned and raced down the hallway, opening doors. Several people were huddled and hiding.

"Stay here, you're safe," she whispered, flashing her badge, and moved on until she found Rita with two people. "Rita, can you tell me how to get to that maintenance room in the lobby?"

Rita nodded. In a quiet voice, she said, "Down the hallway until you see a room marked 'Storage', at the far end of that room is a maintenance door."

Katie mouthed *thank you* and turned, taking off at a full sprint as fast as she could to the storage door. Opening it, she entered. It was noticeably warmer inside and there was a hum of the heating system as dim lights lit the way. There were controls lit up with green buttons, which didn't mean anything to her. She prayed that she wouldn't run into anyone in maintenance because she didn't have time to explain.

She followed instructions straight and then it turned sharply, but it also narrowed to an uncomfortable space. Gasping hard as her heart hammered in her chest; she caught her breath and pushed her focus. There were no sirens yet, but the police would soon be racing into the parking lot and that might push the man to do something he couldn't take back.

Finally she reached the end where the door opened into the large waiting area. It felt as if she had been running for half an hour when in fact it was barely forty-five seconds.

Resting her hand on the doorknob, she felt for a locking mechanism and slowly turned the device. Pulling the door open a crack, she could see the man had his back to her about six feet away. McGaven still had his gun drawn but it was aimed downward, so as to not provoke the distraught man.

Katie pulled the door a little bit wider and hoped that it didn't make a sound.

Three women were huddled in the corner shielding two children. They saw Katie as she slowly showed them her badge. It was unclear if it made them feel better or not.

The man was beginning to get more enraged now, taking aim at various people and things around the room.

Through the large window Katie saw two police cruisers enter the parking lot without lights and sirens—so as to not stoke the pressure and aggravate the shooter. They crept closer and parked. Two deputies got out and began to make their way toward the health center's door.

Katie knew that she had to act fast if they were going to avoid casualties.

She dared to inch out of the doorway a little bit farther. Not wanting to lose her gun in a scuffle, she returned it to her holster and kept moving stealthily closer to the man.

McGaven knew what she was going to do as his body language stiffened.

The man raised the gun and then he swung his right arm down away from McGaven.

It was now or never. She took a deep gulp of air.

Katie sprinted toward the man at full speed just as he turned to see her charging at him. She slammed into his upper body with full impact, taking him down to the floor, landing on top of him; then sliding a few feet before stopping on the hard tile.

CHAPTER NINETEEN

Friday 1615 hours

McGaven was instantly at Katie's side as she wrestled with the man, adrenalin pumping through her veins, but within seconds they had secured the shooter, arms behind back, cuffed, lying face down. Katie made sure that he didn't have any other weapons just as the two deputies burst through the front doors, their guns drawn.

Recognizing McGaven and Katie, the deputies asked, "You guys okay?"

"Yeah," McGaven said as he helped Katie up. "That was crazy," he said breathlessly.

"I improvised." Her arms and legs still feeling weak, she moved toward the entrance to try and catch her breath.

The man's gun had flown from his hand upon impact. McGaven quickly grabbed the weapon between several layers of tissues pulled from his pocket and gave it to one of the deputies as evidence.

They pulled the man to his feet. "Ten-fifteen, one in custody," the officer said into his radio.

"Where's your friend?" McGaven demanded. "Where?"

"She left," the man said in a weak voice. "She's gone, like everyone else."

McGaven turned to the frightened people. "Everyone okay?"

Most of the people slowly stood up and nodded. Some were speechless, while others were still shell-shocked from the incident.

Katie went outside and sat down on one of the benches—her legs heavy. The fire truck entered the parking lot following precautionary procedure for an active shooter call. She watched it park as the loud airbrakes engaged. Two more patrol cars parked as deputies descended upon the Community Health Alliance.

Katie watched as deputies spoke with witnesses. Her breathing began to turn to normal as she focused her thoughts on the interviews with Angela Norton and Virginia Rodriguez. She knew that the chaos of today wasn't a good time to continue talking to the women.

One of the deputies came out and said to one of the paramedics, "We have a middle-aged woman with chest pains."

McGaven came outside and sat down next to her. "When did you get the idea to body slam the guy?" he said trying to lighten the moment.

"About a minute before I did it."

"A whole minute?"

"Had to plan ahead," she said.

"You okay?" He looked at her with a serious expression.

"Yeah, I think so. Nothing a hot bath won't take care of."

"You amaze me. I know guys that wouldn't try that move."

"We were running out of time. I knew that he really didn't want to hurt anyone—he just wanted someone to listen to him."

"Not from where I was standing. He was shooting. Bad guy. Bad news."

"You going to write the report?" she said.

"It's my turn." He sat quietly for a moment. "Did you get anything from the director?"

"Nothing that will push the investigation forward. We still need to talk with Virginia Rodriguez."

"Before the man started shooting, I was eavesdropping on someone I suspect to be Virginia Rodriguez talking to another woman. I was going to intervene but I was waiting for you. She is a brutal gossip. Mandy was right about Jeanine saying there was a hostile environment here."

"The interviews, the background checks, and what we've investigated so far seems weak. We need to dig more."

"I have faith in our medical examiner and forensics," he said.

"You're right. We can't give up in the bottom of the ninth."

"When did you start referencing baseball?"

"When we needed a home run to solve Jeanine's murder. Let's regroup and keep digging."

"That's what we do."

CHAPTER TWENTY
Saturday 0945 hours

Katie felt energized and happier than she had all week as she drove to one of the lesser-used parks for police K9 training. Sergeant Hardy from Pine Valley Sheriff's Department had invited her and Cisco to participate in routine training as the department's own dogs practiced for an upcoming competition. It helped to keep Cisco's energy in check and he would be doing what he loved most—searching for and catching bad guys.

Cisco whined and paced. He knew—most likely by the change of Katie's energy level—that they were going to train.

Katie had called Lizzy and invited her to come and check out the dogs and training. She had sent a text with the location but didn't hear back from her. Their shared military K9 training was one of the factors that had sealed their friendship. Few people knew what that type of bond was like until they trained and worked in police or military K9.

Even though Katie was on her own time and relaxing for a few hours off from the investigation, her mind was never far from the cases.

Yesterday had been intense, but she reviewed in her mind what they had really learned. She felt they understood Jeanine Trenton's life a little better: her work environment was intense due to the workload and the lack of supplies—it was a job that wasn't for everyone, and that was without the harassment that she had suffered. But Katie thought there were clues they were currently missing that would explain why she was murdered.

Katie turned into the parking area at the park where there were several K9 SUVs from Pine Valley as well as some from the surrounding cities.

Cisco amped up the volume of his whining.

"Easy, boy. Save all that energy for the bad guy."

Katie got out of her Jeep and walked through the parking lot until she saw Sergeant Hardy talking with two officers that she wasn't familiar with. He smiled and nodded when he saw her.

"Hi, Detective," the sergeant said.

"Sergeant. Nice to see you."

"Is Cisco ready for some action?"

"Always."

"Good. We're setting up for protection work and then some trailing to find the bad guy." He made some notations on a clipboard.

"Great."

"Are you on a tight schedule?"

"Not really. I'm meeting my uncle later, but he can wait." She laughed.

"Well, it'll probably be about twenty minutes before your turn is up."

"That's fine. Thank you."

Sergeant Hardy added her name and moved on to the other officers.

Katie began watching the impressive teams working with a decoy—there were German shepherds and Belgian Malinois and one black Labrador retriever. She turned and saw a gold Camaro enter the parking lot. Recognizing it immediately, she hurried to the car.

"Lizzy," she said, glad that her friend could make it.

"Wouldn't miss this," she said and shut her car door.

As Katie neared, she saw John get out of the passenger side. Taken back for a moment, she kept her composure. She thought Lizzy and John weren't seeing one another because of the long distance, but they did seem like a good match.

"Hey, John. Nice to see you." Katie smiled.

"Yeah, it's hard to get him to get out in the fresh air," Lizzy laughed.

"I can understand that."

"I've heard so much about Cisco and his abilities, I wanted to watch the K9 teams in action," he said.

"Glad you could come," said Katie.

"C'mon, girl, let's go check this out," said Lizzy as Katie led the way.

The three of them joked and watched the impressive teams in action.

"Well, I have my favorite," said Lizzy.

"The tan Malinois?"

"Nope, Cisco will always be my favorite. I remember him from the beginning."

"Scott, you're up next," said Hardy.

"Go get 'em, girl!"

Katie hurried to her Jeep, opened the back door, quickly snapped on a leash, and led Cisco out. He was poised and ready. Always knowing when it was time to train or catch the bad guys, he waited for his handler's commands. He looked exceptionally shiny in the sunlight.

Katie placed her gun in the holster and secured handcuffs to her belt.

They entered the area where an old baseball field once stood. There was a police car used to make the reenactment as authentic as possible.

"We'll pop the back door when it's needed," said Sergeant Hardy.

Katie nodded. She knew this drill well and it was one of Cisco's favorites. She glanced to the fence where Lizzy and John watched intently. Lizzy gave a wave accompanied by her big smile.

Katie put Cisco in the back of the patrol car and shut the door. She saw him chuff and whine as he paced back and forth.

She got behind the wheel where the keys awaited. Turning the engine over, it roared to life. She was supposed to drive across the field where the decoy—one of the officers in a heavy-duty bite suit—waited to agitate the situation.

Katie couldn't help but flash back to her time on patrol in Sacramento. She wasn't in a K9 unit, but sitting in the police cruiser brought back so many memories.

She put the car in drive and eased it forward. Cisco was barking and wanting to get to work. The decoy stood ahead, facing her and not moving. She shifted the car into park and exited the vehicle.

"Put your hands up!" she said. "Put them where I can see them!"

The decoy obliged and put his hands in the air.

"Turn around and put your hands on your head!"

The decoy hesitated.

"Do it now!"

He slowly turned around and raised his hands, placing them on the back of his head.

Katie walked forward assertively, approaching the decoy. She patted him down and then placed one handcuff on his right hand and then he turned and began struggling with her. He pushed her hard and Katie hit the ground.

"Cisco!" she yelled. "*Fass!*" she commanded in German, meaning "bite".

The cruiser's back door popped open and instantly a black blur flew out of the car and was attached to the decoy's arm, taking him to the ground.

Katie climbed to her feet, watching Cisco.

"Okay," said the decoy, and stopped moving.

"Cisco, *aus*!" she yelled, ordering him to release his bite.

Cisco did so immediately, relaxing his jaws, and sitting to await the next order, but still barking incessantly, never taking his eyes from the decoy.

Katie approached the decoy to secure the other handcuff and he grabbed her forcefully.

Cisco immediately jumped into action again.

"*Aus*!" Katie yelled and the dog let go. "*Platz*." Cisco instantly lay down.

There were a few claps and whispers from the audience due to Cisco's impressive skills of releasing the bad guy in record time.

Katie secured the other handcuff and escorted the decoy to the police car as Cisco obediently walked to heel at her side.

Lizzy and John whooped and hollered. "Good boy, Cisco!"

Katie laughed, feeling a bit winded due to the adrenalin pumping through her body. Taking the cuffs off the decoy, she said, "That was great."

"Hey, sorry about shoving you so hard. I'm used to big guys."

"No problem. Made it more real."

The decoy went back to the exercise location as Katie snatched up Cisco's leash. They walked back to the main area.

"Great job," said Sergeant Hardy. To the rest of the group, he advised: "You could learn something from Detective Scott. Great call-off."

Lizzy hurried to Katie. "Wow, you haven't lost your touch. Cisco is spot on."

"Thanks," she said smiling. Katie loved the work.

"Okay, I'm totally impressed," said John. "That was awesome."

"Thank you. It's a lot of fun, that's for sure. These dogs are all amazing."

Katie went back to her Jeep to give Cisco a rest and spent the next half hour chatting with Lizzy and John, waiting for her turn at the tracking and trailing exercise. She saw a different side to John from the professional forensic scientist side and found out that he was really funny and charming. She still didn't know if Lizzy and John were going to try to make a long-distance relationship work, which made her think about Chad—wondering what he was doing at that exact moment. They had been playing phone tag, leaving text messages and voicemails but never quite connecting.

Katie had secured Cisco in a lightweight harness and a fifteen-foot leash so that she could have control of him as they moved through the forest for the tracking exercise. She waited for the green light from Sergeant Hardy. This particular exercise wasn't a spectator one, which left Lizzy and John to wait at the parking lot until Cisco found the bad guy.

"All ready, Scott?" said Hardy.

Katie focused her attention ahead. The trail wasn't like what she was used to. It was narrow and places were cluttered with low brush and downed tree branches. It was cooler in the dense trees as she gathered her thoughts.

"Cisco, *such*," she said.

Cisco took the lead, keeping his nose down. Every once in a while he would stop and catch some scent in the air.

As the dog led Katie slightly downhill, she navigated the forest as best she could so that she could keep Cisco's pace. It was tricky as branches scraped by her legs. She found herself in a bob and weave move every few feet, keeping small branches and pine needles from slapping her face.

Cisco slowed until he completely stopped. His ears up, he scrutinized the forest as he caught wind of something airborne and unnatural. The scent made him growl—low and guttural.

Katie stopped. She too listened but the only sound she heard was the slight breeze weaving through the trees. There were no birds chirping and nothing sounded in the underbrush. Goosebumps rose on her arms. Taking Cisco's lead, she felt something was wrong. There were no footsteps behind her of the sergeant or any other officer following.

"Cisco, what is it?" she whispered.

Two consecutive gunshots exploded just above their heads. After two seconds, two more gunshots sounded. It echoed all around them.

CHAPTER TWENTY-ONE

Saturday 1145 hours

Shooting wasn't a part of the K9 training exercise.

Katie instinctively lunged forward, grabbing Cisco's collar and guiding him down—they hid in a small ravine, hopefully out of sight as a potential target. She stayed still—listening. There were no footsteps or crunching noises that would indicate someone walking. Who was shooting? A hunter? She didn't think so. She waited for the next round of gunfire.

Luckily, she had her cell phone in her pocket and she had turned it to vibrate. She called Lizzy. It rang twice before her friend answered.

"Lizzy," whispered Katie.

"Katie, are you alright? What's going on? Everyone heard the shots and are responding." Her voice was winded and concerned.

Katie could hear voices yelling back and forth.

"We're fine. We tucked down in a small ravine... but..."

"But what?"

"It's unclear if the shots were meant for us or not. They seemed to be aimed high."

"Did you see anyone?"

"No, but the shots came from the west."

"I'll tell them. About how far are you?"

"We're about a quarter of a mile down."

"Okay. Stay there until they tell you it's safe."

"Okay."

The phone call ended.

Katie waited.

Cisco's rhythmic panting reminded her of all the stressful situations they had encountered together. She and Cisco usually took point to get through rough terrain infested with insurgents and heavily set explosive traps. She thought back to the tiny spaces they had to hide from the enemy fire as bullets pummeled too close for comfort. The battle-torn towns that had once been thriving little communities, where the enemy could be hiding around every corner, waiting to attack.

Her heart pounded, making her feel dizzy. In an instant, her arms and legs felt weakened. She perspired underneath her jacket even though it was cool and comfortable outside. She thought that she caught a whiff of ejected gunfire, but knew that it wasn't real. Consciously slowing her breath helped lessen her symptoms. She was concentrating so hard on listening for signs that someone was sneaking up to ambush her that she wasn't sure if her mind was playing tricks on her.

But then Katie heard real voices coming. The sound of cops communicating and clearing areas as they slowly made their way to her. She breathed a sigh of relief. Of everything that she had been anticipating today, an active shooter in the forest wasn't one of them.

She waited another fifteen minutes—which felt more like an hour—until she heard the word.

"Scott, it's clear!" yelled one of the officers.

Katie slowly crawled up to the makeshift trail with Cisco beside her. She stood up and saw three officers approach.

"You okay?" said one of them.

"Yes, we're fine."

"Go ahead and walk back to the parking lot. It's been cleared for your safety."

"Thank you," she said as she hiked back.

After Katie returned to the main area, Lizzy and John met up with her.

"Are you okay?" they both asked in unison.

"Yes. We're fine. A bit unnerving." She was shaky but held strong.

Sergeant Hardy approached. "Detective Scott, we're going to need your statement before you go."

"Of course." She looked at Lizzy and John. "I'll be right back."

Katie followed the sergeant.

"I'm afraid that I'm not going to be much help. I didn't see or hear anything except the shots."

"You said the shots came from the west."

"Yes, but they seemed to be high in the trees."

"Anything else?" he said. She could tell that he was annoyed that she couldn't help or provide any other information.

"It's just... it seems to me that they were just trying to scare me—not kill me. Otherwise, I would be dead."

CHAPTER TWENTY-TWO

Saturday 1330 hours

Katie was due to meet with her Uncle Wayne. They would usually meet for lunch once a month to catch up without the backdrop of the sheriff's department. They typically would go to a restaurant or an art exhibit, but today had decided to have a nice quiet lunch at her uncle's condo. Katie knew that the transition of moving into a condo from the home he had shared with his late wife was something that took getting used to. It was nice to take some time and enjoy the views.

She stood on the balcony and waited for her uncle to finish preparing the meal. More than anything, she needed family and something to distract her from the current events. It was the healthy thing to do. She had waited to tell him about the incident at K9 training.

Cisco had found a comfortable place on the couch inside and seemed content after a morning of training.

Katie stared out at the eighteen-hole golf course beside her uncle's condo. The view from the balcony was beautiful, with the golf course spread beneath it and the countryside and trees around it.

At first, when her uncle decided to sell his big house in the country after his wife was murdered, Katie didn't know if this type of setting would make him happy. But looking around, she felt now that it seemed to fit him.

Uncle Wayne's three-bedroom condo was spacious, with plenty of room for his hobbies, guests, and any comfort he would need. He could entertain if he wanted and it simplified his life, which was what he needed.

"Okay," he said as he carried out two plates and two bowls.

"Oh wow," said Katie. She eyed the gooey grilled-cheese sandwiches and bowls of vegetable soup, and sat down at the small bistro table. "This was always my favorite when I was a kid—actually, it still is." She laughed.

Taking his seat across from his niece, the sheriff said, "I know you've had a full week and it just seemed like the right meal to have today."

"Uncle Wayne, you always know how to make me feel better."

"It's tough sometimes at work because I want to be your uncle when certain things happen, but I'm the sheriff and that's the way I have to act."

"I know."

"I get the feeling you have something either to tell me or ask me."

Katie took a bite of the sandwich. "Yum, just as I remembered it."

Her uncle eyed her seriously, waiting for an answer.

"It's this…" she began and stopped.

"Is it work or Chad?"

"Actually, it's both, but let's start with work because I'm not ready to talk about Chad yet." She stirred her soup and paused. "I don't understand this case."

"What do you mean?"

"Well, it's a bit unorthodox, wouldn't you say?"

"I don't know about that. Departments and agencies overlap and help each other all the time—especially with high-profile and serial cases."

Katie stared at her uncle, trying to decipher if he was keeping something back from her. She tried to explain from another angle. "Why would the state need help from us—me, especially? I mean, they have so many people at their disposal, including use of the FBI profilers."

"I think it's important that we can help. So if we can, then we do. I would have never agreed to take on these cases if I thought there was something not right."

Katie wasn't completely reassured but she couldn't back up her uneasiness with anything concrete. She decided not to push the issue. "Thanks, Uncle Wayne. I love being able to talk to you."

"Me too. I love you, Katie."

Katie smiled and tried to enjoy the rest of her visit. The conversation made her feel a little better but it still didn't make her job any easier.

Katie feared for what was going to happen next, so she told her uncle about the incident at the K9 training center before he heard it from someone else.

He listened intently, not interrupting, allowing Katie to finish.

"My take is that the shots have something to do with our case, like a warning."

The sheriff hesitated. "I agree. And…"

"And what?" she said softly, knowing what he was going to say.

"And, it seems that your K9 connection with all these cases should be at the top of your list. You need to keep yourself safe, otherwise I will assign an officer to you."

"You don't need to do that. I'm fine. I have Cisco and my house has a top-of-the-line security system."

"I will decide if you need more security or not. I don't want you alone investigating without McGaven. Understood?"

Katie was about to protest but then, "Fine."

"I mean it, Katie. The more you tell me about these cases, the more I think you need to take extra precautions."

CHAPTER TWENTY-THREE
Sunday 0545 hours

That night was terrible for Katie as far as rest was concerned. She had tossed and turned, jolted awake continually by imagined sounds and terrible memories coming back. And then the insomnia set in, where she couldn't get back to sleep. She missed Chad terribly. It was like a part of her was gone. He had been the one constant in her life ever since she was in the fourth grade—no one knew her like he did.

Katie decided to get up to write in her journal before the sun rose to take her mind off things. Her psychologist told her to put pen to paper if something was bothering her—so she did. It had been helpful in the past and it had become easier the more she did it.

Cisco pushed his wet nose at her journal, giving her his usual German shepherd whine.

"Let me finish, Cisco," she giggled, scratching him behind his ears.

The dog padded around the living room and quickly came back to pester Katie.

"Okay, okay. We'll go on a run."

Cisco barked in agreement, bounding around the room in circles.

Katie grabbed a light high-protein breakfast and changed into her running clothes and an all-weather windbreaker.

Heading for the door, she said, "C'mon, Cisco, let's go!"

They drove to her favorite hiking and running area at Break Ridge. It would be near deserted on a chilly Sunday morning, unlike in a month or so's time, when there would be more visitors. She needed to grab as much fresh air as she could and let her mind take a break from thinking about killers. It would energize her brain and she would be more alert to dive back into the investigation again.

Katie parked just adjacent to the entrance and was the only vehicle in the parking area. She adjusted her running pants to accommodate a small Beretta pistol in her ankle holster. Since she was alone and several miles away from any home or business, Katie liked to be prepared. She preferred to take out any unnecessary complications that could arise.

She slipped her cell phone into her pocket along with her car key. Taking Cisco's leash, she wound it around her waist and secured the clasp in case she needed it. After a few stretches, she was ready to go.

"You ready, Cisco?"

Three loud barks was his answer. He was a black blur as he spun around and headed to the entrance, indicated by two large pine trees and a small sign saying "River Ridge."

Katie began her run at the top of the hill and slowly warmed up with a light jog as she increased her speed.

Cisco always knew what to do. He kept up with her ambitious pace: occasionally wandering off the trail, but never for too long, he would then bound back up on the path next to her with his tongue hanging out. He kept a watchful eye for anything out of the ordinary—his main job was to make sure that Katie was safe.

As Katie ran down the path, she steadied her breath and enjoyed the fresh morning aroma of pine and the crisp morning air. There was nothing better. Finally, her muscles eased and her mind softened, as she connected with the beautiful scenery. Even Cisco seemed to be more relaxed.

Katie noticed that in many places the ground was spongy and was holding water from previous storms, although it wasn't yet muddy.

She climbed up to a lookout, slowing her pace a bit to catch her breath. Jogging on the spot, she stayed to admire her surroundings and to appreciate everything that the area had to offer. Sometimes, when she was so focused on a case, she forgot to take a second to be in the moment and enjoy the world around her.

The wind picked up, whipping through the trees. The breeze seemed to switch directions, first blasting her face and then pushing against her back.

Katie realized that a storm was on the way from the change in temperature and the fast-moving clouds. She didn't want to get soaked and have a wet dog in the car, so she decided to turn around and retrace her steps back to the entrance. She had been running for a solid twenty-five minutes at a good pace.

The air temperature dropped further as Katie slowed her pace for the cool down, making her shiver. A strange noise reverberated from above—a low boom and then a sputtering sound. She thought at first it was some kind of thunder, but it wasn't like anything she had heard before. Her instincts told her to leave.

Looking around, she didn't see Cisco.

"Cisco! Here!" she called.

Within five seconds, his large head and perked ears came into view. He ran faster and stayed next to her as she kept her jogging pace.

The strange sounds continued as she decided to up her pace again, still moving down the hillside. She didn't stop to look, suddenly realizing that what she could hear was the sound of—

A massive pine tree with a huge trunk fell in front of her and Cisco, making the ground give way.

Katie stopped abruptly, startled and catching her breath as the tree blocked her path, but it didn't stop there: the trunk kept moving. It made her dizzy, trying to keep her eye on the shifting ground.

Taking hold of Cisco's collar and keeping him close to her left side, there was nothing that she could do except watch the massive tree trunk slowly begin to slide down the hillside.

That's when it happened: her footing crumbled beneath her. Katie jumped up as far as she could toward higher ground, but it was no use. Both she and Cisco began slipping down the side of what was left of the running path. She felt the world collapsing beneath her, as if in slow motion.

Grabbing hold of Cisco with one arm around his neck and the other around his body, she held him as they both began to drop, slowly at first, and then the earth took them as if they were shooting down a slide. Dropping into a sitting position, still holding tightly to Cisco, she shot down twenty feet before there was a large enough place to stop—abruptly.

The groaning and cracking of the tree began to subside.

Katie had closed her eyes tight and held onto Cisco for dear life. She had no way of knowing how their ride would end, but the silence was both deafening and frightening. It was like nothing she had ever experienced or seen before and that unknown moment scared her the most.

She was completely covered in mud and cold earth, making her shiver. Opening her eyes, she checked out Cisco and he was muddy too but hadn't sustained any injuries. Still gripping him tight, she was grateful they were both okay.

Looking around, she saw they were surrounded by branches that had miraculously missed them as the tree's weight finally settled into softer soil.

"Well, Cisco, I guess we're going to have to climb up," she said softly.

The dog got to his feet and headed upward, sliding backward and then pushing uphill again.

Katie did the same. She made progress, but it was slow going, having to climb over branches and then navigate the slippery areas. She had more dirt, mud, and forest debris on her than she would have thought possible as they neared the top.

Cisco stopped abruptly. His tail lowered, along with his body stature. A low guttural growl emitted from him as his hackles rose along his spine, concentrating between his shoulder blades.

Katie knew there was some type of danger. It wasn't insurgents, but she knew how to read the dog well enough that something was terribly wrong—unnatural. She didn't have to wait long before she saw what Cisco had sensed.

Standing at the top, about fifteen feet away, along what was left of the hiking ridge, was a large mountain lion. The sizeable tan cat fixated its yellow eyes down at them. Its strong forequarters were poised, its ears alert against its round head. Katie could see from this range just how powerful were its neck and jaws. She knew it was unusual for them to attack people, but their numbers were strong and more reports of attacks had been documented.

Cisco began to bark rapidly—it echoed around the hillside and down into the valley.

"Cisco, *platz*," she said, trying to get the dog's attention in his trained German command for stay in place. "*Platz*," she said again until the dog obeyed. Slowly he backed down and positioned himself in a low crouch between Katie and the lion with his hackles raised.

Katie had seen a few mountain lions in her life, but they were never aggressive, merely curious or territorial. She could tell that the cat was a male—he was largest one she had ever seen. She moved slowly toward her ankle holster. A warning shot should snap the cat out of its fixation and make it flee. That was the plan, anyway.

The mountain lion opened his mouth and began to pant, but never took its yellow eyes off them.

Gently unsnapping her holster, she was just about to withdraw her weapon when the sound of a gunshot rang out, instantly startling the mountain lion as it disappeared from Katie's view. Shocked that there was gunfire—whether it was friendly or not—she stayed in her position next to Cisco, ready for whatever would come next. Her rapid heartbeat battered her chest. Her hands shook and cold perspiration trickled down her back. Her vision blurred and then cleared. Blinking her eyes rapidly to stay focused, she remained in the same position. Feeling the dog's own rapid heartbeat next to her side, she flashed back as she detected the smell of expelled gunfire—an odor that was forever rooted into her memory.

Her platoon had walked into an ambush because of incorrect intel they had received. Half of the group had made it to safety with sufficient cover and the other half with limited safety, but she and Cisco were caught in between. The last barrage of gunfire had ceased, but the air was filled with smoke and gunpowder, along with an unnatural quiet. It was difficult to see anyone until the dust settled. The next onslaught could mean rockets and bombs, but the silence was more terrifying than bullets. She was in an unknown, foreign place, thousands of miles from home and no help available in the near future. They had to rely on each other, their wits, and calmness to focus on what had to be done. She heard "Katie". It was faint at first, but then it was louder, "Katie"… "Katie"…

"Katie!" the voice yelled. "You alright? Katie!"

Katie tensed. Her hands felt sweaty against the gun grip as she wondered if someone was really calling her name.

Cisco barked three times.

"Katie!"

She knew she heard someone calling her that time. "We're here!" she yelled back.

Carefully, with Cisco following, she managed to get to the top of the hill where there was a small flat ridge and sat down—waiting still with her gun in a prone position. The dog hunkered down next to her side.

"Katie!"

"We're here!"

She still didn't recognize the man's voice. There was some thrashing just on the other side of the downed tree and climbing to the top was Special Agent Campbell.

"Agent Campbell?" she said completely stunned. "Where did you come from?"

"Let's get you out of here first," he said.

"How did you know I was here?" Immediately, she was suspicious: why had he happened to be there just when she needed help to scare away the mountain lion? "Why are you here?" she demanded as her usual senses came back to her.

"A long story," he lamely answered. "Let's get you to safer ground." He was dressed in jeans and a heavy jacket. His blond hair was perfect, considering they were outdoors.

Katie was uneasy about the situation, but she took him up on his assistance.

It took about fifteen minutes for Katie to climb over the tree trunk, but it was much simpler for Cisco because he had trained for all types of agility moves over the years.

When Katie got on solid ground and shook off the thought of that tree sliding down the hillside taking her and Cisco with it, she realized and was grateful that someone knew that they had taken a fall.

She felt one hundred percent better as they walked to the parking lot and she saw two SUVs—one was her Jeep. Turning to Campbell she said, "Why *are* you here?"

"I was following you," he said matter-of-factly.

"What?"

"It's not what you think."

"Oh, now you know what I think?"

He laughed and turned to her. "I had some questions for you. I called you twice. Go ahead and check your cell."

Katie had forgotten all about her cell phone. She pulled it from her pocket, relieved that it was still in one piece, and to her surprise saw that he had called her—twice. "You did call."

"That's what I said."

"Why did you call, and on a Sunday?"

"I needed to talk to you," he said calmly.

She scrutinized him for a moment, trying to decide if he was as innocent as he was making it sound. "You still haven't told me how you found me."

"That's easy. I tracked you by your phone. It's easy these days…"

"Isn't that—"

"Illegal? No, not really. I wanted to know where a homicide detective working my cases was and I found her."

Katie walked to her Jeep, opened the back and pulled out some water for Cisco. She looked down and realized what an incredible mess she was. "Agent Campbell, I don't know what kind of game you're playing…"

He took a breath. "Dane."

"Dane?"

"Yes, that's my name. If I can call you Katie, then you can call me Dane."

"I prefer Agent Campbell."

"As you wish."

She tried to clean her running pants with a towel. "Look, I'm not one that tattles, but you're treading on thin ice. I don't think it's appropriate to spy on colleagues."

"Look, Detective Scott, I'm sorry that this offends you. But I assure you it's in good faith."

Katie was beginning to dislike the agent even more—he wasn't helping his case.

"I followed your cell phone signal and then I thought I'd take a trail. I heard the horrible tree crash, I came across the mountain lion, and well, I scared it away."

Katie concentrated on cleaning her clothes and didn't look at him. She was still deciding whether or not she wanted to speak to him again. She was angry, thankful, and annoyed all at the same time so she didn't want to say something she would regret.

"New Jeep?" he asked.

"Yes, it's actually the second one in a few months."

"I see. What happened to the other one?"

"It was in a… well, it got rain and mud damage, which ruined the engine, dented the doors," she mumbled. The truth was that her car was damaged working a previous missing persons case during a torrential rain storm.

"Look, I have some blankets you could wrap up in. Why don't I give you a ride home?"

"Oh, no thanks. I'll be fine. I don't want to leave my Jeep here."

"Well, let me at least lend you the blanket so you won't wipe out your seats."

Katie was tired and didn't want to play the agent's games. "Sure, that would be great." She forced a small smile.

Agent Campbell went to his SUV and retrieved a gray blanket and brought it to Katie.

"Thanks," she said and wrapped it around her as she was beginning to shiver.

"I mean it. I wanted to talk to you about the cases."

"Can it wait until tomorrow?"

"I know you have quite the schedule, I just wanted to share some information." He kept his focus on her, making her somewhat uncomfortable.

"Well…"

"Unless you're busy for the rest of the day?"

"Okay," she said reluctantly.

"Meet me at Tiny's Diner. Do you know where that is?"

"Yes. In an hour?"

"That sounds good."

CHAPTER TWENTY-FOUR

Sunday 1345 hours

Katie made it home and quickly jumped into the shower to heat up and to relieve her sore muscles. It took several minutes to feel warm and back to her usual self. The heat and steam wiped away any anxious symptoms she had.

She couldn't get Agent Campbell out of her mind. He was acting strange. His explanations were smooth and gave the impression he was honest—but was he?

Was he still following her?

Why did he really want her and McGaven on the case?

The more she rehashed every meeting she'd had with him, the more she thought that things didn't ring true. She couldn't figure out how or why the Pine Valley Sheriff's Department was brought into the cases. Her uncle didn't give her any indication that there was more she didn't know.

Katie quickly dressed and took care of Cisco, leaving him home.

"I'll be back in about an hour," she said as she closed the front door.

Katie drove in the small parking lot for Tiny's Diner and immediately spotted Campbell's large white SUV along with several other cars. She parked and quickly got out, heading to the front door.

It had been a while since she had been to the diner, but it had been around for as long as she could remember. Ever since she was a kid, they'd had the best milkshakes and cheeseburgers.

She pushed open the glass door with an old "Open" sign that had been hanging there for years. It was crinkled and worn around the edges from years of being exposed to the sun. As she stepped inside she was greeted with the smell of coffee and the daily chili special. She saw Campbell right away. He waved to her as she approached the red booth. She quickly rethought the wisdom of meeting him outside of typical business hours. She felt a drop in her stomach and a familiar tension in her neck and back that usually meant trouble—but she was also curious about what he had to say.

"Detective," he said. There were already two menus on the table. "Nice of you to make it. I thought maybe you would stand me up."

Katie sat down. "No, I gave you my word so here I am. What do you have to tell me?"

"No 'Hello, how are you doing?' first? By the way, you look great considering I just saw you barely an hour ago."

Katie remained quiet, staring at him.

"You want to look at the menu?"

"Just coffee."

"Okay," he said and waved over the server. "Two coffees please." Turning back to Katie, he said, "Good?"

She nodded but thought that she was making a mistake meeting him like this. Thinking that McGaven should be there hearing the information too, perhaps she should excuse herself and reconvene the meeting tomorrow. "I think it would be—"

"I have reason to believe," he blurted out, interrupting her, "that we're looking at two killers. Let me rephrase that… an original killer and a copycat."

That was not what Katie had expected. It was like he dropped a bomb on her and the investigation.

"Wait a minute. How long have you known this?" she asked as their coffees arrived.

"We had our suspicions, but nothing solid. That's why it wasn't in the paperwork."

"Suspicions? Did you think about letting us in on it?"

"There was nothing concrete—yet. I don't like spinning tales or spreading gossip that will run investigators down false paths."

"What changed?" Katie kept her composure, glancing around at the restaurant and noticing that no one was paying them any attention—most were engaged in their own conversations.

"I know you have had your hands full," he said. "I wanted to update you as soon as possible so that nothing would slow down the current investigation. It's another angle that you might want to entertain."

Entertain?

She waited to hear more details.

"You haven't spent much time on the first two victims, Nancy Day and Gwen Sanderson."

Katie shook her head. "Just through the military K9 facility, but not much information that would help us." She had skimmed the material but decided to start with the cold case in her county jurisdiction—a decision with which Sheriff Scott had agreed.

"Our second victim Gwen Sanderson killed Nancy Day."

"What?" Katie managed to say. It was a stunning, but an interesting realization. But she didn't know how they could have come to that conclusion. It seemed to be pulled out of thin air.

"A couple of us had our suspicions when Gwen Sanderson was killed. Some things didn't look right with the execution of the murder, despite the general theme being close—the pose, a dramatic scene, and the jewelry being highlighted."

"What convinced you?"

"One of my investigators noticed that Nancy Day's scene was neat and tidy, the makeup was perfect, her hair was styled, whereas with the second and third murders, the makeup was poorly executed and the victims were made to look ugly. Also, the bruising to Nancy's chest looked accidental, but the others seemed deliberate."

Despite her mistrust of the man, Katie was intrigued because she had noticed some anomalies herself.

Campbell added more sugar to his coffee than he should. "We were checking what these two women were doing on the day each was murdered, and a few days before—a victimology timeline. And that's when we noticed some strange things that led us to analyzing Sanderson and what she was doing on the day of Day's murder."

"What made you check Sanderson's schedule?"

"Gwen Sanderson's alibi for the day that Nancy Day was murdered seemed legit—three investigators checked on this. But, everything that she told her friends and family was a lie. She seemed to be leading a double life. When so many small things began to fall apart, we looked further."

"What evidence makes you think that Gwen Sanderson killed Nancy Day? What proof?" she said, still not believing that this was a solid lead.

He leaned back, almost as if he couldn't believe that she didn't immediately agree with his findings. "One, Sanderson had no alibi and she was within the vicinity of the crime scene during the time of the murder. Two, knives were found near her residence that had Day's blood on them."

"Why wasn't she arrested at the time?"

"Her possible involvement wasn't brought to our attention until after her murder."

"Theoretically, the only way that could happen is if the women knew each other. But why the copycat? Who would do that? Someone following the cases?" Katie felt like she was on an amusement park ride with all of the information spinning around her at breakneck speed.

"I knew you'd understand what I'm talking about."

"I think, Agent Campbell, that you are grasping at straws without any solid evidence or link. So now what you're telling me is that Nancy Day's murder is solved because Gwen Sanderson did it. But her murder, as well as Jeanine Trenton's, and the Jane Doe at the fairgrounds are all the work of a copycat?" Katie shook her head in disbelief.

"Look closer at the crime scenes," he urged. "We're close."

"What was the reason or motive for Sanderson to kill Day?" she said.

Taking a sip of coffee, a little too loud for Katie's taste, he said simply, "I don't think we'll ever really know. But, for the other murders…"

"Yes?"

"My theory? And it's a theory, don't forget."

"Please… keep going."

"Someone who is trying to make themselves a household one. Someone who read about Nancy's case and wanted to continue for whatever reason—fame, revenge, or out of hatred."

"I see."

"Look, Detective, I know that you are a by-the-book investigator. And you've proven how good you really are in a short period of time."

Katie still couldn't shake the feeling that she was being set up and was being fed disinformation—her instincts told her to keep to her investigation.

"We're relying on you and your partner to find the killer. The copycat killer."

"I'm working the two cases now in my jurisdiction; however, that's not to say I'm not going to look over the first two."

"Of course not."

Katie slowly digested the information. Her head spun. She needed to verify the new information about Sanderson. "When did you come to this theory?" she said.

"When my entire team couldn't go any further, it pushed me to look outside of the box."

"I see." Although Katie didn't see.

"I can tell you're not completely on board with us."

"I need to see for myself," was all that she could say. She needed to talk to McGaven.

"Absolutely. I know you want the training videos from the military K9 facility and I'll also get you the list of recruits who made the cut—and the ones that didn't."

"I have one question and I really need for you to be transparent—and give me an honest answer. There are many detectives and investigators you could have gone to and you obviously have in the past." She took a breath and felt she needed to brace herself. "Why did you choose me?"

Special Agent Campbell leaned forward and lowered his voice. "That's easy. And that's why we're keeping such close tabs on you. Your proven skills. Haven't you and McGaven solved every case—so far? Well, there's also your military background in K9 explosives training and your above average investigative skills… of course." He watched her closely.

"It almost sounds to me that you're using me as bait because I have the military K9 background similar to the victims."

"That's one possible way."

CHAPTER TWENTY-FIVE

Monday 0835 hours

Katie drove her usual route to the sheriff's department. She could get there faster, but she preferred a slightly longer journey to let her mind wander about the current cases. Plus this route meant more trees, less traffic, the landmarks that hadn't changed since she was a little girl, and a little extra time to enjoy the town she had loved her entire life. Everything that made her life and perspective what it was today.

McGaven had called her at 8:05 a.m. and said to meet him and John Blackburn in forensics regarding the Jeanine Trenton case. Katie had been running behind, since she had overslept. It was rare, but it happened. It had been quite the tumultuous weekend and she still hadn't had the time to update McGaven on everything.

She entered the forensic department and immediately heard laughter—not just chuckles but full-blown hysterical laughter. It seemed odd and out of place in such a quiet zone that was normally deathly silent, but now she could hear two men laughing. No doubt it was John and McGaven.

Katie slowed her pace and hesitated before the forensic exam room door. She peered around the corner where McGaven casually leaned against a work table and John was seated in a chair. She watched them talk about sports for a minute and then she stepped inside the doorway.

"Hi," she said.

"There she is," said McGaven. "We were wondering if your skills were better suited to hockey or football."

They laughed.

"Football," said John. "Definitely."

"I don't know, hockey could really use someone like Katie."

Katie smiled, still feeling her sore muscles from the incident on Friday but not letting the guys know it. "Go ahead, have your fun."

"You know we're kidding, but you've got some serious skills," said John. Dressed in a black polo shirt, leaning back in the chair, he crossed his arms, showing his tattoos. He was always dressed informally, but as if he was ready to go at a moment's notice to attend a crime scene. His experience for eight years as a Navy Seal made him a great asset as the supervisor in the forensic unit and to the sheriff's department.

"I think the army helped," McGaven chimed. "My only regret was that it wasn't on video."

"Let me put my stuff in the office and I'll be right back," Katie said.

She dropped her coat and briefcase on her desk before returning to the exam room. She was interested in what John had to say about Jeanine Trenton's crime scene evidence.

Returning to the exam area, she said, "Okay, what do you have?"

"Well," John began. "All this evidence has already been studied and tested. And by experts in the FBI," he added. His voice didn't give the indication that he was impressed by their findings.

"I want to know what *you* think," she said. She knew what the reports said, but she wanted a new set of eyes on the case.

John smiled. "Okay. Now we're talking. I'm sorry to say that we didn't get anything from the Raven Woods house. No prints near the door, camera, or gas intake. Zip." He pulled up photos on his computer of the comparison and the potential weapons that made the wound patterns. "According to the big guys, an eight-inch blade made the neck wound."

"Like a butcher's knife?" she said.

"It's possible, but I have issues with the jagged cuts in the skin every half centimeter. See here," he instructed as he magnified the image. There were little crescent shapes along the skin like tiny-toothed cuts.

"Hesitation marks?"

"No, more like a dull knife or one with a serrated edge."

"Something that a person would find handy in a kitchen?"

"Could be. But reporting it as a butcher's knife is too generic—besides, it's too flat a blade. Too many variable factors—like the sharpness—to be one hundred percent accurate. The eight inches would seem to be consistent, so it wouldn't be a type of pocket knife." He flipped the screen to a close-up of a tattoo on the inside of Jeanine's right wrist. "I didn't see anything about her tattoo in the report. It's very faint and it appears that at some point there was an attempt to remove it, most likely with a dermabrasion technique, but it wasn't completely successful."

"Didn't know about it." Katie was surprised that they didn't see it initially. "That's where layers of skin are removed?"

"Yes."

Katie leaned in closer to the screen and saw a gold outlined five-pointed star with "K9" and partial solid dog head with two faint slashes making an "X" through it. "It's so small, but it's definitely Army K9." She marveled a moment, wondering why Jeanine didn't continue her training or why she would have wanted to remove the tattoo.

"Maybe she wanted to remove it because of her jobs?" suggested McGaven, studying it too.

"Or she didn't want anyone to know about it?"

"Mandy said that she didn't talk much about her time in the army," said McGaven.

"True. But she might not have been telling the truth—there were some things she said that seemed deceptive and hesitant."

Katie took another long look at the tattoo. "I wonder if we can find out more about it, like the artist. It was probably done when she was in the army. It's blurry and amateurish, so I don't think it was a professional, but you never know. It might have looked better when it wasn't partially removed."

"Maybe a friend? Army buddy? Boyfriend?" suggest McGaven.

"What about the necklace and the makeup?"

"Now it gets interesting," said John. He brought up photos of the necklace. "No prints or fluids were found, but…" He smiled for dramatic effect. "It's not the necklace but the ribbon."

"The ribbon?"

"Look at how it's tied." He zoomed in on the loop. "That is a nautical knot. See how it's a figure eight and the two ends are pulled through? There are many nautical style knots—this one is the more basic."

"It also looks like the beginning of a macramé knot," said Katie. "Why would the killer do that? Why not just tie a regular knot or double knot?" She wondered aloud to herself.

"Maybe the killer is trying to tell us something?" said McGaven.

John wheeled smoothly in his office chair over to a table and took out some rope and cut about three feet. He tossed it to McGaven as he expertly wheeled back to his station. "So you can practice tying knots."

Katie nodded. "We'll have to look at the first two cases to find out if there's anything to the ribbon-tying."

John moved to various photos of Jeanine Trenton's face where the makeup was blurred and clownish, in ghastly colors. The effect was deeply disturbing, like a horror movie. "So, since the makeup was so prominent for the staging of the body, there were tests run and I agree with not only the tests but the findings and the conclusions. The makeup was connected to one of the major cosmetics companies that can be found in any department store, drug store, online store selling makeup—you name it. There was nothing foreign mixed in the makeup used, just the typical ingredients you would find, like pigments for color, waxes, petrolatum oil, lanolin, cocoa butter, aluminum, manganese, and BAK—benzalkonium chloride—for preservative purposes."

"Wow, I'm going to rethink my makeup choices," said Katie with a distinct frown. "So you're saying they were fairly generic, cheaply made makeup items that can be found just about anywhere."

Katie became quiet, rolling scenarios in her mind—preparing herself for what they would pursue next. McGaven and John waited.

"Well, I do have some more thoughts," John said with an upbeat tone cutting through the silence. "I always go the extra mile—you know that."

Katie's hopes raised a few levels as she waited patiently.

"Now, remember how the body looked, posed like a possessed doll from a horror show?" He clicked through several angles of the body. "There was nothing in the crime scene report about the body pose, so... I started searching through covers of horror movies and books with certain specific parameters: body posed, heavy makeup like clown, legs broken, etc."

"And?" she said getting excited.

"I'm afraid that I haven't found anything but the typical slasher movies, but I'm still searching with key words in the database. There were some movies that had scenes that resembled the poses but they were from eighties and nineties. Maybe trying to recreate a time or incident?"

"Oh," she said, remembering those horrible slasher films and hoped that wasn't the inspiration for the crime scenes; again, it was too vague and not specific enough to be a lead.

"I should have some preliminary information about the Jane Doe case soon," McGaven said.

Katie and McGaven returned to their office.

McGaven turned to Katie and said, "What are your instincts saying? What first comes to mind?"

"I don't want to go in the wrong direction."

"C'mon. First thing that comes to mind," he stressed.

"Well, the killer doesn't seem to like the army. It could mean that they don't like the K9 unit or the army in general."

"Keep going."

"The nautical knot could mean that the killer has been trained in navigating boats and it's just a habit to tie a knot like that."

"Good," he said as he made a few notes. "This is fun. You usually make the notes."

Katie imagined the crime scene in her head and everything they knew from the reports as she read the notes McGaven wrote. It suddenly hit her like a sledgehammer. "Why haven't I seen it before? I don't know… It could be possible."

"What? You're killing me here." He sat down to face his partner.

"I think… I think that…" she rambled.

"What? Spit it out."

"We could possibly be looking at a military person or even a veteran as the killer instead of someone who just hates the military."

CHAPTER TWENTY-SIX

Monday 1450 hours

Katie and McGaven made their way to the morgue to speak with the medical examiner, Dr. Jeff Dean, about the findings in the Jeanine Trenton case. They still hadn't heard from him about the autopsy on the body from the fairgrounds, but he had told them they were backed up. Thinking about a morgue being backed up gave her some gruesome images.

As they entered the morgue, Katie's senses were assaulted by an exceptionally strong odor of cleaning disinfectants—more than normal. She fought the urge to pinch her nose so she didn't have to smell it anymore. She glanced at McGaven—he hated the morgue and still had some trouble seeing the oftentimes twisted remains of the dead. Now he was relaxed because they didn't have to view an actual autopsy.

They walked through the doors leading to a row of exam rooms, but this time, Katie didn't divert her attention to glimpse who was lying on a steel exam table, open wide and having their internal organs weighed and counted.

Katie kept her focus on speaking with Dr. Dean.

Before they reached the office area, the doctor hurried out of one of the cubicles, carrying a stack of file folders.

"Hi. My favorite investigators," he said, with his usual upbeat manner. "Please have a seat in my office and I'll be there in five minutes."

He never disappointed Katie with his openness and also his choice of clothing. Some thought Dr. Dean was a bit eccentric, but Katie loved the fact that he wore khaki shorts with a very brightly colored Hawaiian shirt, no matter the weather. He usually sported sandals, but today he'd opted for sneakers and socks.

Katie and McGaven entered the medical examiner's office. It was neat and organized as usual with file folders in arranged piles, brightly colored tabs differentiating categories, and every filing cabinet drawer was closed. There were plastic anatomical parts sitting on top of the cabinets; some were in pieces, while others were put together, along with a full, life-size skeleton in the corner. She didn't remember seeing the skeleton before and assumed it must have been a gift from someone.

To Katie's relief, the smell of disinfectant had subsided and her stomach had stopped churning from the harshness of the odor. She noticed that smells triggered memories—and memories opened a heavy door for anxiety—but she quickly slammed that door and refocused her mind. She had been taught to let her anxious feelings and memories go—float away like balloons. As silly as it sounded, it actually helped Katie to minimize her panic attacks.

McGaven fidgeted in his seat as he looked around the office.

"Do you want to sit this one out?" Katie said.

"Nope."

"Why are you so restless?"

"Three cups of coffee."

"You're making me twitchy."

"Detective Scott twitchy," he mimicked with a half smirk on his face.

"I can't take you anywhere," she softly said.

"Okay," said Dr. Dean as he entered the room and shut the door. "No bodies today, just photos. I had some time to review them last night."

"We appreciate your time. I realize that an autopsy was already performed and reported on the victim, but…"

Dr. Dean made himself comfortable at his desk as he pulled out several files each with a green coded label. Looking at Katie, he said, "Detective Scott, you don't have to apologize to me. I respect your opinion and admire your tenacity when given a cold case. I'll help in any way I can."

"Thank you, Dr. Dean."

The medical examiner put on the reading glasses that he kept on a wide cord around his neck. Flipping open the first file with "Trenton, J." typed on the label, he said immediately, "I respectfully disagree with the senior medical examiner on this case. Actually, partly disagree." His tone was calm and he remained confident in his position, experience, and credentials.

"Really?" she said and leaned forward in her chair. "Why is that?"

"It reads that the manner of death was homicide. I agree. The cause, however, reads neck injury of a sliced throat—loss of blood. However, looking closer, we can see that the knife cut the thyroid and cartilage, and nicked the trachea," he turned the photo image to show the injury, "but it didn't penetrate the larynx, trachea and through the cervical vertebrae to cause instant death."

"Wouldn't she bleed to death?"

"Slowly, unless of course the carotid artery was cut, but in this case, it wasn't. Now look at this photo." He showed a view of the victim's chest, which had extreme darkened bluish-purple bruising, the heaviest being on the left side.

"She had been impaled on the wrought-iron fence. Wouldn't that cause much of that bluish color?"

McGaven took a closer look, studying the photos as Dr. Dean continued his explanation.

"But, what is difficult to see is that the heaviest discoloration is on the left side of the chest almost precisely on top of the heart.

It's not common, but it is possible to be struck with something on the area near the center of the heart's left ventricle. It's the lower left chamber of the heart." He reached for a plastic heart from the shelf to demonstrate his hypothesis. "It's called commotio cordis and it usually happens to young people playing sports—being hit by a baseball or a fist."

Katie and McGaven were both captivated by his explanation. It changed the crime scene dynamics.

"You see, for the blow to the chest to have killed her, it would have had to be during the precise moment of a heartbeat and aimed near the center of the heart's left ventricle. This can trigger ventricular tachycardia. It can cause your heart to stop for a short period of time—or cause a sudden cardiac arrest."

"A heart attack," said Katie.

"Precisely."

"So she could have been having a heart attack, which is what killed her, but the slicing of the throat was secondary. She would have bled to death, but it was sped up by the heart attack. Am I correct?"

"Essentially, yes. If I were to write this autopsy report, it would have read: 'cause of death—primary ventricular tachycardia and secondary hypovolemic shock or blood loss caused from a neck knife wound.'"

"What types of weapons could cause this strategic blow to the heart?"

Dr. Dean thought a moment. "Anything long and slender that could be administered in a jabbing or poking motion. There would have to be some force behind it."

"Like a baseball bat or a heavy tool?" said McGaven.

"Yes. If it were someone that was a master at martial arts or another similar discipline, a fist or foot blow could do the same. But you would have to be quite accurate."

Katie leaned back taking everything in the medical examiner had told them.

Dr. Dean shuffled through several papers. "I have nothing to compare with their toxicology reports, but it appears in order and states that nothing unusual was found in the victim's system."

"Thank you for taking the time to look over this. It was on the condition of the body that we wanted your attention and expertise the most."

"Detectives, it's always a pleasure. You make my job more interesting," he said. "Now, if you will excuse me, I have bodies to tend to, and that includes one for your current investigation."

"Oh, one more thing," she said.

"Yes?"

"Would it be possible for you to look at two other cases, just the autopsy of the injuries to their chests?"

"Of course. Send them over and I'll get back to you when I can." He rose from his desk and was gone.

"What do you think?" she asked McGaven walking toward the door.

"It changes things a bit. I mean, the outcome would be the same but the opportunity and means differ. This type of injury is intentional and also shows that the killer has medical knowledge. This is a game changer."

"I agree."

"I know something is bothering you."

"Why wouldn't Campbell's people have found this? Surely one of them would have caught it. I'm still somewhat skeptical about this case and why we were dragged into it."

Katie's cell phone vibrated as she received a text message from Denise at the department.

You have a package delivered from the army K9 training facility. I left it in your office.

CHAPTER TWENTY-SEVEN

Monday 1625 hours

Katie drove to Ink Tattoo, located in a small strip mall just on the edge of town. She thought about the tattoo and why Jeanine Trenton would want to have hers removed, since it was clear that she loved her time as a military K9 handler and trainer.

"You're sure that this place removes tattoos?" she said to McGaven.

"Yep. And it isn't easy to talk to someone at a tattoo parlor once they know you're a cop. But this place seems more open and they said that they get a lot of veterans and military personnel."

"And they said that they've removed military K9-type tattoos?"

"That's what he said."

Katie parked. She grabbed a file folder with a photo of Jeanine Trenton, since she was local to the area.

They got out of the sedan.

A couple of heavily tattooed men left the shop, giving both Katie and McGaven the once-over before they got into their oversized truck.

"Hi," said McGaven and he gave a friendly wave.

Katie pushed open the door and turned to her partner. "Making friends?"

"Of course, everywhere we go."

Katie stepped inside. She had never been to a tattoo or piercing place before. It was smaller than she had expected. There were three areas where tattoo artists would work on their clients. The chairs resembled a dentist chair, allowing the customer to lie back or on their side depending where the tattoo was placed.

Hundreds of designs festooned the wall from floor to ceiling, featuring everything from cartoons and flowers to faces of famous people and everyday items.

A very large burly man in a white tank top said, "Can I help you?" He had been putting away some ink supplies and wiping down one of the chairs.

"I hope so," said Katie. "You are?"

He turned and looked at her. "I would love to help *you*. You can call me Big Daddy."

"Well, Big Daddy. I'm Detective Scott and this is my partner Deputy McGaven."

His face turned sour. "Cops? Why would I want to talk to cops?"

McGaven had been checking out the designs on the wall and quickly read the mounted business license. "Well, for starters, Mr. Robert Denton, we just want to know about any dermabrasions you've done recently."

"That's a new one."

"Can you help us?" Katie asked, trying to sound more like a friend than a cop. "We're investigating two women who were brutally murdered."

He sighed. "Sorry to hear that. My sister was murdered by her boyfriend. He's doing twenty-five to life."

"At least they caught the person who did it. Would you mind looking at a photo?"

The big man moved toward Katie. "Yeah, sure. It's slow today anyway."

Katie opened the file and showed him a photograph of Jeanine Trenton.

He stared at it for a good minute. "I'm sorry, but I'm not sure." He looked closer at Jeanine and said, "Maybe. What's the design?"

"Military K9. Have you seen or removed anything like that?"

"Well," he said, "it would be in this file." He pulled out a file drawer and fingered through records. "We've done a few of those dermabrasions in the past year."

"How about three years?" she said.

"Hmmm." He kept flipping through pages inside folders. "Here we go." He pulled a file. "I always take pictures of the artwork before removing them, just call it for insurance reasons. And they also have to sign a type of release. I handle all of these types of clients."

Katie scrolled through her phone until she came to a photo of the mostly removed tattoo on Jeanine's wrist.

Big Daddy gave her the photo from the file.

Katie looked at both photos. She turned to McGaven. "What do you think?"

He stared at them. "I would say it's her."

Katie looked up. "Do you remember anything about this client? What's the date?"

He read down and said, "March, two years ago."

"I see. Do you remember anything about her?"

He appeared to really try hard to remember. "I recall the tattoo but the woman… I can't remember exactly what she looked like, even with that photo. Plain Jane, most likely. She didn't complain like so many of them do. It's not a nice procedure."

"One more question," she said.

"Anything for you, little lady," he said and smiled.

"It's 'Detective.' Why do most people get tattoos removed? In your experience."

"Usually it's a boyfriend or girlfriend that's now an ex and they can't bear seeing that name. Sometimes it's just a bad tattoo, muddled, usually from guys that have been in prison." He thought more. "As I recall, this K9 tattoo was something that she didn't want to be reminded of anymore."

"Are you sure?"

"Yeah. She didn't say much. I got the feeling that she was scared. See, usually people who have tattoos removed are very angry."

"You sure about that?" she asked.

"Hey, I deal with people day in and day out… I think I know when someone is angry or scared."

"Noted. Take my card and if you remember anything else about her or someone else comes in asking about her… call me." She handed him a business card.

"Thanks. I will."

"Thanks for your time, Big Daddy."

Katie and McGaven left the premises.

"What do you think?" asked McGaven.

"We know now that Jeanine Trenton was scared about something… or someone."

CHAPTER TWENTY-EIGHT

Tuesday 1055 hours

Katie was tired since she had only slept for three hours, but it was important to continue their investigation on Jeanine Trenton's murder until reports arrived from the Jane Doe homicide. She knew that they would overlap in many ways and waited patiently until more information became available.

Katie spent fifteen minutes talking with Virginia Rodriguez from the Community Health Alliance, the first chance since the distraught man with a gun overshadowed the interview. The woman was difficult to talk to, but was truthful about the friction on the job, as she called it, between her and Jeanine, and admitted to bullying her in the past.

She hung up the phone and sighed.

"Anything?" he asked.

"No, but she was at least honest in answering my questions. Virginia Rodriguez is an unlikely suspect, but we'll keep her on the board just in case."

Katie pointed to a padded envelope on her desk. "Right, shall we see what this is?"

"I was waiting for you to open it," said McGaven with a curious expression.

Katie opened the envelope from the army K9 training facility in Sacramento. She pulled out two flash drives with USB plugs and a handwritten letter.

Detective Scott, please find a few videos from K9 training that I hope will help in your investigations. The sound isn't the best—I apologize for that. These were the only video documentation I could find of Jeanine Trenton, but there were others in which recruits washed out. I thought that would be of interest to you. If I come across anything else, I will send it on. It was a pleasure meeting you. Kindest Regards, Sergeant Anthony Serrano

"Interesting."

"What?" she said.

"'It was a pleasure meeting you'..." he repeated.

"Give it a rest, Gav."

"I'm just saying. He was extremely impressed by your K9 training abilities."

"And Cisco," she added. "Here, plug these into your laptop so we can check them out." She handed him the flash drives.

McGaven took the drives and inserted them. After a few moments, a window opened with ten video images.

Katie rolled her chair closer to McGaven.

He clicked on the first video icon. "Here we go."

There were muffled voices, which Katie assumed was Sergeant Serrano giving instructions. Standing at the front of the group was Jeanine Trenton; she had a regal German shepherd sitting at her left side. There was a group of recruits watching, but it was difficult, if not impossible, to see the identities of the soldiers as the view was of the backs of their heads. There were a couple of women, based on their ponytail or braid down the back. Jeanine was showing basic obedience, and Katie assumed this session would have been the very beginning, or orientation for the training course. Jeanine was cheerful and energetic as she moved through the exercises. She definitely was a good dog handler and clearly loved it.

"We can't see much," said McGaven.

"Maybe not, but we can see Jeanine Trenton alive and happy."

"True."

"And she definitely loved working with the dogs. That's why I can't figure out why she quit and why she never talked about it much." Katie watched the other videos.

There was nothing out of the ordinary until they reached the second to last video. It appeared that Jeanine was arguing with one of the recruits and she was angry. Her words were difficult to make out but she said something like, *"You shouldn't be anywhere near animals and don't know anything about the gift of bonding with dogs."* But the person she was speaking with had their back to the camera. It was clear that it was a woman and there was a man next to her.

"Wow, now there's a different side to Jeanine Trenton," said McGaven. "A little out of line."

"Not really," said Katie. "You don't know the army. It can be a tough pill to swallow if you're not used to criticism. It can be fierce. But I think Jeanine was being passionate and maybe this person wasn't at all cut out for being a dog handler."

McGaven rewound the video a few times. "I can't see who she's talking to or the person next to them."

"I know. Not very useful." Katie was a bit disappointed, but not defeated. There was always something to learn from every clue.

Katie and McGaven watched the videos again.

After the last video, Katie said, "I think I'm going to send an email to Sergeant Serrano and ask if he could identify these recruits, since he sent videos and all."

"It's worth a shot."

Katie quickly sent an email from her cell phone.

She studied the murder board. "So what do we have on Jeanine Trenton's journal? Anything worth mentioning?"

McGaven flipped through his notebook. "Nothing more than about her work nightmare and harassment. I've read most of it, skimming through really mundane stuff. She did mention about the neighbor, Mrs. Caldwell— apparently, she was accusing her of having too many people at her house. She thought the neighbor was weird."

"And?"

"And she mainly talked about day-to-day struggles and if she was going to too many parties. And…"

"Nothing jumped out? Nothing about her K9 training time and how much she loved it?"

"Nope."

"Well, that's unfortunate." Discouragement was beginning to set in. The journal had seemed promising at the storage facility, and now it seemed it was just about boring day-to-day occurrences.

McGaven turned his attention to the board and then back to Katie. "So, assuming that Campbell is right, and the last three are copycat killings, what is the killer's motive? What stands out the most?"

Katie stood up. "Well," she said. "Let's recap what we have so far: we have our killer staging the victims, meaning they want to cause a scene, mock the police, put the vic in view of the public. Basically, making them pay for something that happened to them."

"They took something away…"

"Good point," she said. "It's about control, revenge, and possibly abuse. I still can't get what Sergeant Serrano said out of my mind: 'graduate or wash out'. Could that be what this…" She gestured to everything they had. "What all of this is about? Just a ticked-off person that washed out of military K9 training? It can't be that easy."

"No, but it's central to these cases," he said. "And…"

Katie turned to him curiously. "And what?"

"Well, I didn't think I needed to state the obvious."

"Meaning?"

"The K9 connection is central, but it brings it back to you. Someone was warning you with those shots at the park training.

There was no evidence left behind, but the person carefully fired shots near you."

"What? To warn me? For me to get off the case?"

"No, that you're going to be the next ex-military K9 handler victim. They are giving you fair warning."

"Don't you think that's reaching?" It had occurred to Katie too, but she pushed it aside. Why would anyone want to hurt her?

"Maybe. But what if I'm not reaching?"

"Thanks for your concern, but I can take care of myself." She saw McGaven's expression become clouded and troubled. "Gav, I'll be careful—just in case."

He nodded.

Katie and McGaven spent more time going over notes and lists, and made a few phone calls.

Katie was anxious, her eyes weary, and she wanted to get out into some fresh air to keep moving and recharge her energy levels. She turned to McGaven who had stopped typing on the keyboard and seemed to have closed his eyes for a moment.

"Okay, that's it."

"What?" he said, startled.

"It's Tuesday."

"So, that doesn't really mean anything when working a homicide?"

"This has been a really tiresome week already. And I'm declaring…"

McGaven waited for what she would say.

"Coffee, lots of good coffee and some food too—maybe even junk food." She stood up, slipping on her jacket. "You coming?"

"I thought you'd never ask." He stood up, stretching his back.

"Grab the Trenton file with the interview with the neighbor— Mrs. Caldwell. Let's go pay her a visit."

"Yep, will do. It's shaping up to be a great day now we're getting coffee and a road trip!"

After a quick stop for coffee and bagels with everything on top, Katie felt much better and wanted to get her mind straight about the Trenton and Jane Doe case.

She took a sharp turn too fast, but straightened out the sedan, and sped down the road heading to Raven Woods once again.

"Where's the fire?" asked McGaven, as he was reading the interview of the neighbor. He balanced his coffee and paperwork impressively on his lap.

"There's a fire somewhere right now—I guarantee it."

"Maybe, but I would like to make it to Mrs. Caldwell's house alive."

"Don't be so dramatic. I've driven a Humvee in the desert under heavy artillery fire."

"Not a lot of twisty roads, ravines, and oncoming traffic there," he said and couldn't help but snicker.

"I didn't crash an army vehicle and I'm not going to crash a police sedan."

Changing the subject, McGaven said, "There was a page in here that was misfiled. Missing from her interview. Here, it's page twelve and thirteen is missing. It could be a misfile from copying everything." He continued to sort through the pages making sure they were in order.

"Anything interesting?" Katie sipped her coffee.

"Very."

"Really?" She let her foot off the accelerator and took the next two turns with less speed.

"Mrs. Sadie Caldwell, fifty-five years old, widow, retired correctional officer from Federal Correctional Institution in Lompoc, California. She was caught selling items to inmates including but not limited to, cigarettes, aspirin, mouthwash, arthritis cream, and model airplane kits."

"Model airplanes?"

"I said it was interesting."

"She sounded like the local pharmacy until…"

"It seems that Mrs. Caldwell was helping certain inmates with creative implements that could be made into weapons—not to mention the glue-sniffing thing."

"Was she fired?" said Katie.

"No, she was given the opportunity to quit and take her pension immediately or go to jail for three years. She retired."

"Smart."

"Agent Campbell and his team ran a police report on her and it was clean until after she retired. Apparently, she began harassing her neighbors, acting paranoid, saying weird things, and she secured her home like she was protecting a palace of gold. Her threats to Jeanine Trenton began escalating."

"Are you making this up?"

McGaven laughed. "Nope, not even a little."

"So I'm assuming that you want to take point on this interview."

"Ah, that's a negative."

"Why? You have a way with the ladies."

"Not this one. She has an eighth-degree black belt and has been known to get into fights when she worked at the prison."

"Dr. Dean said that someone with martial arts skills could hit or kick hard enough to damage or stop the heart," she said.

"That is true. Still want to talk to her?"

Katie thought about it. "When did her husband pass away?"

"Six years ago. He was a bail bondsman."

"Interesting couple."

Katie drove past the "Welcome to Raven Woods" sign.

"She's out of my league as an interviewee," said Katie. "She probably wouldn't like me to be in charge and would take direction a little bit easier from you."

"How about we just wait and see after we meet her?"

Katie turned down Fox Hunt Road again, noticing that the road was mostly deserted and how dark it felt, as trees blocked much of the daylight. It was quiet. She found it difficult to believe that no one had heard or seen anything unusual, according to the reports.

"Deal," she said.

The overcast day made it even drearier than the previous visit. Katie immediately recalled their brush with gas suffocation and it made her arms prickle.

Could it have been Mrs. Caldwell who tampered with the gas?

Pulling up to the house next door to the boarded-up home of Jeanine Trenton, Katie parked. Neither of them spoke for almost two minutes.

"You ready?" McGaven said.

"Let's see what Mrs. Caldwell has to say."

Katie got out followed by McGaven and they studied the brown house, which had heavy white shutters and darkened windows and looked well taken care of and tidy. Katie wondered if they were specialized windows to maintain more privacy. There wasn't much landscaping, but some bushes across the front. No pots of flowers. No fruit trees. No ground cover. No doormat. Just minimal and natural.

Katie walked up to the porch and glanced up, seeing a video camera lens. She wondered if Mrs. Caldwell was watching them at that moment, so she shifted her jacket to show her badge and gun.

McGaven waited next to his partner.

Katie knocked three times then stepped back. She noticed that there was a pair of yellow gardening shoes sitting next to the stairs. They had a significant amount of mud and brush from the outdoors.

A static radio sounded, coming from a small speaker. Then a woman's voice said, "State your business."

"Pine Valley Sheriff's Department. We want to speak with you for a moment."

"About what?" The voice was curt and made the cheap speaker crackle.

"Mrs. Caldwell?" said Katie.

There was a pause.

"Mrs. Caldwell?" she said again.

"Yes."

"Can you come out here to speak with us?"

"I can't see your badges. State your names."

Katie sighed and kept her patience in check. "I'm Detective Katie Scott and this is my partner, Deputy Sean McGaven."

"What do you want to talk to me about?"

"Your neighbor, Jeanine Trenton."

"She's dead and gone."

"We have a few questions. Can you come out here to speak with us?" Katie was losing patience as the woman's voice grated on her.

"I don't have to speak with you."

Katie decided to go another route to try to make her open the door—just a bit of deception and pretext. She glanced at McGaven who kept his best poker face. The street was still unnaturally quiet—no cars; no people walking; no dogs barking; no birds chirping; no wind blowing through the trees—just idly stagnant.

"Mrs. Caldwell, the word around Lompoc is that you were selling drugs and stealing profits for yourself."

They waited.

The front door unlocked. It sounded as if three heavy locks disengaged. The door slowly opened a crack as a woman's eye stared out at them. Her short grayish hair was cut in a pixie style with bangs. "That's a lie."

"Just repeating what we heard."

"It's a blatant lie."

"We don't believe in gossip, only in facts. Can we talk to you?" Katie tried to soften her voice and appeal to her as one law officer to another.

"I don't have to."

"We know that, but we're trying to solve a homicide. Any help would be greatly appreciated."

She opened the door wider as her eyes darted back and forth from Katie to McGaven. "Does the big guy talk?"

Katie laughed. "Sometimes."

"We just want to ask a few questions about your previous neighbor," said McGaven. "We won't take up much of your time."

"Here's my card," said Katie.

"Hmmm," she said, taking the card and still eying them suspiciously. She opted to open the door wide and stepped out onto the porch, but slammed the door behind her. Her focus rested on McGaven. "You know, my late husband was tall like you." She seemed to like McGaven and ignored Katie as she stepped further outside.

Mrs. Caldwell was dressed in a running outfit, navy blue, and ill-fitting around her middle. She was heavyset but moved her body much more gracefully than her stocky frame would suggest. It was clear that she'd had some type of advanced physical training.

"Mrs. Caldwell—" Katie began.

"How tall are you? Six foot six?" she asked McGaven.

"And a half," he said, smiling.

"What do you want to know about that hussy?" Her demeanor relaxed as she focused on McGaven.

"Do you remember anything from the night she was murdered?"

"No."

"Anything suspicious or unusual from the days leading up to the murder?"

"Like what?"

"People visiting. A strange car parked on the street or sounds of arguing from the house."

"I didn't hear anything. It was quiet, for once."

"What about you?"

Mrs. Caldwell took several steps toward the street, expecting McGaven to follow.

Katie kept her distance. She noticed a bamboo pole about three feet long lying on the ground next to the house and thought back to what Dr. Dean had said about the injury on Jeanine's chest.

"What about me?"

"Well, I heard that you speak your mind a lot around here."

The neighbor laughed. "That's a nice way of saying it." She turned to Katie. "He has a nice way about him."

Katie forced a smile and nodded in agreement. She watched Mrs. Caldwell's arms moving constantly, twitchy, her fists clenched, as she anxiously moved slowly around in the front yard. She wore a simple gold band on her left ring finger and when she wasn't fidgeting, she spun the ring between her thumb and forefinger of her right hand. There was a slight bulge in her pant pocket that matched an outline of a medicine prescription bottle. It was possible that she could be taking something for anxiety, depression, or even a form of schizophrenia—her erratic behavior began to make sense.

"Mrs. Caldwell—"

"Sadie," she corrected McGaven.

"Sadie," he said. "What was bothering you about your neighbor?"

"It was those parties."

"What kind of parties?"

"I don't know. People would drive up and meet at her house, and then about half an hour later, they would leave."

"Did that bother you?"

"Not at first. But then the parties got louder and they would be out back making more noise. It's just not right."

"Did you call the police?" he asked, knowing that she had from police records he had searched.

"Of course. I obey the law."

"Of course you do."

"They just needed to be taken care of…"

Her words hung in the air.

Taken care of…

"You know, right and wrong. The Lord's wrath."

"And you're sure that you didn't hear or see anything that night?"

"Nope. Wish I did, though."

"Why?"

"Then that would have meant all the bad voices would have finally stopped."

CHAPTER TWENTY-NINE

Tuesday 1325 hours

After speaking with Mrs. Caldwell and realizing she suffered from a form of mental illness, Katie wanted some immediate answers from Special Agent Campbell. There was nothing in the reports they had to indicate she suffered from a mental impairment or that she grappled with voices, real or otherwise. It changed the investigation. It distorted the outlook from a witness and next-door neighbor. It was unclear if the neighbor saw something that night or not—she seemed to slip in and out of lucidness.

Katie felt her anxious energy escalate—sweaty palms, faster heartbeat, and shortness of breath. She wanted some answers and they weren't going to leave Agent Campbell's suite until they were satisfied that they were all up to speed on the investigations.

What else had been kept from them?

Dark clouds moved in from the north and were in typical rain-cloud clusters, ready to spring a leak at any moment. It was common this time of year, before spring laid out its beautiful colors and warmer weather across the landscape. Even the rolling valleys and mountain wooded areas changed and brightened with spring.

Was it all just a game?

Every day she woke up and didn't feel doom looming over her was a great day. But these investigations were increasingly taxing and the anxious fear wormed its way into Katie's psyche, stirring the deep-seated trauma she had suffered and triggering the sneaky symptoms of PTSD.

Katie gripped the steering wheel and concentrated on the strength of the engine performing every time she pushed the accelerator. It gave her comfort and focus on the here and now, instead of what might be. In her mind she challenged herself: *Go ahead, weak arms, shaky fingers, and weird dizziness; I'm not afraid of you.*

"How do you want to approach Campbell?" asked McGaven. His voice was calm but there was a hint of concern to it.

"I want the truth."

"Okay."

"That's all I ever want when I'm working a case—the truth."

"There's some diplomacy needed here, Katie. I know you're upset, but we need to be smart about this. Maybe confronting him like a stampede isn't the best way to get what you want."

"You realize that it's likely he might have sent us into a trap initially at Jeanine's house? I suspect that the missing page on Mrs. Caldwell about her mental illness was deliberately left out of our files."

"You can't say that for sure," he said.

"It's possible, right?"

"Maybe, but the smart way to handle this is to maneuver, not lash out."

Katie thought about what he'd said. "You're saying that we need be smarter to weed out the lies and get to the truth."

"Yeah, something like that."

Katie breathed slowly, feeling the oxygen fill her lungs and then leave her body. She felt a layer of relaxation calm her nerves and begin to soothe her anger.

"Let me know your plan," said McGaven.

"We're going to Agent Campbell's room at the Hobson Inn & Suites."

"And?"

"And… I know you're right, but I'm still mad. How are we supposed to solve a case when information is conveniently left out? Who does that? This is the third time we've found something missing."

They were a few minutes away from the motel.

"It's like we have a mystery within a mystery," she said. "I don't know why Uncle Wayne approved this arrangement."

"You'll have to ask him."

"I know he has his reasons. He wouldn't give his okay if he thought there was anything hinky about it. If there's one thing I know about our sheriff is that he is by the book—he told me so on the weekend. No exceptions."

"Would that include having his niece head up the crime scene unit with little experience?"

"Do you always have to do that?"

"Do what?"

"Make sense all the time and call me out."

"That's what partners are for."

Katie stood at the door of room 212 at the Hobson Inn & Suites once again. This time she had a purpose that overrode everything else, but she couldn't let Campbell know.

It began to drizzle—lightly at first and then more of a shower. The drops were large and dappled the foliage around them, making a calming sound.

She knocked on the door.

It was difficult for her to focus and keep her reaction calm and professional but she was determined not to let her anger get the better of her.

Katie knocked again.

No answer.

"He's not home?" said McGaven, with a hint of sarcasm.

"It looks like his car is here."

"Maybe he left with someone else? That agent…"

"Agent Haley?"

"Maybe. Call him or we can come back tomorrow."

"No," said Katie.

"No? What do you suggest we do?"

She tried the door and surprisingly found it unlocked. It seemed odd because usually at motels, doors automatically locked when you left. Agent Campbell must have deliberately unlocked the door, which seemed odd with the equipment and confidential information inside.

The doorknob turned in her hand and she hesitated before pushing the door open. To her surprise, McGaven didn't say anything.

"Agent Campbell?" she said. "Anyone home?" She tried to make her voice sound casual.

Katie and McGaven stood at the threshold, not entering the suite. They could see the command center with photos and reports on the wall. The computers were humming, and there were stacks of various paperwork, file folders, and bankers' boxes filled with even more information.

"Oh hi, Detective," came a voice behind them. It was Agent Haley carrying a sealed container that had some type of meal inside and a drink with a straw.

"Is Agent Campbell here?" asked Katie.

"No, he's doing some errands—I believe personal in nature. Can I help you with something?" She forced a smile.

Katie noticed that the perky agent assistant was different, more solemn. Based on the darkened areas under her eyes, she had probably been working all hours.

"We're waiting for the results from forensics and autopsy report for the victim at the fairgrounds. I wanted to double-check some information that we received for the Trenton case—I think there might be some missing."

"Of course," she said. "Come in." She walked past them and paused a moment to catch McGaven's eye.

"Thanks," said Katie and gave her partner a look, raising her eyebrow.

McGaven shut the door.

Agent Haley put down her food and went to one of the computers. "What are you looking for?" She sat poised with her fingers on the keyboard.

"Trenton case. There was an interview with Mrs. Sadie Caldwell. We seem to be missing some pages."

"Oh?" she said. "Let's see here…" She keyed up the case and scrolled through files. Then she opened a desk drawer, rummaged around through various office supplies and retrieved a flash drive, inserting it into the computer. "This will just take a few seconds."

"That's great. Thank you," said Katie as she slowly skimmed the room again. Nothing had changed since their last visit.

The computer hummed as it transferred the information.

When it was done, Agent Haley pulled the flash drive out and handed it to Katie. "There you go. I just went ahead and copied all the reports. Sorry for the inconvenience. I'm a new junior agent, promoted from administrative executive assistant, and it's been a bit overwhelming, but I'm getting there," she rattled on then finished with a sigh.

"Thank you," Katie said and then decided to ask, "Is there anything new on the Trenton case?"

"Not that I know of. Everything is there in your hand." She popped open her container and began to eat. "Maybe we can keep this a secret? I don't want Agent Campbell to know that I messed up."

"Don't worry about it," said McGaven.

"Thanks, I appreciate that." She smiled as she ate a large forkful of salad.

"Are you sure there isn't anything new we need to know?" Katie gently pushed.

"No…" The junior agent shook her head. "I don't think so."

"Well, if something new comes in, please don't hesitate to give us a call."

"Of course, Detective Scott," she said.

Driving back to the office, McGaven's cell phone chimed. It was a text message from Dr. Dean:

We have an ID on the vic.

CHAPTER THIRTY
Tuesday 1600 hours

Katie and McGaven were directed to wait inside the exam room for a few minutes while Dr. Dean finished up some other business first. There were no chairs in the room except the round rolling stool that sometimes was used by the examiner when making notes as it allowed them to navigate around the table easily. As they waited, they felt the suspense build.

It was difficult to look away from the body lying on the metal table—but there was nothing else to keep your interest as you waited. Usually, bodies were covered with a sheet, but this time the nude, battered body of Jane Doe was not protected from view. Her lifeless eyes stared at the ceiling. She had been washed, the blood cleaned off in preparation. The purple-grayish body lay motionless, almost resembling a rubber doll.

Katie noticed that her right hand was darkened and the fingers were black from the inking for print identification. The room was colder than normal—at least that was how it felt to her. She struggled with the urge to cover up the young woman.

Katie glanced to McGaven who had a stern and stoic expression, his eyes studying everything in the room except the body.

Dr. Dean dashed in, his white smock covered in bright blood. "Sorry I'm late. Still a bit behind with bodies—busy weekend, I'm afraid." It was a new look for him since it covered his usual cheery Hawaiian shirt and khaki shorts. Now he looked like a spunky hero who had run the gauntlet of the zombie apocalypse.

"No problem," said Katie, trying to keep her eyes on the medical examiner's face.

"Nice to see you both, as always, but it's always under such stressful circumstances." He grabbed a file folder from the table. "Ah yes, your Jane Doe now has an identity. This is Darla Winchell, thirty-four, who worked for First Community Bank of Pine Valley. The next of kin is Dorothy Winchell, her mother. She's been contacted and will be here later to make an official identification."

"How did you find out her identity so quickly?" she said, making a few notes.

"Luckily she had been fingerprinted when she applied for the First Community Bank. It's common for anyone who works for banks. An FBI background check is always done." He effortlessly zoomed around the body. "And for professional purposes, I deem this to be a homicide—primary cause of death is blunt force to the chest causing sudden cardiac arrest and secondary would be extreme loss of blood, or hypovolemic shock."

"Now we can begin our investigation," said Katie. It was stating the obvious but she was relieved that they had something to work with to chase down clues.

Dr. Dean adjusted his glasses and stood next to the body. He pointed out the markings on her chest. "I knew that you would be interested in this right away. See those two markings—circular in shape and darker than the other bruising?"

"Yes," she said. They were round like something had pressed up against her or hit her. "Is that similar to the blow that hit Jeanine Trenton?"

"Yes and no," he said.

Here we go again...

Katie knew that the medical examiner loved to give both the positive and negative about injuries. It kept her on her toes and made the examination that much more accurate, but still, Katie became anxious, wanting the information.

"In my opinion," he began, "those are test impacts."

"As if the killer was trying to see the minimum level of pressure they needed for whatever they wanted to accomplish—like stunning before killing the victim? Testing and improving his technique?"

"That's the way I interpret it. This time, the killer appeared to do a test—actually two tests—first, incapacitated the victim but it wasn't enough to cause a full cardiac arrest. And then the final strike of the cutting of the throat allowing the bleed-out was what completed their procedure."

Katie thought about that for a moment and realized that this was a brutal signature. "There isn't a way to tell if the same person committed both murders by the way they incapacitated the victims and then sliced their throats?"

"I see what you're getting at, Detective, but I can only give you the cause and manner of death. There were quite a few defensive wounds, as well." He adjusted his glasses, turning his focus on her. "But I can tell you that the same technique was used—whether it was the same person who used it against Jeanine Trenton or someone who was taught the same method, you'll have to figure that out."

"I see."

"Otherwise, I would be stepping into your territory."

"What else can you tell us?"

"She was in good health, appropriate weight, didn't appear to have any diseases or disorders."

"Toxicology?"

"Still waiting on that, but I don't foresee anything. I'll be sending you the official report after the autopsy is complete." He smiled.

"I noticed at the scene she had some broken fingers and toes."

"Yes, her left hand had breakages on the pinky and ring fingers of the middle phalanges and the middle metacarpal bone." He picked up Darla Winchell's hand, moving the fingers for documentation. Turning to the X-ray light box, he showed the broken hand and foot bones. "Also the left proximal phalanges on the outside toes."

Katie studied the X-rays. "Thank you, Dr. Dean."

McGaven gave a nod.

"She also had a faint tattoo on her left arm right here," he said and brought their attention to the inside of her left wrist.

"What is that?" she said.

"It looks almost as if it's a… K and a 9."

It stopped Katie cold. Could it be another K9 handler?

"Detective?" said the medical examiner.

"Yes?"

"If anything unusual comes up, I'll be sure to contact you right away."

Katie smiled before she exited the room, followed by McGaven. Now their work really began. Who was Darla Winchell? Was she a military K9 handler? Why did she end up at the fairgrounds?

CHAPTER THIRTY-ONE
Wednesday 1015 hours

Katie was relieved and excited to receive a text from John saying that he had some things to update her on relating to the Darla Winchell investigation. McGaven was still researching names and doggedly cross-checking them. It was something that he did well, so he wasn't going to be with her at the forensics reveal.

She stood at the forensic exam room door, which was, unusually, closed. She knocked twice softly.

"Come in," said John.

Katie opened the door and walked into the darkened room. The overhead light was off and there was just a dim light in the corner where John hovered over a large microscope. She wasn't sure what type it was—usually he used a scanning electron microscope for the evidence comparisons, but this one looked different and more specialized.

"Uh, you seem busy. Should I come back later?" she said, feeling a bit awkward, not knowing what she should be doing. "What do you want me to do? You want me to come back?"

"Hang on a minute. Have patience."

Katie looked around and noticed that everything had been choreographed a bit differently. The larger computers and screen were in the corner area and the exam tables were in the middle, which made it easier to move around each side.

"I like how you rearranged everything."

"Makes more sense. We've been busy, so the more we can organize and automate, the better." He was still studying something, making notes on a piece of paper.

Katie tapped her small notebook on the exam table.

"Okay," said John as he straightened up and closed a binder. He was wearing a white lab coat, which was also unusual, and he stripped it off, revealing his typical black T-shirt. "Are we waiting for McGaven?"

"No, he's buried in paperwork."

"Okay. Here's what we have so far."

That didn't sound hopeful to Katie, but she waited to see if John found anything she and McGaven could run with.

"Let's start with the fairgrounds first. Specifically the Ferris wheel. Okay, the blood was over the top, meaning that it actually contaminated the entire car. If there was anything that could have told us about the killer—hair, fluids, anything—it was covered by the bleed-out of the victim. There was also some type of mechanical oil and what appears to be remnants of old food."

"Okay."

"Now, that being said, there were indications that the killer wore gloves, but this particular type of glove wasn't just the pharmacy-store type. The smudges were found on the controls of the ride, the car door, the overhead metal bar, and the black ladies' shoe—size seven and a half."

"Anything fingerprint-related?"

"No, but the gloves were what I was interested in. They were nitrile exam gloves…"

"And you know this because…"

"They are made from nitrile butadiene rubber, another synthetic type of material, making them an alternative for people with latex allergies and they have a longer shelf-life than the typical latex gloves." He moved to another computer. "Nitrile is three times more resistant to punctures, but if they do puncture they create a noticeable tear, it's easily visible. You have to order them through specialty places and not a hardware store or pharmacy."

"Aren't they the most expensive type of exam gloves? More than latex and vinyl?" she said.

"Yep."

"This could mean that the killer is in some kind of industry that requires them, like agricultural, chemical, laboratories, medical, and even our industry." Katie's mind began to reel events quickly, like a movie screen. "So you said if there's a tear, you can see it. Does that translate into impression evidence? Can you actually see the tear?"

"Great observation. On the left side of the Ferris wheel car, there's a bloody impression of a hand—no visible prints, but you could clearly see a tear area where the index finger is located. It would be my guess that the killer injured their right index finger—most likely nothing entailing any medical care, but worse than a paper cut."

"Okay," said Katie. The evidence was interesting, but didn't really help unless they had a suspect to look at.

"I know it isn't much but it might give a better understanding of the kind of person who would use those types of gloves." He smiled. "So, I know that you're wondering about the similarities of the injuries between Darla Winchell and Jeanine Trenton." He moved aside so that Katie could see the computer screen. "Here are the victims' chest injuries. See the round indentations, like something cylindrical? Now look when I change the lighting source: ultraviolet, and then, infrared. You can really see how many times each victim was struck. At first, it looks like twice or maybe three times, but it appears that there are many blows, some in the same places. Darla was clearly struck more times than Jeanine."

Katie watched, intrigued by how the impressions on each victim's chest could be clearly seen with a different light source. It meant that the killer was slowly bruising the heart, knowing just how much would incapacitate them, or even eventually be the death blow.

"What about the knife that cut their throats?"

"That's actually tricky."

Katie waited. She knew John's style and she wasn't going to push him. He would explain everything in his way, and in his own time.

"The cuts were different. Jeanine's was more precise and Darla's was more ragged. It could be that there were two different knives, one sharper than the other."

"So you still think it was a butcher's knife?"

"It's consistent."

Katie jotted a few notes down for her own reference. "I wish we could find the murder weapons," she said, more to herself than to John.

"The heavy makeup is basically a cheap brand that is available everywhere, as before. There's no way to trace it. I also had it tested and there are no foreign chemicals, either natural or otherwise."

"I know you've probably not had enough time to test the blood…"

"We did a preliminary test from several places to confirm that it is human, and the ABO type, which is AB negative. The DNA process will take a couple of weeks, I'm afraid."

Katie was exhausted thinking about all the possibilities.

"Okay, stop," he said.

"What?"

"You look frustrated. Sorry, but evidence doesn't lie. It can be sneaky and hide sometimes, but it can't be untruthful."

"It's just difficult when there are several cases. It's a juggling act."

John stood up and faced Katie. He studied her for a moment. "I've never seen anyone so committed."

"It's my job," she said, taking a step back.

"That was impressive watching Cisco tracking the killer and victim's steps at the fairgrounds."

Katie smiled, still feeling a bit uncomfortable.

"I'm still working on the knots on Darla's hair and the ribbon holding the size six garnet ring."

"Anything about the ring?" she asked.

"It's a high-quality garnet, older facet but there was some trace residue that I'm trying to track down. It's a type of grease, but I'm not sure yet what its origin is."

"Could it be from the makeup?"

John went to another computer station and took a moment to pull up the files and clicked on the garnet ring. "It appears to be a type of soap grease with the properties of a simple soap—rather than the anti-bacterial kind. The reason I say grease is because the main thickener used in grease is a metallic soap substance. These metals include lithium, aluminum, sodium and calcium."

"Did someone try to clean the ring?"

"You know how a ring could get stuck on your finger? Maybe the killer, or someone, could have soaped the finger to get the ring off?"

"More than likely; maybe the killer used a particular soap to clean the cut on their finger."

"I also found traces of these chemicals on the body, forearms, and her hair."

"Why would the killer clean the victim?"

"That, Katie, is your job," he said and smiled. "I'll have final reports to you tomorrow or the next day, but I wanted you to have the preliminaries."

"I appreciate that. Thanks, John. Can you email the photos?"

"Of course. You'll get them later today." He turned around. "Oh, by the way…"

She walked back toward him.

"I was able to compare the impression evidence at the fairgrounds to the oversized screwdriver. That's how someone gained access, but there weren't any fingerprints or anything identifiable on the tool or the lock. Sorry."

"It's okay. At least we know how someone, most likely the killer, got into the fairgrounds."

He nodded.

Katie left and quietly shut the door behind her. She was standing in the hallway when her phone alerted her to a text.

She quickly glanced at the cell phone screen from McGaven.

You're the bait.

CHAPTER THIRTY-TWO
Wednesday 1045 hours

Laughing to herself at McGaven's bad sense of humor, Katie hurried to the office, eager to get to work. The text from McGaven angered her at first because she felt he was making light of the investigation, but then she realized he was most likely trying to lighten things a bit. She pushed it from her mind. There was so much to do that she didn't want to stop and think about how overwhelmingly complex this investigative puzzle was—they had so many pieces and now they had to figure out how to put it all together, to lead them to the killer. After she updated McGaven on her chat with John and the forensics findings, they moved forward and tracked down Darla Winchell's background.

Katie's cell phone rang. ·

"Detective Scott," she answered. "Yes, hello, Dr. Dean." She listened intently for a minute. "Thank you so much." She ended the call.

"What?"

"Dr. Dean said, having looked at the files for the first two victims' autopsies—Nancy Day and Gwen Sanderson—he is confident that while Gwen's chest injuries are consistent with those sustained by Jeanine Trenton and Darla Winchell, Nancy's seemed to have been caused more by a fall, perhaps."

"That's a signature for the last three murders. And it backs up the theory that Gwen killed Nancy."

"Yep. I think we're closing in," she said. "Slowly, but we're getting somewhere."

"So what's your take on Agent Campbell now?" McGaven asked.

"I don't know… sometimes I think he's just desperate to get a lead to close his cases after having so many investigators work on them. But…"

"But you still have that gut feeling that something's not right?"

"Yes."

"I'm with you. What do we have?"

Katie picked up the marker and began to make a list. "Okay, we have the Jeanine Trenton and Darla Winchell cases. And here's what we know."

Jeanine Trenton, 27, brunette, blue eyes, born in Wisconsin, single, lived alone, no boyfriend, worked as a health care specialist at Community Health Alliance, gifted her home in Raven Woods, no debts, no health issues, no family, harassed by next-door neighbor Sadie Caldwell who has mental health issues, had get-togethers, people coming and going from her house, harassed by co-workers, found murdered with chest impression and throat cut, found by best friend Mandy Davis because missed party. *joined army—K9 trainer

Persons of Interest:
Mandy Davis, best friend, Jeanine hooked up with her boyfriend
Sadie Caldwell, neighbor, mental dysfunction
Co-worker, Virginia Rodriguez
Ex-boyfriend
Family member
Stranger—someone following her fixated
Unknown or K9 training facility

Darla Winchell, 34, executive, First Community Bank, found at the fairgrounds on the Ferris wheel, chest impressions, throat cut.

Crime scene characteristics in common:
Bodies posed, drama, heavy makeup, like characters in a play or on a game board, throats cut, impacts on chests before death, jewelry hanging by a ribbon (trophy?), nautical-style knots?

Crime scene differences:
Level of ability, brunette versus blonde victim, knife incision neat versus ragged, one left in place where she would be discovered quickly, other on private land, crime scene getting bigger and more complex. Same killer? Possible copycat?

"Was Darla Winchell reported as a missing person?" she asked.

"No," he said.

"What do we have for her? Place of residence, family?"

He searched through their accessible police databases. "I have an address: 1616 12th Street, apartment 21."

"Is there a person listed as an emergency number or next of kin? I'm assuming it was her mother?"

McGaven's fingers pounded at the computer keyboard at an impressive speed. "Yep, looks like Dorothy Winchell, her mom."

"Any other family you can find?"

"No. Wait—there's a Cynthia Winchell, but it shows she died three years ago."

"And how's that list coming for the fairgrounds?"

"It's going to take a while, searching my parameters. I have one list that's more broad in particulars and another that's very specific."

Katie grabbed her notebook and jacket. "While the computer is crunching that list, let's go check out her apartment."

"Road trip."

"Are you going to say that every time?" She smiled.

"When we get to go to places of interest and help to solve a murder. Then yeah, I'm going to say 'road trip.'"

CHAPTER THIRTY-THREE
Wednesday 1310 hours

Katie drove with purpose and hit the accelerator a little too much. She felt they finally had some new information that would lead them closer to the killer. They needed to find out who Darla Winchell was and why she would be targeted by the same person that had targeted Jeanine Trenton. She speculated that they were connected through the army, but there had to be more to it.

"There's something we're missing," she said.

McGaven was texting on his phone. "You say that every time, but we seem to find out the next clue when we're supposed to find out the next clue."

"Is that something from one of those TV shows?" She tried to keep her giggles to herself. "When it's coming close to the end and everything wraps up nicely and even the killer confesses. Ta-da!"

"You've been in an exceptionally good mood today."

"What do you mean?" She took the freeway heading downtown, accelerating and passing several cars.

"Oh, I don't know…"

"Talk about anything but relationships. Just do me that one favor…"

"Okay, okay."

Katie merged into traffic and the cars were slow-going. "Looks like we've hit rush hour."

"Car accident."

"No, it's just too many cars causing congestion."

"Accident."

Katie maneuvered between vehicles, changing lanes as they headed up first and second streets. On the side of the road there was a four-door car broken down. A tow truck was finally making its move and was about to hook up the distressed vehicle.

"See."

"That's a breakdown, not an accident."

"Could've been an accident."

Ignoring his remark, Katie took a left and drove through several signals before finally reaching 12th Street. "Okay, what's the address?"

McGaven looked at his notes. "It's 1616 12th Street, apartment 21."

"Okay, here's the fourteen hundred block and the fifteen hundred block…" she said as they slowed and passed small houses and duplexes.

McGaven watched for the address.

There were sidewalks and well-manicured trees, tidy front yards and common areas. The street had been recently resurfaced, making the ride feel like gliding.

Katie spotted a sign for 1616 out in front of an apartment complex consisting of several buildings with four apartments, two upstairs and two downstairs. Light brown structures with white trim, they were independent four-plexes and were situated around the property. It reminded Katie of vacation rentals because of the trees, walkways, and gates.

She pulled up and parked along the street. Taking a moment to turn off the ignition, she scrutinized the property. "What do you think?"

"These are nice apartments. I had a call here once, prowler."

She cut the engine. "Let's go see what we can find."

Katie exited the vehicle, followed by McGaven.

They walked around several of the apartment buildings until they found number 21.

"It's upstairs," she said and climbed up the stairs. Someone was cooking something mouthwatering. It made her stomach growl because she hadn't had anything to eat since breakfast.

"Smells good," said McGaven.

Katie laughed. It was untimely, she thought, since they were going to the apartment of a murdered woman, but her stress had been elevated. And sometimes, police officers laugh at inappropriate times.

They approached the apartment. It had a small potted plant on each side of the door in desperate need of water and a cute welcome mat that said "Wipe your paws." It struck Katie for a moment because it made reference to dogs. Could Darla Winchell have been connected to a military K9 at one time? She needed to verify with Sergeant Serrano.

Katie decided to knock, expecting that no one was home, but thinking there may be a roommate or boyfriend. She rapped three times.

No movement.

McGaven walked around to the side of the apartment and casually peered inside.

"Anything?" she said.

"It's difficult to see through the curtains, but it looks like a light is on. And something dark. I can't tell what it is."

Katie glanced down at the doorknob, noticing something dark next to it. She gently touched it with her index finger. It appeared to be dried blood. Scrutinizing it more closely, she saw more dark smudges that seemed to have been wiped with something.

"What's there?"

"Looks like dried blood. I'm not sure. And here, it looks like someone wiped something clean recently."

McGaven inspected it. "It does look like dried blood."

Katie walked to the railing and looked around at the apartments all over the property. She saw one with an "Office" sign. "Let's try the office," she said and hurried down the staircase.

They dashed across the property to apartment number eight, which displayed the "Office" sign. Katie knocked.

They didn't have to wait long before the door was opened by a nice-looking, middle-aged woman, and a smell of something delicious wafted out. The woman poked her head out and said, "Yes? Can I help you?"

"Is this the office for the complex?" asked Katie.

"Yes, it is."

"I'm Detective Scott and this is my partner, Deputy McGaven."

"Oh," she said, eying their badges and guns. "Is something wrong?"

"We're here about one of your tenants—Darla Winchell."

"Oh really? Is she okay?"

Katie looked around to see if anyone was nearby and within eavesdropping distance. "May we come inside?"

"Oh dear. Yes, of course," she said and opened the door wide for them to enter.

After shutting the door, she turned to them and said, "I'm Rene Cross."

"I'm so sorry to tell you this, but I'm afraid that Ms. Winchell has been found murdered."

It was clear that the news shook her. The color drained from her face and she wobbled a bit in unsteadiness.

"Ms. Cross, are you okay? Why don't you sit down and catch your breath," said Katie as she guided the woman to the couch.

The living room was open and spacious with two big windows that looked out at the trees. A white fluffy cat with bright blue eyes jumped up on the couch and immediately went to the woman's lap. "Oh, you silly boy," she said.

Katie knelt down beside her. "Beautiful cat. What's his name?"

"Simon," she said as the color flooded her cheeks again.

Katie petted the silky cat. "Can I get you a glass of water?"

"No, dear, I'm fine now."

"I'm sorry to have to tell you about Ms. Winchell's death so abruptly."

"How? When?"

"I'm sorry, again, but we're in the middle of the investigation and we can't divulge anything right now." Katie stood up. "Would it be possible to get a key to her apartment?"

"Oh, yes, of course." She got up and went into the kitchen and came right back. "Here you go." She gave the keys to Katie.

"When was the last time you saw Ms. Winchell?"

"It must've been… last Monday. She was on her way to work, so it was around 8:30 a.m."

"Did she happen to confide in you about anyone bothering her? Did she have any problems that you knew of?"

"Oh no. She was a wonderful woman. So kind. Friendly. Always paid her rent on time. I didn't notice anything out of the ordinary."

Katie handed her a business card. "If you think of anything, please don't hesitate to call me."

"Thank you."

"We'll get the key back to you soon," said McGaven.

"Okay," she said and walked Katie and McGaven to the door.

After the door shut, Katie and McGaven hurried back up the stairs to the apartment.

Katie stood at the front door staring at the number 21. Her nerves were twitchy and an annoying prickle ran up the back of her neck. Her instincts and experience told her to push forward. Inserting the key, twisting and pushing the door open, she stepped over the threshold.

Inside was dark except for a table lamp which emitted minimal light. The curtains were partially closed, allowing very little daylight in. Katie waited for her eyes to become accustomed to the dim lighting.

Katie and McGaven stayed at the entrance, surveying what they could see. There was a distinct stench of urine and feces that was a bit overwhelming.

There was a large sectional couch in the middle of the living room, but that was the only thing that looked undisturbed. The coffee table had broken glass scattered across the surface. Magazines were strewn across the floor. Two chairs from the dining-room table were overturned, one was broken. There were more bloody handprints around the wall entering the hallway.

"Wait," Katie said. "We need gloves and booties before we go any further. Maybe something for that smell too?" She pushed the front door as wide as it could go hoping that the sealed-up stink would mostly escape.

McGaven instinctively retraced his steps and backed out of the apartment. "I'll be right back."

"I'm putting a call in to John," she said, dialing her cell phone.

After Katie hung up, she created a game plan for searching the apartment.

A *meow* and purr sounded as a cat rubbed up against her left leg.

Startled for an instant, Katie looked down to see a thin yellow tabby with a few black marks circling her. "Oh, you're the cutest." She bent down and picked up the cat. "You're friendly," she said, eyeing the round ID tag that said "Tigger."

She heard McGaven storm up the stairwell, taking two stairs at a time. He appeared in the doorway. "Making friends, I see."

"Maybe I should take him to Ms. Cross for now?" she suggested, looking down at the cat who was purring madly in her arms. "I bet you're hungry too."

"Good idea. Don't think Cisco is going to like that you smell of cat."

Katie carefully retraced her steps to outside the doorway. She quickly descended the stairs and brought the cat to the office and into Ms. Cross's care. She was happy to take care of Tigger.

Upon returning to the apartment, she donned the booties and slipped on the gloves. McGaven patiently waited.

"You want to lead the search?" she said.

"Ladies first."

"John should be here anytime, probably an hour given the traffic."

Katie looked outside at the horizon and estimated that they had two hours of daylight left. "It would be a good idea to see if Darla Winchell's car is in her allocated parking slot."

"On it," he said and ran back down to the parking lot.

Katie turned back to the apartment and took a moment to focus her entire energy on the examination. She made her entry slowly and decided to search in a clockwise motion. Again, she saw the beige sectional couch with three pieces. It was big enough to fill most of the living room area with the shattered coffee table in the center. Two small tables, each with a western-themed lamp, were positioned one at each corner of the room. One lamp was on, but the bulb flickered, as if it were getting ready to burn out. The effect was unnerving and even disturbing—as if Darla Winchell was trying to communicate from the great beyond.

Katie focused her attention on details and pushed silly thoughts from her mind. She surveyed the room from the bottom, to the walls, and up toward the ceiling as she walked.

There were signs of a struggle in the living room, and when Katie stood at the doorway to the hall there were three handprints on the wall, two of which were overlapping, making an abstract of blood. One print was clear enough for a good comparison, she thought.

Before going down the hallway, Katie walked toward the small open kitchen. There was a coffee cup, glass, a small plate, and bowl in the sink. A fork and spoon lay on the counter. Everything seemed normal, but Darla Winchell hadn't cleaned up yet. One of the cabinets was open a few inches. It seemed to contain dry goods—cereal, rice, coffee, and some canned goods. She theorized that the victim had a bowl of cereal, piece of toast, and coffee. It told Katie that she was here during the morning.

Could the killer have been so brazen as to confront her during the day?

Looking for any of the weapons, such as a knife, she didn't see anything that might have been used.

Katie then moved to the hallway, detecting the bloody hand-prints once again. The apartment was a two-bedroom unit with one bathroom. The hallway was narrow with a bedroom at each end. The small bathroom was in the middle. There were dark smudges along the walls, but Katie couldn't tell if it was blood or some other substance. The first bedroom she approached had sections of long blonde hair stuck to more blood along the baseboard.

She paused, looking closer at the strands of hair. It was difficult to see with the naked eye but it appeared that there were pieces of scalp still attached to the roots, suggesting it had been pulled out by force. Piecing together what happened at the apartment, Katie worked backwards.

She took a couple of cleansing breaths before entering the bedroom. The door was half closed with several holes indicating someone or something had tried to force it open. The room was about ten-foot square and contained a double bed, small dresser, a nightstand and an antique wooden chair in the corner. The sliding closet door was open and revealed an overcrowded rail with clothes squeezing outward.

But Katie couldn't take her eyes away from the bed. The sheets and comforter were white, but now soaked with blood. The crimson stain was nothing short of horrifying. The bedding was twisted and pulled from the four corners. It looked as if the items from the nightstand were on the floor between the bed and the table.

It was clear to Katie the attack had begun in the bedroom. She surmised that the killer caught Darla Winchell off guard and a fight ensued. It was where the defense wounds on her forearms had originated, and from the bloody handprints, the killer must've dragged her out of the bedroom, down the hall, and into the living room.

But the most disturbing aspect of the bedroom was the three-foot-long bamboo cane, spattered with blood. It was similar to the bamboo at Mrs. Sadie Caldwell's front porch. There was no doubt in Katie's mind it was the weapon that led to Darla Winchell's death.

CHAPTER THIRTY-FOUR
Wednesday 1835 hours

Darla Winchell's apartment was now the official primary crime scene—the fairgrounds were the secondary crime and murder location—and an investigation was in progress. Two patrol deputies roped off the apartment building and the parking area where the victim's car was located.

McGaven was searching the car and assisting the forensic technician Rob, as Katie was inside the apartment with John. The two deputies were keeping residents away from the area and not allowing anyone into the building.

Katie watched as John documented the apartment, recovered fingerprints, and other forensic evidence including blood samples. He carefully retrieved and boxed the bamboo tube, the potential murder weapon. Its size and diameter were consistent with the wounds found on Darla Winchell's body.

"Thanks, John," said Katie as she exited the apartment. She was confident that John would do his job with exceptional ability. She wanted to double check the files on the other victims to find out if there was a bamboo pole or something similar found at the crime scenes. She didn't recall, but it was due diligence. Flashing back in her mind to the three-foot bamboo pole on Sadie's porch, she suspected it had to do more with gardening than murder, but she wasn't going to rule it out.

Just as Katie walked out the door, she was confronted by Special Agent Campbell.

"Hello, Detective," he said.

Katie hid her surprise and immediately thought of what he had said during their meeting on Sunday at the diner.

She hid her dislike for the agent; she was a professional and would do her job.

"You look great," he said. "You would never guess that you slid down a mountain recently."

"It was a small hillside, but nonetheless." She glanced down at the parking lot and saw Agent Haley speaking with McGaven. "What brings you here?"

"Anything new and potentially important about my cases, I want to know."

"I see."

"No worries, Detective. I won't get in your way and I look forward to your report." He forced a smile that looked predatory to Katie. As he stood in the early evening light, she felt less sure of him than ever. It wasn't just his presence, it was his demeanor, his stare, and how he seemed to have all the right answers.

"We might have recovered the murder weapon."

"The first or second?" he asked, clearly trying to test her knowledge of the case.

"Weapon?"

"Yes."

"The autopsy report—which I'm sure that you have read— suggests that the victim, Darla Winchell, was hit forcibly with a cylindrical implement—forcibly enough to induce a heart attack or serious arrhythmia."

"I see. So you think the victim was struck hard, like you described, enough so that she was compliant and the killer could get her to the fairgrounds."

"At first I thought the struggle began in the living room, but I believe she was initially in her bedroom when the killer entered. Most likely getting ready for work—maybe she was partially dressed. That could account for her scant clothing at the fairgrounds. She was struck in the bedroom—at least once. There was quite a struggle in the hallway near the bedroom entrance. Maybe she tried to get back to her bedroom to secure the door to call for help. But you can read my report." She turned to go down the staircase. "I need to get back to work."

The agent watched her leave and didn't offer any other suggestion or question.

Katie couldn't help but feel incredibly uncomfortable around Campbell. Even after they'd had that conversation at the diner, her instinct still inhibited her feelings. She hated to have feelings drive her investigation, but there was something amiss about his motivations. She had relied on her instincts before and they hadn't proved her wrong—yet.

Katie walked up to McGaven. "How's it going? Anything?"

Agent Haley walked by. "Hi, Detective Scott. Nice to see you."

Katie forced a smile back.

McGaven leaned in to his partner. "Something wrong?"

"Not a thing," she said, clenching her teeth.

"We found her wallet and jacket, but nothing else. Her car appears to be untouched, but Rob is going to dust for foreign prints inside and out." McGaven paused and a serious expression crossed his face. "Can I talk to you for a moment?" he said, glancing up on the deck.

"Sure." Katie led her partner to the other side of the complex near a group of trees. The darkness began to settle over the property, but she could still see McGaven's grave expression. "What's on your mind?"

"I saw you talking with Campbell."

"Yeah, he was just making sure we're doing our jobs." She tried to make light of it, but in truth, it bothered her. His attitude. His insinuation.

"You know that I'm not one to ring the panic button."

She smiled. "C'mon, Gav, spit it out. What gives?"

"After you told me what he discussed with you at the diner the other day, the more I think about it, something seems fishy to me."

"Fishy?"

"Yeah, I don't like how we were roped into this situation and how he sits on his throne watching us—you know what it reminds me of?"

"What?"

"It's like he's… it's like he's pulling the strings. Everything in my gut says so. Especially after I saw him today."

Katie began, "I know—"

"Just do me a favor, take extra precautions, okay?"

"Okay," she said.

"I mean it. Otherwise, you're going to have someone sleeping on your couch until this investigation is over."

Katie laughed. "I'll be fine." She had her own concerns, but now hearing McGaven's voice, she was apprehensive. "Really, I'll be *fine*. And I'll be careful."

CHAPTER THIRTY-FIVE
Thursday 0915 hours

"Okay, thank you," Katie said as she pressed the end button on her cell phone. "Just confirmed with Mrs. Dorothy Winchell we can talk to her this morning, she will be home until 1 p.m."

"How did she sound?" McGaven asked.

"Strong, but a bit weepy—but that's understandable with what she's going through." Katie shuddered, remembering what it was like when her Uncle Wayne came to the house to tell her that her parents had died in a car accident. So many emotions erupt and keep coming, but you find strength somehow. "She wants us to do whatever we need to do to find her daughter's killer." She read through her notes. "Mr. Winchell died four years ago from cancer. There are no other family members. She's still in Darla's childhood home. We might be able to find out more about her and maybe how she might've come into contact with her killer."

McGaven was printing out lists from his database, trying to corral names and people that could be of interest from the fairgrounds.

"You ready for a road trip?" She tried to sound upbeat. In reality, she'd had a difficult time sleeping last night. She kept running through the strange conversations she'd had with Agent Campbell, thinking of the times she now knew he had been following her, and wondering how many other times he might have been watching her without her knowing.

"Always ready."

"How are those lists?"

"Long and tedious. Breaking them down, running down backgrounds, crossing some off. And I know there must be aliases mixed in the group."

Katie stood up and slipped on her jacket. "I still think there could be a reason that the fairgrounds location was chosen to display the body. Some connection. It could mean something to the killer—whether it's a fond memory or a terrifying one. Something... having to do with the Ferris wheel in general, maybe an accident or something that happened near the ride?"

"There are all types of people on this list, every age and background; it makes you wonder if people work carnivals and fairs because they are hiding from something."

"You know, Gav, that's a great point. How far did you get with your search on accidents at fairgrounds?"

"Not far. I didn't have time to check on the fire you mentioned," he said, following her out of the office.

"We need to look for something that isn't regular fair or carnival stuff. Something that is life defining."

"That might be a great assignment for Denise. She likes digging for that kind of stuff."

"Great idea."

"I'll call her on the way."

Katie was relieved they didn't have to drive to another small town, since it looked like it might storm soon. Darkened clouds resembling fantasy creatures loomed overhead. It reminded her of a metaphor for all things looming over the investigation that she couldn't control.

They easily found Mrs. Winchell's house, since she lived in a cul-de-sac located on Bridge Street. It was a nice two-story home, dark brown with white shutters, with two willow trees in front. The landscaping, part lawn and part flat stones, was meticulously organized.

Katie parked on the street in between two houses. As she got out, she was struck by how quiet it was, reminding her of Jeanine Trenton's home.

Katie and McGaven walked up to the front door, which had a large oval stained-glass window featuring flowers, vines, and robins, and rang the doorbell, which emitted a beautiful chime. Within a minute, she saw a woman coming down the stairs to the foyer. She appeared younger than Katie would have thought. Slim and blonde, she moved with ease.

Mrs. Winchell opened the door.

"Mrs. Winchell?" said Katie.

"Yes?"

"I'm Detective Katie Scott and this is my partner, Deputy Sean McGaven."

"Please, come in," she said as she led them into the living room.

Katie noticed that Darla resembled her mother. She could also see that pain infused Dorothy's expression and her words. Losing a loved one was something that changed you, defined you, and nothing would ever be the same again.

"Thank you," said Katie. She marveled at the décor—high-end couches, tables, chandelier, baby grand piano, and exquisite paintings on the wall. The modest exterior of the house gave no clue to the beauty and meticulous decorating within. It was stunning, but felt lonely too.

Mrs. Winchell took a seat on the sofa as Katie and McGaven opted to sit across from her.

"First, we and the department would like to convey our sincere condolences. We are so very sorry for your loss."

She nodded. "Thank you."

"Would you mind answering a few questions? I promise we will not take up too much of your time."

"Of course. I want to do whatever I can." She took a breath and seemed to brace herself for what Katie would ask.

"When was the last time you talked to Darla?"

"It was about a week ago. She would always try to make sure that she called me at least every week, usually in the evenings. I did wonder when she didn't call me this week, but I assumed she was busy."

"Did she seem worried about anything?"

"No, not at all. She was the same cheerful person she always was." Her voice caught in her throat, but she composed herself.

"Had she ever said anything to you about someone bothering her at work or at her apartment?"

"No. But then, if there had been anything like that, she wouldn't have wanted to burden me with her concerns. Darla was like that—considerate of everyone else's needs."

"Was she dating anyone?"

Mrs. Winchell thought for a moment before answering. "No one special. I think she dated a young man at the bank on and off."

Katie saw the photographs along a table. She stood to see them clearly. There were photos of Darla and her parents in exotic places. "Such amazing photos. You traveled a lot."

"Yes," she said and smiled.

Katie came to another photo. It was a smaller black-and-white shot of Darla with a German shepherd. It was familiar to Katie and she could barely contain her amazement and excitement. "This photo," she said as she picked it up for McGaven to see. "Where was this taken?"

"Oh, Darla was in the army for two years. She wanted to earn her way through the military, and didn't want us to pay for her college."

"Was she a military K9 officer?" She wondered if the victims overlapped their time in the army.

"Yes," she said. "Darla loved dogs. We had several while she was growing up. We thought she might be a veterinarian, but she decided to go into banking because she wanted to start a business of her own."

Katie set the photo down. It brought back her own memories with Cisco. She realized how lucky and blessed she was that her uncle had had the connections to allow her to bring Cisco home. It made her transition much easier and she couldn't imagine doing it without him. "She sounds like she knew exactly what she wanted to do."

"She did. She always made lists, ever since she was about eight years old."

McGaven watched Katie and then turned his attention to Mrs. Winchell. "Did Darla ever have any issues with the bank?"

"No. She said it was difficult at first. They expect a lot out of their employees, but then, like Darla always did, she settled in and excelled."

Katie came back and sat down next to Mrs. Winchell. "I don't want to make this any more difficult than it already is for you."

Mrs. Winchell fought back the tears as she touched Katie's hand. "Nothing is more difficult than identifying your daughter's body. Please, if I can do anything…"

Usually Katie was able to get through interviews with family members who had lost a loved one, but this time it was difficult.

McGaven must have sensed Katie's unease, as he asked, "You said this was the house that Darla grew up in?"

"Yes. We bought the house just before Darla was born thirty-four years ago. Darla still has a room here."

"Would it be possible to see it?" asked Katie. "Anything that might help us to know Darla better would be helpful."

Standing up, Mrs. Winchell said, "Of course." She climbed the stairs and stopped at the top landing. "Please excuse me, but

I'd rather not go into her room right now. It's the last door on the right. Stay as long as you like." She turned away and went back down the stairs.

Katie and McGaven went directly to Darla's room. For some reason, Katie had imagined the room to be that of a little girl, decorated in pink with a canopy bed. But instead, it was modern, almost like the rest of the house, but with personal touches. There was a double bed with a white comforter and lace pillowcases with two blue velvet pillows, much more luxurious than her apartment furnishings. There was a nightstand on each side of the bed with Tiffany-style matching lamps. A glass desk with a closed laptop sat on the other side of the room. A white bookcase was filled with old books from her childhood and some new business textbooks. It was tidy and organized. A large rug with a woven gray-and-blue design covered most of the light wood floor.

"Okay, I'll start over here," she said, referring to the nightstands. Standing in Darla's childhood room, which had been updated through the years, made Katie feel the loss as well. Maybe it was something from her own childhood, but it was difficult to stay neutral to the situation.

"Okay," said McGaven and he began his search at the desk. He sat down and opened the computer.

Katie had learned from experience to check the bed and mattress first. She slipped her hand in between the mattress and box springs hoping to find a journal, but found nothing. She checked the pillows carefully for any secret pockets. Again, nothing.

There were two small drawers on each nightstand. She opened them, but there wasn't anything of interest inside, only items like lotion, gum, an old magazine, two novels and some earplugs, but nothing that would help them.

The other nightstand had similar items in the top drawer— empty notebooks, pens, keys and perfume. When Katie tried to open the bottom drawer, she found it was stuck fast. She finally pulled it out and inside, there were envelopes with letters addressed to Darla Winchell at her apartment address. It seemed odd. Why would they be here?

"Hey, I think I might have something," said McGaven. "Check this out."

Katie put the letters down, joined him and peered down at the laptop. "How did you get into her email?"

"She had her password checked to remember each time she logged in." He clicked on the envelope icon. "Look at this," he said and clicked on a file folder marked "Military." There were many emails from people she met in the army, from dog trainers and military police to people in her training class. There was one email in particular from someone signing themselves just "DH." Look at this." McGaven clicked open the message.

The subject line read: *Liars Reap* and the message was three short sentences: *You know what you did. You can't take it back. The finale is coming.*

"A threat?" she said.

"Looks like it."

"Look at the date. It's from a year ago."

"And there are a few more, but they won't open."

"Can you figure out where it came from?" said Katie.

"It looks like it was a temporary email—like those generic ones you get in spam. I can't tell where it came from." He clicked on a few more things without luck.

Katie wrote down the message in her notebook with the date and initials so she wouldn't forget it: *You know what you did. You can't take it back. The finale is coming.*

"Now we need to find out what Darla did—or what someone thinks she did."

"We need to check the emails of the other victims." Katie was hopeful—finally, they had a big break.

CHAPTER THIRTY-SIX

Thursday 1410 hours

Katie was quiet at the lunch break with McGaven. They had stopped at her favorite burger place before visiting the First Community Bank of Pine Valley where Darla Winchell worked, but she was preoccupied with the email message and being in Darla's home. It was as if she were connected to her, and the other victims, due to the military K9 link. She wondered if she was too close to the cases to be completely objective. She had skimmed through Darla's personal letters, but there wasn't anything that stood out or was connected to her time in K9—most were just letters from an old boyfriend. She would have McGaven take a look at them back at the office.

"Are you going to eat your fries?" asked McGaven.

"What? Oh, go for it." Her appetite wasn't what it usually was when she was working on a case.

"I know that I'm not one of your gal pals but if you have something on your mind, you know you can trust me." He looked at Katie with a sincere expression.

Katie knew how lucky she was to have a great partner—they had been through so much together and she knew she could trust him. But sometimes she just had to let herself work through things in her own time. "I'm fine, really. I appreciate the concern."

"Is it Chad?"

Katie couldn't lie. "Yes, but… we'll just have to see."

"I know the cases are difficult, but we are moving nearer to a closure." He dipped another French fry into catsup. "It always feels like this in the middle of wading through everything—trying to figure out what's pertinent and what isn't. It's the game we play."

"It's true."

McGaven looked at his watch. "We should probably head over to the bank."

The First Community Bank of Pine Valley was a medium-sized bank located in the main part of town and was a popular place for most of the local residents. Darla Winchell had worked for them for six years, working her way up from a teller to an executive, handling business accounts.

Katie and McGaven entered the bank and hovered around the entrance trying to figure out where to go to meet with the president. The security guard immediately spotted them and made his way over to greet them. Katie opened her jacket to reveal her badge. He made a waving gesture with his hand, indicating he understood, and went back to his post.

Katie saw the various desks behind partitions and walked over to ask if she could meet with Michael Raines, the president of the branch. A young woman wearing a burgundy dress went to alert Mr. Raines that two police detectives wanted to talk with him.

They didn't have to wait long. A serious-looking, dark-haired man wearing glasses and a dark suit with a red tie headed toward them. He moved with purpose and projected an all-business attitude.

"Hello, I'm Michael Raines, the president of the bank."

"I'm Detective Scott and this is Deputy McGaven."

"Pleased to meet you both," he said and shook their hands. "Let's talk in my office."

They followed him through an area where there were four desks. The employees looked at Katie and McGaven with some interest, but mostly concern.

The big corner office was where they were headed. It was sparsely decorated, with a large desk, comfortable leather chair, and two smaller chairs for customers to sit down.

As soon as they were seated, Katie began.

"Mr. Raines, thank you for seeing us on such short notice."

"You said it had to do with Darla Winchell."

Katie shifted in her chair, knowing she would not only have to break the news of a death, but of a brutal murder. "Yes. I'm sorry to inform you that Ms. Winchell is dead."

He sucked in a gasp. "What?" he whispered. "Dead? But you are detectives so that means… she was murdered?"

"Yes, that's correct." There was never an easy way to break the news. It always sounded harsher than it needed to be under such trying situations. "I am so sorry to have to share such horrible news about one of your employees."

"Oh my… how?"

"We're not able to discuss any details at the moment," she said. "It's an active investigation."

"Of course. What can I do to help?" he said, obviously upset. His mind was clearly reeling from the news.

"We would like to ask a few questions about Darla. If that's okay."

"Of course. I'll try to answer if I can." He looked back and forth from Katie to McGaven and then settled on Katie.

"How would you characterize Darla's work here?"

"She was what every employer dreams of. I mean that. She was one of those employees that always wanted to learn more, strive more, and move up whenever she could." He paused a moment to gather his thoughts, as if it had really sunk in that she was dead.

"Whenever there were classes— whether it was better ways to work with co-workers or new computer systems in dealing with business accounts—she was the first to sign up."

"Did she ever confide in you that something was bothering her at work? Like another employee or a customer?"

"No, never. But I'm not the best person to ask, being her boss. Some of the other employees would be better suited to answer that question." He leaned back in his oversized chair. "I know that she was close with Daniel Harper; he's in charge of new accounts and investments."

"Is he here today?" asked McGaven.

"Yes."

"Just a couple more questions and then we'd like to speak with him, too," said Katie.

As Mr. Raines waited, he tapped his right index finger on the arm of the chair.

Katie thought he was holding something back. She was curious and suddenly remembered what John had said about the killer receiving an injury to the right index finger. "Mr. Raines, can you show us your hands?"

He looked confused, but slowly moved his hands forward with his fingers and palms facing upwards for Katie and McGaven to see. There was no indication of any injuries.

"Thank you," she said, changing tack quickly to hide her disappointment. "Did you ever have to reprimand Darla for anything?"

The president appeared to think about it. "No, I don't think so. She is... *was* one of my best employees... and I still can't believe that she's gone."

"I would suggest informing your employees so that they don't hear it from some other source. Please give them time to grieve and whatever support they need. Everyone is different." Katie made sure that the president understood.

"Yes. We have a company that helps with crisis situations and I will have them be available to anyone that needs it."

Katie felt relief wash over her. "That's wonderful. Would it be possible to speak with Daniel Harper?"

"Uh, yes. Please stay. I'll bring him in and you can use my office."

The president left the office and Katie waited until the door was closed and he was out of view.

"What do you think?" she said in a low tone.

"He's genuinely shocked. We've seen it many times, but did I detect some deception?"

"I caught that too. He was too nervous, but that could have something to do with things going on in his own life—not with Darla."

"True. There's a high percentage of nervousness among people who interact with police."

"Daniel Harper," she said. "I didn't see any photos in the apartment or her parents' home with him. Is that odd? Or maybe she didn't want to be reminded of him."

"We'll just see what he has to say."

The president returned with a man in his early thirties, dark wavy hair, suit and tie without the jacket. His eyes were wide and he was obviously confused about why he was being ushered to the president's office to talk to police.

"Detectives? This is Daniel Harper." He held the door for the man. "Nice meeting you both." He shut the door and disappeared again.

"I'm Detective Scott and this is Deputy McGaven. Please have a seat."

He sat hesitantly in the president's chair, looking uncomfortable. "What's this all about?" he said in a quiet voice.

"I'm sorry. This is always difficult," she said. "I'm sorry to tell you that Darla Winchell is dead."

"What? *Dead?* How? When?" His voice became an octave higher as his eyes darted from one detective to the other.

"She was found murdered."

"Murdered... what... what happened? Did you catch the person?"

"The case is currently under investigation so we are not able to give you details, but we wanted to get some background information from you. Is that okay? You up to it?"

"Uh, yes, of course. I... can't believe she's gone." His eyes welled up with tears, but he was holding them back.

"What was your relationship with Darla?"

"We were friends and co-workers."

"Did you date?" asked Katie, watching him closely.

"Well... yes, technically, we did."

"What does 'technically' mean?" said McGaven.

"When we first met about six years ago, we flirted a lot and we went out a few times."

"And?"

"And we felt we are better as good friends," he said, not making eye contact.

Katie leaned forward. "Mr. Harper, I can see you have feelings for her. Anyone can see that you have feelings for her."

"So? It's not a crime."

"I take it that Darla was the one suggesting that the two of you be just friends."

"Yes."

"How did that make you feel?"

"What do you mean? I was upset but I got over it. You don't think I..."

"Mr. Harper, we're trying to piece together her life and timeline before the murder to figure out who might have wanted to harm her."

"I can't imagine…" He couldn't finish his sentence.

McGaven shifted in his chair, moving it closer to the man. "Can you think of anyone who would want to hurt Darla? Someone she had trouble with?"

"No. I can't think of anyone. She is… was… a great person and everyone loved her."

"Did she ever confide in you about something or someone that was bothering her?"

Daniel Harper thought for a moment. "No, I can't think of anything. That's what makes this so incredibly heartbreaking."

"Mr. Harper, here's my card." She handed him a business card. "If you think of anything—

anything at all that might help us—please call me."

He took the card and put it in his top pocket. "Of course." He stood up.

Daniel Harper? D.H.

"Oh, just a couple more things. Could I see your hands, please?" He held them out before him, mystified. There was no injury to be seen. "Thank you. And did you ever send Darla emails?"

"Sure."

"Did you ever sign them 'DH'?"

He thought about the question and shrugged. "I don't think so. Sometimes if I sent her a quick message, I might just sign it 'D'. I don't remember."

"Okay. Thank you, Mr. Harper. We appreciate your time."

He rose and then quickly left the office.

McGaven looked at her.

"I just had to ask."

"You think he's the one who sent that email?"

"No. But we have to run down all the leads."

"I'll run background of the employees to see if anything pops up."

"But, Gav, it is a coincidence. Someone who was close to Darla but wanted to be more just good friends, whose initials just happen to match up to our emailer?"

"I see your point."

You know what you did. You can't take it back. The finale is coming.

CHAPTER THIRTY-SEVEN

After interviewing Mrs. Winchell and Daniel Harper, Katie felt there was more beyond their answers to her initial questions; she felt they were telling the truth, but not offering up any other information.

She added to the board the new persons of interest and case characteristics for Darla Winchell:

> *DH left threatening emails/harassment. Was she hiding it? Is DH Daniel Harper?*
> *Daniel Harper—boyfriend to friend. He wanted more.*
> **Spent 2 years in army as military K9 handler.*

"I keep coming back to the military K9 aspect," she said. "How could we not? I'll call Sergeant Serrano about the list of names and ask him about Darla Winchell as well."

McGaven turned and said, "Well, I have good news."

"Oh great."

"I have two lists from the fairgrounds," he said and fished out the papers from the printer.

"Let's see," said Katie as her mood began to elevate.

"I also have bad news. On the more general list, I have a little over three hundred names. The more specific searches turned up seventy-nine names."

Katie read down the shorter list but not one name even made her pause. She sighed. "What are the asterisks for?"

"An arrest report."

"Track those down." She handed the list back to him.

"I thought you'd never ask."

There was a soft knock at the door. It opened and Denise poked her head in, "Knock, knock."

"Hi, Denise," said Katie. She was like a breath of fresh air, always upbeat.

Denise stepped inside. Her arms were loaded with two file folders.

"Hey, babe," said McGaven. His face was a bit flushed with embarrassment due to the fact that Denise was his girlfriend.

"Oh, what do you have for us?" said Katie, eyeing the paperwork.

"Well, this is for Gav." She put down the bulging paperwork on his desk.

He picked up it, pretending to shake it.

"No, silly. I copied some articles about fair and amusement park stories. Here you go."

"Wow, you got all these?" he said, amazed.

"Denise can do anything," said Katie.

"I wish. I found the subject matter on this site that specializes in out-of-date and difficult-to-find articles." She handed Katie the other folder. "This is for you. I searched through newspapers, internet sites, and circus and fairgrounds newsletters."

"They have newsletters for circuses?" McGaven said.

"Now you know," said Katie. She opened the file and began thumbing through. There were articles included about accidents, famous people visiting, creative features for amusement park rides, and other miscellaneous topics that proved interesting enough to be written about. "Thank you. This is great stuff. Eye-opening."

"Look at the back section. I filed articles pertaining to the local fairgrounds here in Sequoia County. Did you know it's haunted?" she laughed.

"Great. Like our job isn't difficult enough. Now we have to add a ghost as a suspect," said Katie.

"That's cool," said McGaven. "Any murders?"

"One."

"Really?'

"A woman was brutally raped and murdered. The case was solved—the son of one of the maintenance workers did it. But I thought it was worth including in the stack."

"Thank you. You have a knack for finding information."

"My pleasure. It adds a little fun to my boring days in records." She blew McGaven a kiss. "See you later."

"Bye."

"Is it me or does she just keep getting cuter?" said McGaven.

Katie laughed. "I know. Does she ever have a bad day?"

"That was her bad day."

Katie opened the file and began organizing the articles. Some were a year old and the oldest went back forty years. They were interesting to say the least, but the more she filtered through them, the more she began to feel like she might be looking for a needle in a haystack. But she pressed on, reading headlines and skimming articles, looking for anything that might break the investigation.

Katie's cell phone buzzed with a text. She hoped it was John saying he had some news.

It read: *Dead and gone. Now the house is going too.*

The text was from Sadie Caldwell.

CHAPTER THIRTY-EIGHT

Thursday 1815 hours

Katie and McGaven raced to Raven Woods to meet up with Sadie Caldwell after notifying the police department, fire, and the county mental health services. They didn't know what they would find, but made it to Fox Hunt Drive in record time.

As soon as Katie turned down the usually quiet road, they were greeted with the flashing lights of the first responders as smoke billowed from the house.

"She did it," said Katie, breaking the silence.

"She killed Jeanine Trenton?" asked McGaven.

"No. She burned the house to get rid of the voices." She sighed. "I should've informed health services to do a welfare check."

"You didn't know that she was capable of arson."

"I feel bad for her, you know? With the homicide investigation aside, I think there should be some type of investigation into her previous workplace."

"That will go over well," he said with emphasized sarcasm.

Katie parked a few houses away from the scene. She and McGaven hurried to the person in charge, which was the fire captain.

"How bad is it?" asked Katie, watching the firefighters continue to shoot water into the windows. "Sorry—Detective Scott, PV Sheriff's Department."

He looked at her badge. "Nothing left. As soon as the smoke subsides, it will be just a shell. She started it with gasoline and a lighter."

Katie looked at him.

"She left everything in the backyard. All the evidence is there for the fire inspector."

"Where is she?"

He pointed to the front porch of her house.

Katie looked at McGaven and they both went to see Sadie.

The woman was sitting on the porch step as one of the deputies stood nearby. "I told you... I told you," she kept murmuring, wringing her hands.

"Sadie," said Katie as she sat down next to her. "What happened?"

"Thank you for coming, Detective Scott. Thank you... thank you..."

"Why didn't you wait for me?"

"I knew you wouldn't want me to do it, but I had to get rid of it. Bad things there... such bad things." Her face had softened as if she were a little girl watching the flames and smoke.

"Sadie, do you know who killed Jeanine?"

"Such bad people... they are everywhere... they tell me things... dead and gone."

"Sadie, look at me," Katie said softly. "Sadie."

The woman turned and looked her in the eye.

"Did you see who killed Jeanine?"

She took a deep breath. "It was dark. He was dressed dark. There were no screams."

Katie glanced up at McGaven, who stood staring down at them.

"Had you ever seen the man before?"

"No man, no woman, bad things..."

Katie saw two county mental health officials approaching—a man and woman. "Sadie, I want you to do me a favor. Okay?"

She nodded.

"I want you to go with these nice people."

"Is it okay? They aren't *those* people?"

"No, they are good people. They want to help you."

"Good," she said and stood up. Looking at the mental health professionals, she said, "Detective Scott says you're okay."

Both county health workers gently took her arm to guide her to the car. Sadie looked back and said, "Thank you. Be careful too… there are dangerous people out there."

CHAPTER THIRTY-NINE

Thursday 2135 hours

Katie kept warm curled up on the couch with a cozy plaid blanket. The day had been long and she just needed quiet and security. Missing Chad was an understatement. She had even thought about driving to Los Angeles for a couple of days to be with him—but his schedule was so intense that they wouldn't have any time together even if she was there.

Looking at the framed photograph of her and Chad, she had begun to realize how much she missed having him around whenever she needed him. It was clear that she hadn't realized how much she had until it was in limbo—whether or not they would be together was still in question.

She couldn't go to sleep right away and didn't want to watch a movie or read a book. The soft rhythmic ticking of her mantel clock helped to slow down her pulse. She just wanted solace—to be quiet and think. Being well aware stressful situations brought on her symptoms of anxiety, she decided to let them come if they wanted.

Cisco was ecstatic that she was home even though her uncle had visited him earlier and fed him. He was a lucky dog that so many people cared about him when Katie had to work late. He snored softly next to her.

It didn't take long for her to start thinking about everything that had happened during the day. Interviewing Mrs. Winchell and Daniel Harper. The clue McGaven found on Darla's computer. The DH coincidence? Could Sadie be the killer?

It occurred to Katie that the victims were hard-working and strong personality types. They seemed to excel at military dog training. Was that what had triggered the killer?

Everything whirled around in her mind like a winter storm and there were signs that it wasn't going to end any time soon.

Her phone beeped to alert her that a text message was waiting.

Katie picked up her phone. Reading the text, she sucked in a breath. It was from her friend Lizzy, but that wasn't what disturbed her.

It read: *Dead and gone.*

Katie thought it was strange and creepy. Why would Lizzy send that? She pressed the dial button and after three rings, she answered.

"Hey, I was just thinking about calling you!"

"Why did you send that?" said Katie.

"What?"

"Why did you send that text message?"

"I didn't. Katie, are you okay?"

"Lizzy, I'm looking at this message you sent a minute before I called. It says, 'Dead and gone.'"

"I never sent it, Katie. You sure it's from my number?"

"Yes."

"I would never send something like that."

Katie knew in her own mind that Lizzy wouldn't have sent it, but she felt that all of a sudden she couldn't trust her own judgment. Who sent it? And why?

"I'm sorry, Lizzy. I was mistaken. It's been a long couple of days. I'm sorry." Even though she knew the message came from Lizzy's phone number—or did it? There was more going on and she was going to get to the source, but she didn't want to worry her friend so she made light of it.

"Katie? You doing okay?"

"Yeah, just a rough day, that's all. I'll call you later. Okay?"

"Sure. Talk to you soon."

The phone connection went dead.

Katie sat there with her phone in her hand for several minutes still looking at the text message.

Dead and gone.

CHAPTER FORTY

Katie burst through the office door. "I almost forgot about this until last night. I know that you're concerned about me, but sending a text saying, 'You're the bait' isn't funny." She had forgotten about mentioning it to McGaven—thinking he was joking with her—but now this one from Lizzy confirmed there was something going on.

McGaven looked up from his screen. There were more papers scattered across his desk than before. "What are you talking about?"

"This," she said, showing him the text with his cell number ID.

"I didn't send that."

"Who did? It's your cell number."

"I'm telling you, Katie, I didn't send that text. Why would I do that?"

"How is this possible?" she said and put her phone down like it was radioactive. "What's going on? Who is sending these?"

"What do you mean 'these'? Have there been more?" he asked, clearly concerned.

Katie calmed her nerves. It was just a text. "Well, yes. Last night I received a text, which I thought was from my friend Lizzy. It has her name and cell number ID."

"What did it say?"

"It said, 'Dead and gone,' like the email at Darla Winchell's parents' house. Sadie said it too."

McGaven picked up Katie's phone. "Can I look?"

"Of course," she said.

He examined her contact list, phone numbers, and texts. Then he pulled up his name on the contact list and sent a text to himself. "Everything okay." Taking his own cell phone, he sent a text to Katie. The message came in. Examining it, he said, "I think your phone has been cloned or spoofed."

"How? I have it with me all the time. I never set it down."

"I'm not sure—this isn't my area—but I know that you would have to be in close proximity of the person and phone that it needs to be cloned to."

"What's spoofed mean?" she asked.

"It's when a person falsifies their caller ID and then submits it when dialing your phone—it's more common than you might think. Just about anyone can do it with a criminal mind and motive to do it. It's usually done by spam callers to make someone answer their phone so they can do some phishing techniques."

"Can you trace it to find out what phone it came from?"

"From what I understand, you can call your cell phone carrier and put in a complaint. It's a long process and doesn't usually render any solid results."

"So I have to take this crap? Never knowing if my friends are really sending me a text?"

"You could change your phone number. Or, you could speak with a security expert and see what they say."

"Maybe John can check it out," she suggested.

Katie's mind spurred through several scenarios that might explain this happening to her phone. The first person who came to mind was Special Agent Campbell. He would have the right software on his phone to do that, know all the ins and outs of cloning and spoofing, and he had been in close proximity on several occasions. Katie grabbed her jacket. The anger was rising. It wasn't just anxiety symptoms, it was real annoyance and she was going to get to the bottom of it. And it was going to be right now.

"Wait. Where are you going?" he said.

"To the source."

"Wait a minute."

"I'm not going to tell you where I'm going because you'll stop me."

"C'mon, Katie, sit down and tell me what's going on."

Her cell phone rang.

She didn't recognize the number and answered, "Scott."

"Is this Detective Katie Scott?" said a woman's voice.

"Yes?"

"My name is Ruth West and I'm a nurse at the County Health Care. One of our patients, Sadie Caldwell, wanted me to call you."

"How is she doing?"

"She's doing much better. She's asked if you could visit her today."

Katie thought for a moment. Her anger was subsiding, and her curiosity was piqued so she agreed. "Yes. I can do that."

"Wonderful. I'll tell her. Thank you."

The call ended.

"Who was that?" said McGaven.

"The health facility. I guess Sadie is lucid and she wants to talk to me."

"Maybe she'll give us some insight into the killer?"

"Maybe. Let's go."

"Road trip."

Katie drove in silence; she eased her anger and frustration, determined to be professional and keep a clear head. That didn't mean she wasn't still steaming about the phone cloning or spoofing, but McGaven was right that she shouldn't go to Agent Campbell's suite spewing anger.

"I've been thinking," began McGaven. "What would be the reason for someone to spoof someone's ID to text your phone?

To get your personal information? Send you information about the investigation? What?"

"Think about it, Gav. Who would want my personal information? To see what I'm doing, who my contacts are. To keep an eye on me?"

"It could be anybody."

"No, what's been a change in our work? What's different?"

McGaven thought about it. "I'm so dense. Of course, it's the elusive Agent Campbell—he has the means and has been in direct contact with you several times. But why would he be sending those cryptic messages?"

"I can say that he's got some serious issues. I should probably call and talk to his supervisor or someone else that helped to work these cases with him. Not to tattle on him but maybe get more perspective?"

"I don't know, Katie… that's a thin line you're walking."

"I don't want to say anything to my uncle yet."

"What if you're wrong?"

"Then I'm wrong. I just want to find out more about him and these cases. Get some insight."

Her cell phone rang.

Hands free, she pressed the speaker button. "Detective Scott."

"Hey, Katie," said Lizzy with an upbeat voice.

"What's up? You're not mad, are you?"

"What? About last night? Nah, it's going to take more than that after what we've been through."

They laughed.

"I don't mean to keep you, I know you're busy," she said. "You want to meet at the bistro downtown for drinks and dinner? Just us. I'm only going to be in town for two more days and then I have to return to the coast. I don't know when I'll be back."

"You know what, Lizzy? That's sounds perfect. Seven thirty?"

"See you there."

The call ended.

"I like her," said McGaven. "She's solid. And very cool."

"Yeah, we went through some serious stuff in the army. She's always been someone that I can really count on as a friend."

Katie pulled into the health services parking lot and searched for an empty place.

"I'm curious to see what Sadie wants to talk about," said McGaven.

"Me too. I feel bad for her, wrestling with this mental problem. I think she thinks that she's doing the right thing." Katie knew what it was like to cope with psychological issues that pulled the ground from beneath your feet.

"We'll see."

They got out of the car and headed into the building. Walking through the double glass doors, they came to a front desk where an older woman with short grayish hair sat.

The woman looked at them and removed her glasses. "May I help you?"

"Yes, I'm Detective Katie Scott, to see a patient, Sadie Caldwell."

The woman keyed up the computer and searched. "Yes… But the appointment is just for you." She gestured to McGaven. "Not you, I'm afraid. It's policy."

"We're police detectives. Can you make an exception?" asked Katie.

"I'm sorry. They are very strict, only allowing one person in."

McGaven touched Katie's arm. "Don't worry about it. Go."

"Oh, and you'll have to check your firearm."

Katie sighed and removed her Glock from its holster, handing it to her partner. "Thanks."

McGaven left to grab a coffee and wait as Katie was instructed to go up the stairs and turn right until she saw room 111.

It seemed deserted as she climbed the stairs and walked down the hallway. She didn't see a doctor or nurse. There was just the hum of the heating system keeping her company. Not having any real expectation as to what Sadie Caldwell had to tell her, she pushed on to work every potential lead.

Katie stopped at room 111. It was a white door with no other identification except the number. It wasn't open or ajar—it was shut. She knocked. Finally she heard a faint, "Come in."

Katie pushed the door open and walked inside. It was similar to a regular hospital room with the adjustable medical bed, two uncomfortable-looking chairs, and a small table in the corner.

Lying in the bed was Sadie Caldwell. She looked lifeless, like a doll propped up, but her face had color and her eyes looked bright. It was clear that she was on some kind of medication that made her tired and lethargic.

"Hi, Sadie," said Katie, trying to sound upbeat.

"I'm glad you came."

"Of course. How are you?" She sat down in a chair near the bed.

"Oh, you know—hanging in there."

"Do you need anything?"

"You're sweet," she said and touched Katie's hand. "I'm fine. Where's that handsome tall partner of yours?" She smiled.

"They would only let one of us in at a time. Strict orders."

"Oh well, I wanted to talk to you."

Katie waited patiently. She could sense that Sadie had something important to tell her, but was struggling with the words.

"When I first realized that I was having trouble remembering things, I was still working the block. You know… And then I had strange feelings, like someone was watching me, and the feelings turned into whispers… and then voices…"

Katie remained quiet and let Sadie get out what she needed to say. Her compassion ran over; she knew what it was like, struggling with something that wasn't real, but no one could really understand unless they had experienced it. PTSD was like a ghost she carried around with her—and it was never really gone, only hiding and waiting for the right moment.

"And… well… after I retired and my Sam died, things began to get worse. I heard voices coming from next door at Jeanine's house. I saw people come and go…"

Katie nodded but remained quiet.

"You see, I don't know if what I saw and heard was real or in my head."

"What are you trying to say?" said Katie.

"I saw this dark figure. I thought it was one of those black mass things I sometimes see, but now as I'm sitting here with you…"

"It's okay. You can tell me."

Sadie pulled up the blankets as if she felt a chill in the room. "I remember the night that poor girl was killed. I saw someone wearing dark clothing sneak between our houses and go into the backyard."

"What did they look like?"

"I couldn't see a face. They were wearing all black, I think, with the hood pulled up around their head. They weren't too tall. Slight build."

"Do you remember what time it was?"

"It was dusk and almost dark."

"Did you notice a car?"

"No. The street had been quiet without traffic."

"Do you remember anything about the person?"

She flopped her head back on the pillow in frustration. "I was having a difficult time that particular day," she said. "But I remember thinking that they moved in a certain way."

"How is that?"

"You know, like they had some type of formal training. The way they moved."

"Formal training? Like law enforcement?"

"Yeah, you know. I've been around cops and correction officers my entire life. And many of them move with purpose, careful, stealthy... it's the way they hold their upper body and place their feet... oh, I don't know..."

"It's okay," said Katie. She knew that Sadie was trying to be helpful but was confused about whether what she saw was real or not. "Just tell me what you think you saw."

"The person was lean, moved along the side of the house like they were hunting someone, getting ready to capture their prey."

Prey was an unusual description to use, thought Katie. "What else?"

"I... I don't know... I'm sorry."

"It's okay. You've given me some new information," she said, trying to make her feel better.

Sadie closed her eyes. Her breathing became low and rhythmic as she fell into a deep sleep.

Katie waited a moment, rehashing what she had told her. She believed that Sadie believed she was telling the truth about what she had seen—whether it was real or not. She got up and took one last look at Sadie peacefully sleeping.

"Sleep well, Sadie," she whispered.

CHAPTER FORTY-ONE

Friday 1200 hours

Katie stirred her fruit smoothie with a straw as she thought about Sadie's information. She picked at her salad. Not saying much, her mind rattled back through Jeanine Trenton's and Darla Winchell's crime scenes. The injuries, the heavy ghoulish makeup, the settings. What was she missing?

Her thoughts were interrupted by a call from John.

"Scott," she said.

"I just wanted to give you a preliminary report on Darla Winchell's apartment."

"Okay."

"The blood on the walls and hallway has been identified as Darla's, but we haven't been able to identify any fingerprints except for hers. Many areas have been cleaned and scrubbed. I'll keep you posted," he said.

"Thanks, John."

He ended the call and Katie slowly put her cell phone down.

"Want to clue me in?" asked McGaven, who was eating a large club sandwich.

"The blood in Darla's apartment is hers and all other fingerprints have been cleaned. Nothing yet."

"And?"

"I've told you everything that Sadie told me at the hospital."

"No, I mean, what's bothering you?" He held her gaze.

"I'm just digesting all of this—and no, I'm not talking about my food. Everything that we've seen and investigated. It's like a dizzying maze."

"And?"

"Doesn't it bother you that Campbell brings us in to investigate and then he goes to his suite, following everything we've done?"

McGaven stuffed another bite in his mouth. "I'm worried more about your safety at this point. He's got some kind of agenda. There are too many coincidences and strange occurrences.

Katie didn't say anything. She let her thoughts run.

"Because two of the cases are ours—in our jurisdiction—and they all connect to cold cases." He finished off his iced tea. "Let's do our job and forget about him—for now. And pray that the killer doesn't decide to kill again tomorrow." He tried to keep everything upbeat, but Katie could tell he was really worried.

Katie had downed most of her smoothie, giving her an ice headache. "You know, Gav, I never have to worry why you ended up with me. It was meant to be—and no force was going to stop it. Thanks for being my rock."

"Anytime." He high-fived her.

Katie pulled out her small notebook and flipped through the pages, searching for a phone number.

"What's up?"

"I'm looking for a number in Sacramento… here it is." She dialed. Waited. "Yes, I would like to speak with Special Agent Campbell, please. Oh? Yes, Campbell." Pause. "Could you put me through to his manager, please? Hello? Yes, I was looking for Special Agent Dane Campbell. Could you repeat that? And you're sure. Thank you." She ended the call.

"What did they say?" McGaven asked.

"I knew something was off. Now I know why." She stared at McGaven. "The California High Crimes Task Force in Sacramento said that Special Agent Dane Campbell is on an extended leave and is not in charge of the serial cases anymore."

CHAPTER FORTY-TWO

Friday 1345 hours

Katie found herself standing in front of Special Agent Campbell's suite at the local inn—once again. The sun was out, warming her back, and there were very few clouds in the sky. She stood for several seconds enjoying the warmth and formulating her thoughts, determined to prioritize her reason and not her emotions. She wanted to talk to the agent before she reported the situation to her uncle, but she wanted to get some answers first.

McGaven stood next to her, not quite knowing what to expect, but he was her partner through good and bad situations—this was no different.

Katie knocked on the door loudly three times.

The door opened and Agent Campbell stood there. "Detectives. To what do I owe this honor?" he said and smiled.

Katie pushed her way inside. "We need to talk."

"Okay," he said, looking confused.

McGaven followed Katie inside.

Rookie Agent Haley was sitting at one of the computers. "Hello, Detective Scott," she said cheerfully. "Nice to see you and McGaven." She took a moment to make eye contact with him.

"Would you mind giving us a few minutes?" Katie asked the younger agent.

"Uh, of course. I have an errand to run anyway." Turning to her superior, she said, "It might take a bit longer."

He nodded to her.

Katie waited until the agent had left and she'd heard her walk away.

"Do I look stupid to you?" she demanded.

"Of course not. What's this all about?"

"Let's just start with… how long have you been on suspension from these cases?"

"Now, it's technically not a suspension—"

"You're working cases on your own terms," she said, gesturing to the command center he had created. "Without anyone to report to. You've scammed Sheriff Scott. You've been tracking me like I'm some type of prey for your serial cases. Are you really who you say you are?"

Campbell waved his hands in "calm down" motion. "Take it easy. There are simple explanations."

"I would have every right to report to Sheriff Scott right at this moment. Tell me why I shouldn't. Tell me." In the heat of the moment, Katie wanted to rip all the photos off the wall and shred the file folders. She stopped herself from letting her emotions run wild—taking two deep breaths.

"First, let me explain. I was in charge of these cases and when my team reached a dead end, everything started to go sideways. Due to politics and pressure from people in high places, I was given an ultimatum: either I bring in a viable suspect or I take a leave of absence. Simple as that."

"Why would they do that?" she said.

"You don't understand. This case was high profile and our overall case closure rate was down—even lower than the state's average." He sat down.

Katie's anger lessened, but she still didn't trust him.

"There were internal problems. Supervisors that were taking advantage of cases and more interested in climbing the ladder than finding killers."

"Why didn't you come clean right away?" asked McGaven.

"I know how this must look to you both. But my career was on the line. I had no more leads, no more help except for Dawn and she's more of an administrative assistant than another agent. She took her own personal time to help me—she knows the cases backwards and forwards. I had nowhere to turn. I ran out of options."

"I don't know what to say," said Katie. She understood wanting to solve a case and bring closure for the friends and family of the victim. She understood that better than most, but still, she didn't know what to do about Campbell.

"I thought it was all over for me, my career, until Dawn showed me some articles on how you'd solved some of the toughest cold cases in Sequoia County. So I started to shadow you—to find out for myself if you would be what these cases needed. And I was right—I still think you're the right person—both of you—to solve these cases."

Katie couldn't keep her focus away from the cases plastered all over the walls and around the room—the connections, subtle differences, and the lives these women could have had. She perused the photos of victims, headshots, crime scenes, and thought about the fact that they were all connected by one common thread—military K9 handlers. Then she saw the photo of herself at the Jared Stanton crime scene near the pond—it tugged at her heart and her soul how important it was to close cold cases—now, more than ever.

"I have one important question," she said, not bothering to turn around to look at Agent Campbell. "No more games. Tell me the truth. Understand?"

"Of course."

The room went quiet. The tension built and both men waited, their focus on Katie, for her to defuse it.

"Did you clone my phone, or spoof it, and have you been sending me text messages purporting to be from people I know?"

She turned around. "I want the truth, Agent Campbell. Professional to professional."

He shook his head. "No, I did not do anything of the sort." His look was solemn but it was difficult to tell if he was speaking the truth or not. "I did not clone your phone. Why would I?"

"I guess we have to take you at your word." She still didn't completely believe him.

"What are you going to do?" he asked.

"I'm going back to work and then I'm going to dinner tonight with my friend. I'm not making any decisions on this right now."

Katie didn't say another word or look at the agent as she walked out the door.

Once the door was shut and Katie had descended the stairs, McGaven spoke. "You made a good decision."

"Think so?"

"Yes, I do."

"Good."

Katie opened the door of the police sedan. "Let's get back to work. We need to figure out what's going on with my phone. I wanted to ask Agent Campbell, but I'll wait." Glancing up, she saw Agent Campbell standing on the balcony watching them. He gave a subtle nod. To Katie, it was either a nod of respect and a thank you—or it was a warning.

CHAPTER FORTY-THREE

Friday 1555 hours

Katie and McGaven drove back to the sheriff's department and were mostly silent. There were some strange anomalies that had embedded themselves into the investigations—and it weighed heavy on them: the way the homicide cases were brought to her and McGaven; another police agency tailing Katie's investigations and crime scenes; the unusual signature of the killer; the differing styles of makeup application; the spoofed text messages taunting Katie; the possibility of a copycat. All these things meant something specific to the killer, they were trying to communicate something in their own way, and each piece had to be deciphered. Katie struggled with telling her uncle about what was going on—her gut instinct told her to wait, and that it would play itself out, and soon.

As they reached the forensic department, Katie felt relieved that she was entering her sheltered haven. It was her private, quiet place to be the most productive. Nothing would ever happen that would endanger anyone. She looked at the forensic area as her safe cocoon. That was the only way she could describe it—as silly as it was: it was her safe place.

Walking past the main forensic examination area, Katie glanced inside to see if John was working but it was empty. All the computers were running. One of them looked to be running through AFIS, searching for an identity.

Katie followed McGaven into their office. He didn't say anything until he was in front of his computer, then he finally spoke.

"The more I think about this, the more I think that you need to talk to the sheriff about what's going on."

"I've been thinking about it too… but," she said as she cleared part of her desktop, cluttered with papers, files, and notepads, "I think we need to wait. Something weird is going on, but we don't know what it is—yet," she stressed.

McGaven rubbed his forehead with his middle and forefinger. She knew it was a sign of agitation for him, which was rare. "This time, Katie, I'm not in agreement with you. There's something not right about this case. I don't think we should wait. You can see where I'm coming from."

"Give it until tomorrow. Let's move forward on these cases and come back on Monday, then decide. It'll be clearer with time to think over the weekend."

He thought about it. Reluctantly, he said, "Okay. We'll discuss it then."

"Good." She stood and walked up to the whiteboard. "It's not as impressive as Agent Campbell's command center, but I have some things he doesn't."

McGaven straightened his pile of lists of the fairgrounds' employees and miscellaneous workers. He had already worked through half of the names, checking them off apart from a couple of questionable ones. He leaned back in his chair as it squeaked under the stress. "Bring it on."

Katie smiled. She loved the fact that even though McGaven disagreed with her, he still held their friendship and working relationship in a higher regard. "Okay… When I'm having a bit of trouble with a case, or in this instance, cases plural, I go back to the beginning."

"The crime scenes?"

"Even further than that. The killer's motivation." She paused in her usual stance with her hands on her hips. "There's a big clue with the crime scenes. Why such flashy in-your-face displays? What is the killer trying to convey to us?"

"A life-changing event? Something they can't get over?"

"Think about the thread that ties them together?" she said.

"Besides the makeup and poses? It would be the military K9 aspect."

"Was it someone that had a bad experience with a K9 team? Washed out of the program and now wants revenge? We saw some indication of that."

"That would make sense of the threatening message: 'You know what you did. You can't take it back. The finale is coming.' It was signed DH."

"That brings us to Daniel Harper who was Darla Winchell's friend. But it doesn't fit with his background—and why kill the other victims?"

"To throw law enforcement off the trail?" he said. "I don't follow the whole copycat angle."

Katie made a few notes. "There's something about the word 'copycat' that makes me cringe. How common is it, really? Five percent of serial murders? Ten? One percent? It's more likely one tenth of one percent." She pulled out some of her papers. "But it does seem as if Gwen Sanderson killed Nancy Day, for whatever reason. And someone has been copying her MO, possibly for fame and attention." She thought about it. "Fame and attention," she repeated. "And that brings me to a theory. Bear with me, it's a theory. It was something that Sadie Caldwell said, about when she saw a person sneaking over to Jeanine Trenton's house, they reminded her of someone in law enforcement."

"Or military. But we would have to assume that Sadie really saw something that night—it could've been in her mind."

Katie tapped her pen. "I think she really saw someone."

"Maybe," said McGaven. "But maybe she was mistaken on the day or the time even though she did see someone."

"One thing we can agree on: Sadie was in law enforcement as a correctional officer, so she would know all the common mannerisms of a cop." She thought more about it. "What if it *was* someone from a law enforcement background? And many police officers have been in the military."

"Like you."

"Like me. But this person has an axe to grind—for whatever their personal perspective or experience."

"I see where you're going with this. Someone who would have access to military information—specifically military K9 members." He studied the investigation board. "I don't know, Katie. Isn't that a reach?"

"Hang in there… Could it be something so far out that it's actually right in front of us? The military dog training is central to all of these investigations."

"Yes…"

"The message said, 'the finale is coming' and now I'm getting cryptic messages that pertain to this case. C'mon, Gav, you know what I'm thinking."

"I don't know…"

"Let me run this by you: who has access to law enforcement information, military files, and would have the software to clone my cell phone? And moves like a cop?"

"Short answer: a cop, and the long version…"

"The long version would be the same person that's watching us investigate these cases. The same person who is pulling the strings… making the scenarios work their way."

"But what for? What's his motivation for all of this?"

"A killer is a killer for their own reasons—even if it's to make themselves look like a hero. To right a wrong. They generally feel as if someone has wronged them. Who would know how to keep suspicion away from himself? And watch us so closely?"

"But Sadie said the figure she saw was slight—nothing like Campbell. I think we need to talk to the sheriff tomorrow and bring him up to speed on what has happened... everything." McGaven was adamant. "We need to talk to him and let him know our concerns. He'll know what we need to do—if anything."

"Yes, okay, you're right." She glanced at her watch. "I need to get out of here so I can get ready to meet Lizzy tonight."

"Go home. Take your mind off this... it's all theory, remember?"

"It's profiling in order to make the pool of suspects smaller so we can pinpoint a few."

McGaven began sifting through his lists, intending to keep plugging through them.

Katie tidied up her desk and put everything in a pile with her yellow steno pad on top with Special Agent Campbell's reports. "I'll talk to you later," she said.

"Blow off some steam and have some fun tonight."

"I just want a quiet nice dinner with a friend," she said and smiled, leaving the office.

CHAPTER FORTY-FOUR

Friday 1945 hours

Katie sat at a table in the bistro waiting for her friend Lizzy to arrive. She was looking forward to having some one-on-one time with her, so they could chat about the army days. Although Lizzy had relocated to the coast, she had visited Pine Valley a few days every month or so. Katie needed to relax and chat with someone close to her and push the investigation aside, even for just an hour or two.

The server brought Katie a glass of white wine as she waited. It felt great to be out and not wearing her typical work pant-suits; instead, she had opted for a navy dress and heels. One thing she never skipped was carrying a small Beretta pistol that she stashed in her purse. It was something that she had become accustomed to doing even though she was officially off duty. She chalked it up to being a police officer—basically you were always a cop, whether on or off duty.

Katie glanced at her watch and saw that Lizzy was fifteen minutes late. It was unusual for her; she was a stickler for being on time. She checked her cell, but there was no message from her either.

Katie dialed her phone and waited. No answer. The phone kept ringing. No outgoing message. She wondered if Lizzy could be in an area that didn't have a signal, but then realized that the recorded message should cut in if that were the case. Odd.

The server approached the table. "Would you like to order?"

"I'm still waiting for my friend, but yes, I would like to order a chicken Caesar salad, please."

"Of course," he said and left to put in her order.

Time kept ticking by and Lizzy was a no-show.

Katie knew that her friend wasn't a flaky person so she must've had a good reason for not showing up, calling, or even sending a message. It was a nice, quiet evening so Katie decided to enjoy her salad and wine. It was good to push the investigation from her mind—even if it was only for a little while.

As Katie was leaving, she tried to call Lizzy again and the same thing happened. No answer. She decided to go to Lizzy's motel.

She slowly drove into the motel parking lot, which was more than half filled. Lizzy's gold Camaro was there. Katie parked and walked to Lizzy's motel room, which was around the back in a quieter location. The air was much cooler than it had been an hour ago. When she got to the door she found it was slightly open and light peeked out around the frame.

"Lizzy?" she said and pushed the door open wider. "Lizzy," she said again.

No answer.

As Katie entered, a familiar icy shiver ran up her spine. Solid cop instincts told her to be vigilant and careful. She saw that the double bed was unmade; the white sheets were folded back and there was a nice outfit laid out—a pair of black pants and a cream blouse. A pair of black pumps was neatly placed on the floor.

She could smell a slight fragrance of Lizzy's favorite perfume. It was light with an undertone of roses.

"Lizzy?" she said again.

There was a blue suitcase in the corner. Several textbooks were lying on the TV console next to her purse, keys, and sunglasses. Walking toward the bathroom, Katie saw a white towel lying on the floor near the shower, which was still damp. Her toiletries and makeup were spread out on the counter.

Katie thought maybe she'd gone to get some ice and waited a moment. But Lizzy wasn't there and wasn't returning soon. All of Katie's instincts were screaming at her that something was wrong—very wrong.

"Where are you, Lizzy?" she whispered. Deciding to wait another ten minutes just in case it was a silly misunderstanding with a perfectly logical explanation, Katie paced in the room. Her breath shortened and remained shallow. Heat rose up in her chest and flushed her face.

No, don't even try it…

The anxiety symptoms had a way of showing up at the least opportune time. Katie quietly berated herself, she had been doing so well and keeping the PTSD monster at bay. She knew that when stress crept up, so did the usual symptoms.

With no sign of Lizzy returning, and Katie's anxiety building, she knew that she had to take action. Trying to figure out where Lizzy might be, Katie decided to call John, hoping that he was still at work.

"John Blackburn," he answered to her relief.

"John, it's Katie."

"Katie, what's up? You sound stressed."

"Have you heard from Lizzy?"

"No, why?"

"When did you last talk to her?"

"Katie, what's going on? I talked to her yesterday. Why?" His voice became strained. "Katie?"

"Thanks, John. I'm sure it's nothing."

"Katie what's—"

She ended the call. As she walked out of the motel room, she closed the door.

Her cell phone chimed, alerting her that she had a text.

The message was from Lizzy's number.

Welcome to your crime scene. If you don't play, Lizzy dies. If you call anyone, Lizzy dies. You have ten minutes to get to the Trenton crime scene. Yes, this is real. Tick Tock.

CHAPTER FORTY-FIVE
Friday 2115 hours

If you don't play, Lizzy dies.

Katie had no doubt that the text message was real—everything in her gut told her so. She had no other choice but to get into her Jeep and drive as fast as she could to Jeanine Trenton's house—or what was left of it after the fire. Katie knew that whoever had cloned or spoofed her phone could use the GPS to see where she was going. Her every move was being closely scrutinized and she wondered if her new Jeep with all the latest technologies was being monitored as well.

As she sped as fast as she dared to Raven Woods, she thought about who was behind this façade. It was definitely someone connected to law enforcement or military—maybe both. Everything teetered on the fact that the women who had been targeted were in the military as K9 handlers. Everything came back to this one thread connecting them all to each other—and it led to her.

If you call anyone, Lizzy dies.

Katie took the turn into Raven Woods too fast and the Jeep fishtailed, but she fought to keep it on the road, gripping the steering wheel harder. Tires squealed. Her body slammed into the door. An oncoming car blasted its high beams at her and honked the horn, speeding past.

"Think, Katie! Think!" The thought of Lizzy being in the snare of this killer made Katie want to break down.

The victims were all connected by military K9, and by the fact that they were all women. Each one was a pawn, presented in an outlandish crime scene. The crime scene characteristics were amateurish and planned, with planted evidence that didn't mean anything—or did it? The jewelry. The makeup. The presentation of the victims was designed to humiliate them, mock them... making them pay. But pay for what? What was the horrible defining moment in the killer's life? Why the production?

You have ten minutes to get to the Trenton crime scene.

Katie finally turned onto Fox Hunt Road, barely reducing her speed. She looked at the clock on the dashboard. Two minutes left and counting...

Screeching to a stop, flinging open the car door, Katie jumped out. Realizing she was still wearing high heels, she pulled them off and tossed them into the car. Grabbing her cell phone, she slipped it into her bra. Taking her gun and a flashlight, she was on the move.

Katie ran as fast as she could in her snug-fitting dress between the burned-out Trenton house and Sadie's darkened home. The weeds, sticks, and rocks pressed hard against her bare feet, but it didn't slow her down.

"Lizzy!" she yelled.

The area was dark and eerily quiet.

Katie stopped. She tried to calm her heavy breathing so she could listen. Her senses strained to hear... A snap of twig. Movement through the trees. The unsettling silence enveloped her.

She ran toward the backyard, flashing the light beam from end to end. Nothing. There was no sign of anyone on the property.

"No," she lamented.

Not knowing what to do next, she walked around the land, frantically searching—for her friend, for clues, for *anything*.

Her phone chimed with a text message from Lizzy's phone.

Find the key in the rubble. If you don't play, Lizzy dies. Tick Tock.

CHAPTER FORTY-SIX

Friday 2010 hours

McGaven was about to leave after a long evening reading through more names and backgrounds. He'd reread Katie's theories, suspect list, and killer profile. He would have left earlier, but he had an early dinner break with Denise. Full now and getting sleepy, he still wanted to skim through the articles she'd brought them.

McGaven picked up the pieces about the fairs and circuses. He shuffled through them and also the articles about new exhibits. There was one in particular showing realistic mannequins with an uncanny resemblance to the crime scene victims—the broken pose of the body, slumped torsos with the arms and legs bent in difficult positions resembling a broken doll. It was an advertisement for a fun house which had been advertised and proved to be one of the biggest attractions that year until there was a tragedy. Something piqued his interest. He continued to read more articles about the mannequins with renewed energy.

CHAPTER FORTY-SEVEN

Friday 2145 hours

Katie tore the remains of the house apart looking for the key, not sure if it was a regular house key or something more substantial. She kept looking. She looked under everything, moving the burned-out two-by-fours. Soot covered her dress and the lingering smoky smell got into her lungs, making her cough.

"Where's the damn key?" she said aloud out of frustration and fear.

Katie kept looking desperately, lifting every piece of lumber. She looked along the outside of the foundations. Inside. Up high. Underneath. Nothing.

She stopped, knowing that her phone would soon chime with another incoming text. She couldn't call or text the police, McGaven, or her uncle. The killer would know it and she couldn't risk Lizzy's life.

Think...

Looking out at the densely forested property, she thought about how the killer liked to display and hang jewelry. And...

"That has to be it," she said and ran toward the back of the property.

Trying not to cry out in pain from the rocks and sharp brush underfoot, she made it to the back fence. Looking along the line until she got to the area where Jeanine's body was found, Katie shone the light up and down. Nothing. But then something flashed in the light; the key was dangling by a yellow ribbon on the lower part of the fence. She almost missed it.

Katie grabbed the key.

She limped back through the forest until she reached the house. The text arrived like clockwork.

Find the circus place that we like to play up high. If you don't, Lizzy will die. Tick Tock.

"Crap! I hate rhymes and riddles. Play up high? Circus?" She thought about it. "Of course, the fairgrounds."

She ran as fast as she could back to the Jeep, jumping inside and revving the engine, and sped off back down the street.

The finale.

Katie prayed that Lizzy was still alive—she would never forgive herself if something happened to her.

Her heart sped up to a scary level. Her hands and feet felt sweaty. The road ahead looked peculiar to her—her vision became fuzzy and the lane seemed to be rolling like incoming waves. She boosted her high beams, to help her see the road. Her chest was heavy, as if a huge weight was pressing against it, making it difficult to breathe.

No, please no.

Swerving on the road as oncoming lights blasted what was left of her vision, she began hyperventilating. Katie couldn't drive anymore and pulled over to the side of the rural road. With the engine still running, she lowered the windows to feel the cool air whipping across the front seat.

It seemed that she was losing everything and everyone in her life that she cared about. She couldn't make her breathing normal. It was out of control—the pressure against her chest felt like a heart attack. Was she dying?

Her memory was bombarded with every gunfire shot and firefight she had endured. The smell of expelled gunfire wafted into her Jeep. She knew it was only in her imagination, but that wasn't comforting at the moment.

Dr. Carver's voice came to her mind, reminding her that when she was having trouble she should go to a time in her memory that was happy and uplifting.

She would say, *"Cling to someone that you love, whose love makes you happy."*

Chad's smiling face came to mind and all the places they had been together, whether it was hiking on the many wonderful trails in Sequoia County or staying at the beach in a motel. So many memories engulfed her mind once she calmed a little and let them flood in. Sitting on her porch watching the sunset. Playing ball with Cisco. The memories flooded on.

Katie's breathing began to slow and normalize. All she could smell now was the fragrance of the pine trees just outside her window. Her sweaty hands and bare feet were cold and she shivered in her sleeveless dress.

As she looked down the deserted road, she could see the lane clearly and everything had returned to normal. Her hands shook as she wrapped her fingers around the steering wheel, clutching it tight. She closed her eyes and counted down in slow breaths from ten to one.

Suddenly her phone buzzed with a new text.

"No," she said, terrified about what it would say. Instead, she saw it was an email from Sergeant Serrano from the army K9 training facility.

Katie snapped back into investigative mode with her typical curiosity. She clicked on the email to find a list of eight names from the videos:

R. Rodriguez, S. Davis, D. Haley, R. Ramos, G. Simpson, J. Trenton,
A. Crowley, and P. Frear. Note: Yes, D. Winchell was trained here
during the same time as J. Trenton.

Katie studied the names. She couldn't concentrate and the only name that meant anything to her at that moment was Jeanine Trenton's name. She put away her phone, took another breath, and mustered all her focus to concentrate on the safety of her friend Lizzy.

Her mind was almost clear and her vitals were returning to normal, so she eased the Jeep onto the road again and raced toward the fairgrounds. She hoped that when she got there it would be clear which lock the key would open.

The journey would take her almost a half hour. She braced for another text message. Feeling like a pawn being moved around on a game board, Katie focused on who could be behind this escapade.

The more she relaxed, the more her mind cleared and she picked up back where she had left off, thinking about the identity of the killer. The killer had given her another clue; it was obvious they knew who Katie was and, more than likely, her background as a military K9 handler. Now they were toying with her.

Her thoughts sharpened and Agent Campbell came to mind again. He had been shadowing her and McGaven. He had asked for her on purpose. He had the means and the opportunity to have cloned her phone; he had even told her in a roundabout way she was *bait*. What the hell? And what about his theory that Gwen Sanderson had killed Nancy Day and that a copycat was now killing the other women? Was he manipulating the investigation? Could he be pulling the strings? And, crucially, he had been taken off these cases. So he didn't have the authority to request Katie and McGaven's assistance.

One thing about working in law enforcement was that you didn't want to think that one of your own could be a killer, but Katie knew it happened.

Katie increased her speed as fast as she dared, and was coming up to the main road leading to the fairgrounds. She felt the prickly sensations warning of another anxiety attack and used her techniques of steadying her breathing and keeping positive thoughts in mind until she saw the billboard that read "Sequoia County Fairgrounds NEXT RIGHT."

She drove past the main entrance and towards the east gate. Unless the key fit, it would remain locked, and she would have to scale the fence.

Pulling into the driveway, she parked the Jeep. Katie knew she was a mess. Her outfit was entirely unsuitable for climbing or running, and she felt vulnerable as it slowed her down. She didn't have her gym bag in the car, so she had no clothes to change into.

The only thing on Katie's mind was Lizzy's safety. She pushed forward. She tried the key, just in case, but it was no use. Securing her gun and cell phone—underneath her armpit and inserted in her bra—she put the key between her teeth and climbed over the fence, tearing the hemline of her dress.

Hitting the ground running, she was aware that the killer could be watching her, and if so, she would be a perfect target. She ran as fast as she could. The pavement was brutal on her feet, scraping at her soles, but she only thought of her friend as the horrible images of the crime scenes rushed through her mind.

She got to a maintenance building and paused in the shadows to catch her breath and give her feet a rest. There was silence and no sign of anyone or anything happening. Was she in the right place?

Katie inched her way in the shadows along the buildings so that she wasn't a bright target, undeniably aware that she was going in without knowing where the killer or Lizzy was. Not completely certain what she was looking for, she tried to make her way to the Ferris wheel.

Up ahead she saw something dark on the ground. As she inched closer with her gun directed out in front of her, she realized it was a body.

Not moving any faster, but maintaining a steady pace, in case it was a trap, Katie kept her cool and continued on. It was a man dressed in dark clothing. She could see he had white or blond hair. Finally close enough to see the man clearly, she realized it was a security guard. He was lying sprawled on his back with his arms out from his sides. His utility belt was empty, no baton, no flashlight, and no gun.

Katie rushed to his side and knelt down next to him. She could see that he was in his mid to late fifties. The side of his skull was bloody as if he had been hit with a sizable object, but it had stopped bleeding. Gently she picked up his wrist; there was a faint but steady pulse.

She leaned into him. "Can you hear me?" she whispered. "Sir, can you hear me?"

He moaned and moved his head.

"Who did this to you?"

He continued to moan and his words were incoherent.

Katie patted down his pockets looking for a cell phone and found nothing.

She noticed a nasty gash on the side of his forehead where he was knocked out. She inhaled deeply, calming her nerves and keeping her concentration.

If you don't play, Lizzy dies. Tick Tock.

He moaned something unrecognizable.

"We need to get you out of the way—safe."

Katie wrestled with him for a minute and managed to drag him near the maintenance area and out of immediate view. "Stay here. I'll get you help. You understand?" she said.

He looked at her and nodded weakly.

Katie didn't want to leave him and she needed to call an ambulance.

Suddenly breaking the silence and darkness, loud carnival music blared through speakers and the bright lights of the Ferris wheel lit up the area.

CHAPTER FORTY-EIGHT

Friday 2130 hours

McGaven was still deeply engrossed in the articles, his instinct telling him that they might be key to the cases.

A knock at the door interrupted him.

"Hey," said John poking his head in. "What are you still doing here?"

"Catching up on my reading and running endless reports."

"Oh. Is Katie around?"

"No, she left at the regular time. Did you need something?"

John opened the door wider. "I just got a call from Katie a little bit ago looking for Lizzy. She seemed stressed and abruptly hung up."

"What did she say?"

"Just that. She wanted to know if I had heard from Lizzy, which I haven't."

"Katie was supposed to be meeting Lizzy for dinner tonight."

John paused and thought a moment. "Did she happen to mention that text problem with her phone? She got some strange texts, supposedly from you and Lizzy."

"Yeah, we thought you might be able to trace the sender."

John frowned and stepped inside. "I did some checking about cell phone cloning because I really don't know much about it. Spoofing someone's number is more accessible and it's a common tool used by telemarketers these days. Someone could do that, but there are some software programs out there that you can use to clone from one phone to another but you generally need the SIM card of the phone you want to clone. There is more sophisticated software which allows you to clone a phone within a minute—but it's generally used by the FBI or other law enforcement agencies."

"Really?"

"Yeah. You worried?" said John.

McGaven picked up his phone and called Katie. He waited for her to pick up, but it rang out. "Huh, no voicemail," he said.

John called her number on his phone. "Same. No pick-up or voicemail." Turning to McGaven, he said, "You look worried."

"I am."

"What's been going on?" John remained solemn and listened intently to McGaven explain about Agent Campbell and the circumstances surrounding the investigations.

"I see," said John. He was a man of few words but he spoke up when he felt it was necessary. "We need to find her."

"What makes you think she's not at home and just not answering her phone?"

John smiled. "We are talking about Katie."

"You're right." McGaven picked up the department phone landline. "Patch me through to patrol near the ninth RA." This referred to the responsibility area of a specific police officer. He patiently waited. "Sarge, it's Deputy McGaven. I was wondering if you would check on a detective. Yes: Scott. It's 8788 Spruce Drive. Thanks." He hung up.

"And?"

"He'll call me back."

"Where was she going after work. Home?"

"Yes, and then she was going to meet Lizzy at seven thirty at the bistro."

"Okay." He dialed Lizzy's number. "Same thing," he said. "It rings but no answer." He looked up a number on his phone and then dialed. "I'm calling the bistro. Let's make sure they— Yes, thank you. Two of my friends are having dinner tonight and I was wondering if they had already left or not? Katie Scott or Lizzy Cromwell." He waited. "I see. Thank you."

"Were they there?" asked McGaven.

"Only Katie, but Lizzy didn't show up."

The phone rang.

McGaven snatched up the receiver. "Deputy McGaven. You sure? Thank you." He slowly hung up the phone.

"What?" said John.

"Not home. We have a problem."

"I have an idea."

CHAPTER FORTY-NINE

Friday 2245 hours

Katie left the security guard in the safest location she could find and moved toward the Ferris wheel. She kept out of sight as best she could while the annoying music blared. It was difficult to concentrate as her head throbbed with the annoying tune.

Her phone alerted with an incoming text.

> *If you don't play... today... Lizzy dies. Tick Tock. Tick Tock. Tick Tock...*

Katie was frustrated. She needed to find Lizzy and who was behind this.

She finally reached the Ferris wheel, which was slowly circling in its revolutions. She stood in the shadows, watching the wheel. After a few moments a blue car came down and she saw, to her horror, that Lizzy was inside, tied to the bars. She wore barely any clothes—obviously she had been ambushed as she was getting ready for dinner. Her eyes were closed and her head and torso gently bobbed from side to side as the rotation of the ride came and went.

"Oh, Lizzy," she barely whispered. Closing her eyes momentarily, she prayed that she wasn't too late. Katie wanted to yell out to Lizzy to let her know that she was here and was going to get her out of this nightmare, but it was best to be as quiet and hidden as possible.

She searched for the controls, only to find that some of them had been destroyed. Feeling a sickening lurch of dread, she forced herself to concentrate, and think through the problem logically. She realized she would have to find and cut the electricity supply—without being seen. Scrutinizing every building and structure, she first made sure that there weren't any cameras. The GPS on her phone would just give a general area and was not as accurate as an actual camera on location.

Katie needed to find the utility area so she could turn everything off. Remembering the map she had used when tracking the site with Cisco, she recalled that it was near the food stands. She moved stealthily and quickly, watching from every direction.

Cautiously approaching the group of food kiosks where there was a small brick building, she noticed two doors marked "Do Not Enter—Employees Only," along with a sign depicting an electricity hazard. She tried both doors but they were locked. Taking the key she had been instructed to find at the Trenton house, she tried the first door. Nothing. Hands trembling, she tried the second door and it unlocked.

Katie looked behind her and up and down the food walkways. She was alone. Pushing the door open, she felt the warm air hit her skin.

In front of her were several electrical panels with fuses and switches—some were huge while others were smaller. They were lit up in green and there were dim lights along the bottom of the wall, so she didn't have to use her flashlight and risk attracting attention.

As Katie's eyes adjusted to the weak lighting, she could read the plastic labels affixed to each panel. She quickly fought the potential to become overwhelmed with the unfamiliar equipment and steadied her nerves. Keeping her focus and hands steady, she forced herself to read each label and mentally imagine where it powered in the area. Most were associated with different food booths. Then there were breakers in the subpanels matching the different rides. She searched for the Ferris wheel and couldn't find it. Panic filled her. Taking a quick breath and methodically reading the labels again, she came to realize that there was one label missing from a panel with three sub-panels and several breakers in the up position.

"Here we go," she said softly and flipped the switches to the breaker downward.

Suddenly the music stopped.

Katie hadn't realized how loud and irritating the sound was until it was silent. She paused a moment to enjoy the quiet and stillness before leaving the warmth of the utility room.

She opened the door partially and stepped into the darkness of the night. Strong arms forcibly grabbed her from behind, around her neck and waist, pulling her firmly, causing her to drop her weapon. The gun hit the ground next to her feet. The person's body was heated and sweaty as they pressed up against her.

A desperate voice whispered into her left ear. "*Don't* move or say a word."

CHAPTER FIFTY

Friday 2245 hours

McGaven followed John into the main forensic examination room. John pulled up a chair and began searching through a database that was unfamiliar to McGaven. He watched as the forensic supervisor clicked in and out of programs until he came to what looked like a type of GPS program.

"Okay, we can put Katie's cell phone number in and it should tell us by pinging off of the cell towers where she is—or at least a close proximity."

McGaven watched the screens eagerly, waiting for the outcome.

"Here we go," he said and pressed the enter key.

Both men watch the screen search through large areas of the county and then begin to narrow the pursuit until finally it pinpointed a specific area.

"Where is that?" asked McGaven.

"Looks like the outskirts of town."

"It's rural. Lots of farmland. What's in the vicinity?"

"Of course," said John. "It's near the fairgrounds."

CHAPTER FIFTY-ONE

Friday 2310 hours

Katie knew that whoever had grabbed her wasn't going to kill her because they would have done it by now. His arm was wrapped tightly around her neck and she clawed at it with her fingernails and began to struggle. She broke free, falling to the ground and grabbing her gun at the same time. Aiming it at her attacker, she said, "Back up! Who are you?"

The man stepped into the light and she saw his face clearly—it was Agent Campbell. He looked frazzled and skittish. His clothes were torn. There was blood on his face and now on his arms. His eyes darted back and forth as though he was expecting to be ambushed.

"Campbell?" said Katie.

"You have to believe me, I didn't know."

"What are you talking about?" She stood up, gaining her bearings and taking control of the situation. "I have to save Lizzy."

"I knew you would flush out the killer. I knew it…"

"Start talking right now. What are you doing here?" She scanned around them in all directions. Spotting a garbage can, she saw some rope inside.

"Keep moving. Now!"

"Detective, you have to believe me." He moved as she ordered.

"I don't have to believe anything you have to say. You've lied to me from the beginning. You're not going to hurt anyone else.

Understand me?" she said, reaching for her cell phone. Pressing a familiar saved number, Katie dialed McGaven. Nothing happened.

"You're going to release Lizzy, now."

"You don't understand," he stammered.

"You set up this entire thing—it's obvious that someone in law enforcement set this up. That was your mistake. The victims. The crime scenes. Stalking me. Setting this entire thing in motion. Beating up the security guard. You've gone too far. Are you setting me up now? You are despicable." She detested him and everything he had put the victims through.

"I didn't do any of these things."

"Why are you here, then, huh?" Katie tried to keep her wits. "If you didn't do it, which you did, why are you here?"

"I got a text from you."

"What?" she said, blinking in surprise.

"You sent me a text saying to meet you here."

"I don't believe you," was the only thing she could say. "Turn around, now!"

"What are you doing?"

"Turn around so I can secure you and get to Lizzy… and I'll let the police sort all this out." Katie pointed the gun directly at his head. "Believe me, I know how to use this and won't hesitate."

He complied as Katie tied his hands behind his back using the rope in the trash can.

"Why are you so sweaty?" she asked.

"My car broke down and I hurried here." He turned around to face Katie. "I didn't do this. I may have done some things that I'm not proud of, but I didn't kill anyone or set anyone up."

"I have to say the text messages were a nice touch," she said sarcastically. "I'm the bait," she mocked.

"I don't know what you're talking about—I haven't sent any texts. You don't understand, this is all I have. This job. When they put me on suspension my life was over. I found you, Katie Scott, I knew that you would find the killer."

Katie patted him down and found he had a gun. "What's this?" she said and took it.

"Think about it! I have no reason to track down female military K9 officers!" He turned to her. "Why would I do that? I have no connection to the military. Why, Katie? Ask yourself!"

Katie really studied Campbell and saw him as a scared and desperate man. She believed him about his job, but… he fit every part of the profile for the killer. The military K9 connection had to be something from his past—something they weren't aware of yet.

"You do believe me," he said. "Don't you?"

"If it's true what you're saying, who else would have the same access as you, the skills, capability, knowing what the next steps were?" Her mind raced in several directions. For some strange reason she thought of Jared Stanton and how his parents were the closest people to him, but they were the ones who had killed him and disposed of his body. These cases and victims were close—like family? Close like friends? K9 handlers and trainers—a close-knit group. She saw the crime scenes and Darla Winchell on the Ferris wheel—why? Why was it this particular location? Did it hold something personal to the killer? The murder location wasn't just a convenience like in the Stanton case. Katie guessed it was someone who had either an abusive past and wanted someone to pay that took something from them—based on the humiliation of the posed victims. Everything in her gut dismissed Agent Campbell as the killer as she studied him.

It had to be someone who knew everything that Agent Campbell knew…

The list of names that Sergeant Serrano had emailed from the training videos… R. Rodriguez… S. Davis… D. Haley…

Katie flashed back to when she arrived at the fairgrounds crime scene and approached her uncle. Of course! He had introduced her to Agent Campbell's rookie agent.

"I want you to meet Agent Dawn Haley," said Sheriff Scott.

"It can't be… but…" Her mind whirled with everything she had read in the reports, the crime scenes, the autopsies with the layered bruising on the chests, the victims' backgrounds, military K9 training, and what Sadie Caldwell said describing a person with a slight build moving onto Jeanine Trenton's property. As Agent Haley beamed with enthusiasm at the fairgrounds—obviously a perfectly planned pretext—Katie suddenly remembered seeing a Band-Aid on her right index finger which she carefully tried to keep from view. Of course! Someone who was close to Agent Campbell and knew everything about the cases—watching and waiting. Someone who knew everything about Katie. Watching. Waiting. The pieces of the murder puzzle were steadily being put into place. "DH stands for Dawn Haley," she said.

Several shots rang out in succession. The bullets ricocheted from the buildings and pinged from metal parts of the rides making a variety of musical noises.

Katie instantly hit the ground and began crawling, army-style, away from the shots. The guns still held aloft in her hands, she commando-crawled on her elbows, moving to a covered area underneath a food kiosk with oversized pictures of hotdogs and iced drinks painted on the side.

"I know it's you, Agent Haley," Katie shouted and took aim in the direction where the shots originated. She remembered her fake smiles and overenthusiastic gestures.

Glancing to Agent Campbell, she saw he was bleeding out from being hit in the neck—no doubt the carotid artery. She had seen soldiers bleed out in less than a minute before on the battlefield but she couldn't let it slow her down or stop her from saving Lizzy. There was nothing that she could do for him. Another unnecessary death.

Katie rolled onto her back and inched away even further. To her best estimation, the bullets were coming from the west and from a higher elevation—probably from a ride.

"What's the matter, Dawn? You wash out from military K9? Is that what this is all about?" Katie kept moving, skinning her exposed legs against the asphalt. She could now see the Ferris wheel and Lizzy about halfway up. The ride was now stationary, which meant that she was safe for the moment until Katie could safely get to her.

"Someone a victim in your family? Something horrible happened to them at a fair?" called Katie as she searched her mind through the articles Denise had brought her. There was a murder at one of the new fun house exhibits.

Two more bullets struck the building just above her.

"Wow. You figured that out all by yourself. I thought you were supposed to be a better profiler than that. Fairs and carnivals were supposed to be a place for family and fun," Dawn said.

"But not for you. Who was it, Dawn?" Katie tried to gain more time keeping her talking so that she could get to Lizzy.

"She was my mother," Dawn said with hatred. "A miserable, abused drug addict. I would watch her apply hideously heavy makeup that she thought looked beautiful before she went to do her sex business. But... nobody should be a victim to rape and murder. May she and her killer rot in hell."

"So she didn't take care of you—love you—is that what this all about? C'mon, Dawn, you're a walking serial killer profile. And the wash out at the military training. Poor you. That's so boring. Tell me something that I don't know."

"You don't know anything!" she yelled and her voice cracked. *Got her...*

Katie knew that now Dawn was emotional, she could make a mistake. That's where Katie's strength would come from—the killer's mistake would give her the upper hand. It was the way it had to be.

"You weren't cut out for K9. It takes special, intelligent people with a true bonded relationship with a dog." She waited for the next bullets so she could see the muzzle flash. Bracing herself on her back and holding her aim steady between her knees.

Like clockwork, two shots fired again in her direction with a fiery flash.

Katie fired back with three shots in quick sequence.

It was unclear if she had hit Agent Haley or not. It was quiet and then finally…

"I didn't wash out!" the agent yelled. "It was taken from me. They lied! I never washed out! If it wasn't for the precious Jeanine and those others, I would have made it without any problems. It was because of *them*. I didn't wash out!"

"Seems to me you did," said Katie as she moved closer to the ride. There was another ride near the Ferris wheel that flung people up and down that she could use as her cover.

"Once I found out you solved cold cases *and* were a military K9, I couldn't resist. That was my only mistake. I should've killed you a long time ago. It would have been so easy—and your death would remain a cold case."

Katie thought that Dawn was getting closer and moving in on her. She slipped her cell phone from her bra strap and pressed McGaven's number, clumsily typing with a bloody hand, *911 fairgrounds.*

Katie had to move fast. The thought of that height on the Ferris wheel made her nauseous and weak in the knees. By her estimation, she could climb up to Lizzy and free her, with the other ride covering her for about a minute, maybe two. It would have to be long enough and she would have to make the climb hoping that the ride would shield her.

Katie got to her bloodied knees, stayed low, took the moment, and ran as fast as she could. Bullets sprayed all around her, hitting the metal ride. It sounded like a massive slot machine reverberating. There was a reprieve as the bullets momentarily ceased as Dawn was taking the time to reload another magazine.

With luck as well as strength, Katie made it to the Ferris wheel. She crept to the side of the ride. She knew that she couldn't take both guns and climb at the same time, so she tossed Agent Campbell's gun up to where Lizzy was helplessly waiting. She heard it clatter as it dropped inside the cab.

"Lizzy," she said softly.

To her relief, Lizzy moved and nodded down toward her. "I'm okay. I can't get loose." Her voice was weak and Katie knew that she was hurt, but would never concede to the pain or defeat. Lizzy was one of the toughest people she knew.

Katie could see that her wrists were tied to the metal pieces next to her head. She wouldn't be able to free herself without Katie's help.

A bullet whizzed by, seeming to come from farther away from her than the previous ones. Dawn must be circling around and trying to come up from behind—in an ambush.

Katie took the opportunity to climb. It was difficult barefoot and in a dress, but she finally got her rhythm hand over hand on the metal pieces that spread out like a spider, making it easy to get to the cab. She ordered herself not to look down. Heights were one of her fierce enemies and it invited a host of unwanted feelings to bombard her. Fighting her lightheadedness and dropping stomach, she continued with fortitude.

When Katie reached the cab, she climbed over and sat down next to Lizzy. She knew she had only seconds, not minutes, to free Lizzy. The knots were complicated, like the nautical ones from the Darla Winchell crime scene.

Lizzy was only wearing jeans and a bra and Katie could see that her friend's chest was already bruising—her mind flashed back to

Darla Winchell's chest in the medical examiner's office. She knew that they didn't have much time and that Lizzy needed medical attention immediately. Her breathing was erratic.

"I can't untie these knots," said Katie as she began to panic.

"In my... pocket... that stupid penknife..." she said weakly.

"You still have that?" Katie quickly retrieved it and began cutting. It was slow going and she was only able to get one of Lizzy's wrists free.

The gunfire began again. This time coming from the opposite direction from before. Dawn was on the move.

Katie knew that the only way she could save Lizzy and get out alive was to leave her friend and divert Dawn away from them both in order to take control of the situation.

"Lizzy, I'll be back, okay?"

She smiled weakly and nodded.

She hated leaving Lizzy in that condition and tears welled up in her eyes, but there was no other way to defuse the situation. Climbing over the side of the ride, Katie began to climb back down—which was harder than she'd expected. Her feet were numb, making it difficult to feel the metal bars. Her arms were weakening and she could feel her heart race in her chest.

Two more gunshots sounded—getting closer.

Katie hurried.

In her haste, halfway down, she took a misstep, losing her balance and dangling precariously. She made the worst mistake and looked down. The ground wavered and appeared to be more like an abyss than fifteen feet. Her hands were sweaty and her grip was weakening by the second the lower she got. As she reached out, she missed the bar and plunged. Her left wrist hit a piece of the ride on her way to the ground. She hit the pavement hard, reverting to a tuck-and-roll method she had learned in the army, her head dizzy, making it impossible to see her surroundings clearly. The ground acted like a magnet, keeping her body pinned to the asphalt. Her stomach dropped and became queasy. No matter how hard she tried, she couldn't get up so she rolled over onto her stomach, attempting to push herself up. Her head was heavy and her ears still rang from the impact, but she was relieved that she was on the ground.

"Not so fast, Detective," said Agent Haley. "Pretty pathetic, but that's what all you military jerks are—at least in my eyes." She stood over Katie with her gun pointed down at her.

Katie realized she had lost her own gun when she fell and had no idea where it was.

"You want to know why I killed those women?" she sneered.

Katie couldn't turn her head to look at her, but she wasn't going back down or give in to the enemy.

"Huh? You know why? Because I could—that's why." She laughed. There was no cutesy voice and wannabe agent of law and order now; there was only hate, rage, and revenge on her mind. Agent Haley was a shell of a person and wasn't interested in finding herself.

"That sounds more like a coward to me," said Katie holding her ground.

"Oh, I know I'm not high-minded like you, but now I get to rid the world of special army princesses who always get what they want," she crowed and managed to give a chuckle. "But I got my revenge before I killed them. Terrorizing them to remove their tattoos, to remove everything related to their K9 time. They didn't deserve it. It wipes everything away. I know I will sleep better."

Katie managed to turn her body to face the agent. She was dressed in army fatigues despite not being in the military—more than likely having been expelled on a dishonorable discharge. She didn't know for sure, but it didn't matter at this point.

"That's good. You should look at the person who's going to shoot you in the face."

"No matter how hard you try, you're never going to change your past. It is what it is... you're the daughter of a murdered drug addict."

"She had me when she was addicted and on the street." She stepped closer. "When I was taken away, she never looked for me. She always told me that I would be nothing. She just left me there so that those monsters could have their way with me in foster home after foster home. Her demise was an inspiration to me. It was only fitting that those women got what they deserved in that way. Publicly."

"You have a chance to rise above that situation, Dawn. You can do it right now. Show the world that you are stronger and better than all the others..."

She shook her head adamantly as if she tried to convince herself that she never got a fair shake. "I am better than the others, my mother, and I'm better than you. Goodbye, Detective Scott."

A shot was fired, but not from the agent's gun; it had come from above. Lizzy had shot the junior agent with Campbell's gun.

Katie leaned back against the ride, relieved, tired, and glad that everything was over. She looked at the woman who could've had a life, but let her past overtake and corrode her. Her wide open, lifeless eyes stared upward to the stars—she was dead. The bullet had pierced her chest and blasted her heart into pieces.

Sirens approached.

"We're going to be okay, Lizzy," she said. Closing her eyes, she tried not to let the tears fall but they did.

Katie could hear voices yelling and the sound of police-issue boots hitting the pavement and heading in their direction.

"We're here!" yelled Katie. "It's okay..."

McGaven finally appeared with John at his side followed by several deputies. They rushed to Katie and helped her up. "You okay?"

"I think so," she said, feeling dizzy as her surroundings whirled like the nearby merry-go-round. "Get Lizzy to the hospital... and there's a wounded security guard near the employee area... Oh, and Agent Campbell is dead."

The officers and John began to rescue Lizzy from the ride, gently lowering her to safety.

"We need a couple of ambulances," McGaven ordered the deputies. "Now!" He turned back to Katie. "C'mon, let's get you out of here."

"I never want to go to the fair again," she said. "Ever."

McGaven wrapped his arm around her, to help her walk. "Nice dress. What happened to your shoes?"

"A funny story..."

CHAPTER FIFTY-TWO

Two weeks later

Friday 1600 hours

"I, Sean Patrick McGaven, do solemnly swear that I will support and defend the Constitution of the United States and the Constitution of the State of California against all enemies, foreign and domestic; that I will bear true faith and allegiance to the Constitution of the United States and the Constitution of the State of California; that I take this obligation freely, without any mental reservation or purpose of evasion; and that I will well and faithfully discharge the duties upon which I am about to enter."

"As sheriff of the Pine Valley Sheriff's Department in Sequoia County, California, you have been officially promoted from deputy sheriff to detective." He handed a detective shield to McGaven and shook his hand. "You've earned it."

"Thank you, sir," he said.

Cheers erupted from the audience.

McGaven turned toward the crowd with his shield held high in the air and let out a whoop and holler.

It was a beautiful day. Spring was near and nature beginning to bloom. It was a perfect day to celebrate McGaven's promotion. Katie whistled along with the group from the department, and with Denise, John, and Lizzy.

Her friend Lizzy had been convalescing and Katie had been enjoying this longer visit. Lizzy was expected to make a full recovery from her injuries and planned to return to the coast and begin her new job in another two weeks.

McGaven said, "Hey, we're all going to Danny's. You coming, Katie?" He had Denise in tow with her young daughter.

"Wouldn't miss it. See you all there," said Katie smiling, but feeling a bit melancholy and lonely. Her shoulder and wrist still ached causing her to recount the events at the fairgrounds. They were beginning to fade and would soon only be a distant memory. She wasn't sure if she was up for a party but it was overdue for McGaven to be promoted to detective and she wanted to support her partner.

Everyone left the area, laughing, along the way to their cars.

"You okay?" asked her uncle as he caught up to her. This time he sounded like her uncle, and not the sheriff.

"Sure, I'm fine."

"You take care of yourself. Understand? You've earned some more time off and I'm going to make sure you take it." He squeezed her hand and then disappeared into the group.

Katie walked to her Jeep where Cisco waited for her. His large head stuck out the window, getting some good air scents.

"Hey, big guy," she said and petted him. "It's you and me." She continued to pet him for a few moments.

"Hey, can I get a ride?"

Katie turned in surprise and couldn't help herself as she ran up to Chad, hugging him tightly. "I missed you so much," she said, kissing him. "How... I mean, why are you here?"

"What? I can't go to a friend's promotion party? Besides, when were you going to tell me about everything that went on at the fairgrounds? I had to hear about it second hand."

"I'm fine. Everything is okay and we closed our cases." She couldn't look directly into his eyes as she recalled the last images of the events at the fairgrounds.

"Can you forgive me for being so stupid?"

Katie loosened her hug. "For what?"

"I wasn't thinking."

"You mean about your fire investigator training? But that's your dream. I would never stand in the way of that."

"I'm truly sorry how I sprung it on you and then left. That's not fair. There's going to be a training program in Sacramento later this fall where I can go during the week and come home to Pine Valley on the weekend."

Katie was relieved and so happy he was home. "That sounds great." Something was missing in her life without him—now things were back the way it was supposed to be.

"I'm home now. I will always be with you."

"I like the sound of that," she said.

"Home or being with you?"

"Both."

He kissed her. "Let's get to that party."

A LETTER FROM JENNIFER

I want to say a huge thank you for choosing to read *Pretty Broken Dolls*. If you did enjoy it, and want to keep up-to-date with all my latest releases, just sign up at the following link. Your email address will never be shared and you can unsubscribe at any time.

www.bookouture.com/jennifer-chase

The Katie Scott thriller series has continued to be a special project for me. Forensics and criminal profiling has been something that I've studied considerably and to be able to incorporate it into crime fiction has been a thrilling experience. This series has been one that I've wanted to write for a while.

One of my favourite activities, outside of writing, has been dog training. I'm a dog lover, if you couldn't tell by reading this book, and I loved creating a supporting canine character for my police detective. I hope you enjoyed Cisco's appearances as well.

I hope you loved *Pretty Broken Dolls* and if you did I would be very grateful if you could write a review. I'd love to hear what you think, and it makes such a difference helping new readers to discover one of my books for the first time.

I love hearing from my readers—you can get in touch on my Facebook page, through Twitter, Goodreads or my website.

Thanks,
Jennifer Chase

AuthorJenniferChase

JChaseNovelist

authorjenniferchase.com